Faerie's Don't Exist!

Faeries Don't Exist!
by Brian Clopper

Printed in the United States of America
Published by Behemoth Books in September 2022

Visit https://www.brianclopper.com

a novel by
BRIAN CLOPPER

Acknowledgments

A big thank you to Keith, Arantza, and Ashlea for pouring over my first draft. Your comments and suggestions always make the book so much better.

Chapter 1
Skipping Stones

Donovan Strong flung the stone at just the right angle to have it skip across the lake four times before it sliced into the water. He picked up an even bigger one and again used the sidearm technique his uncle had insisted he perfect. The projectile bounced twice before sinking into the murky depths of Lake Ocho.

Skipping stones, together with rock and tree climbing, were his gym class. His uncle had the weirdest ideas about what was appropriate for homeschooling.

Uncle Drexel prided himself on making the outdoors Donovan's classroom. Tree and mushroom identification counted for science. Journaling on the wooden bridge that connected their small island haven to the slight Maine peninsula and the town of Slip Knot Harbor fulfilled the writing requirement. His uncle was a real stickler for grammar and made him edit his stories before they could go fishing. Reading on the shore or in their rowboat was Donovan's exposure to literature. His uncle's personal library overflowed with fantasy and mystery reads. He also made regular trips to the public library for other genres. And who wouldn't love history spun the way his uncle told it high up in a pine tree clubhouse!

Donovan couldn't complain. He liked being outside as much as possible. Although, he desperately wanted to be around other kids his age, and for something, anything, to come along and break him out of his routine.

Twice a month, he accompanied his uncle to town for a supply run. While their garden was impressive, they still needed to stock up on other groceries. The townies always eyed him with suspicion. And no wonder. They made an odd couple—his uncle with his long brown beard marred by a pair of white lightning bolt streaks, and Donovan with his own disheveled red hair, which his uncle insisted he keep long. Right now, it was well past his shoulders and quite shaggy. It didn't help that he'd walked into town on several occasions with dead leaves and other forest debris tangled in his mane. One onlooker had even given him the nickname of 'mountain boy.'

Donovan had so wanted to correct the gangly teen, countering that he was more a lake boy or forest hermit, as the nearest mountain was miles away.

He skipped another stone, getting five bounces before it hit a wave and disappeared.

Deciding west was as good a direction as any, he resumed his stroll. Walking along the shore required him to be mindful of his foot placement. The beach was more rock than sand. He paused to watch two crows gliding over the water. They soared up into the higher branches of a nearby pine and screeched at him in protest.

"Sorry, fellas. Don't let my presence *impede* you from your hunt."

He always tried to use the word of the day in conversations with the local wildlife. The fox from yesterday evening had been more impressed with the use of the word *oscillating* than these two bird brains were today.

"Go on. The vocabulary lesson for this morning is done with. Fly off to hither and yon." He smiled, pleased he'd worked in an idiom from earlier in the week.

Donovan stopped to sit on a large rock, staring out at the opposite shore. The sky was streaked with oranges and purples. He closed his eyes and listened to the sounds all around him—the gentle lapping of the waves, the distinctive bird call of a Cape May Warbler, the creaking complaints of swaying pine branches, and even the twittering chitters of what seemed like a whole family of argumentative squirrels. This close to winter, they were likely scolding each other about how behind they were in hoarding nuts.

He cleared his mind and sought out a pleasant memory of his parents. Meditation was another mainstay of his homeschooling and one Donovan would never admit he truly enjoyed to his grouchy uncle. Meditating wasn't a normal interest of most fourteen-year-olds. While he'd not been around others his age much, he at least knew communing with nature like this would earn him harsh looks. Imagining himself meditating atop monkey bars at recess while all the other students heckled him produced a snicker. He'd watched enough television to know such an activity should be kept secret.

Donovan concentrated, summoning his last birthday with his parents. His eight-year-old self was scrawny and perpetually sunburnt. They lived along the shore then, a beach house on stilts that he always imagined could crabwalk away from any threatening storms. In the memory, his dad held their birthday gift to him, a boomerang. Donovan had been way into marsupials at that time, and everything was about Australia. His father wagged the boomerang as he instructed him on the best way to throw it.

His father's green eyes gazed at Donovan with pure love. "So it's all about the flick of the wrist."

His mom chimed in from a blanket farther up the beach. She withdrew her nose from her book long enough to add her own advice. "Fling it with love in your heart, and it will always come back to you."

Young Donovan laughed. His dad threw the boomerang, and it flew out over the water and swept back toward them, landing at the edge of the churning surf and not quite back into his dad's open hands.

With an excessive grin, the man pinched his fingers and thumbs together like a crab and offered up a sad face. "I really thought it would make it back into my hot little hands this time." He scrambled over and scooped up the boomerang before it could be pulled out by the next receding wave.

His dad handed it to young Donovan and tousled the boy's long hair. Even at eight, his hair was out of control. Had no one in his family heard of a barbershop before?

Gripping the boomerang with his left hand, the little boy swiped downward as if he were going to karate chop the sand with it, a test swing. Satisfied, he then reared back, and let the toy fly. It made it four glorious feet before veering toward the ground and smacking into the sand.

His mother laughed as her husband fetched the boomerang and stowed it out of sight behind his back. He waved for Donovan to join his mom. "Let's have our snack and then go hunting for shells. Sound good?"

Young Donovan's frown evaporated at the mention of food. He scampered toward his mom and dove on her, wrapping his little arms around her thin torso. She dropped her book and made a show of fretting over where her bookmark could have gone. The threesome playfully dug at the sand until Donovan found the prized bookmark. He held the cardboard giraffe high and beamed with pride.

His mother kissed his forehead and brushed the sand from his hair as the memory dissolved.

Feeling distant, Donovan sat on the rock for a long time. He so wanted his parents to come back but knew they never would. That wasn't how life, or death, worked.

Squeezing his eyes shut to hold back his tears, he jumped off his perch and grabbed a rock. Life was so unfair. Why did he have to lose his parents? Why did he have to live such a lonely life with an uncle who avoided the world? Why him?

Frustrated, Donovan flung the stone at the lake. It bounced twice, then did something utterly surprising. Instead of disappearing into the water, it veered upward and curved. It skipped across the water four times as it wound back toward him along a wide arc.

His jaw dropped as the stone skipped one last time off the water and then bounced off the shore on course toward him.

Despite how fast it raced toward him, Donovan flung out his right hand and caught the stone. It was surprisingly warm to the touch. He peeled open his fingers and stared at the rogue projectile. How had it done that? Stones traveled in straight lines, and no amount of wind could make it behave the way it had.

What was going on here?

Donovan pulled out his phone to take a picture of the strange rock and noticed the time. It was almost eight o'clock. History class waited for no one according to his uncle. He pocketed the stone and raced into the woods, intent on not being late for today's lesson on the Revolution.

Chapter 2
A Gravel Situation

Gritting his teeth, Donovan shoved his shoulder hard against the truck's door. It popped open on the second try, and he almost spilled out of the cab but caught himself. He slipped onto the blacktop and slammed the irritating door. It creaked in protest but did shut.

With a casual air, Uncle Drexel exited on the driver's side, encountering no trouble whatsoever in opening his door. He smirked at his nephew. "Sorry. Really do mean to fix her one of these days." He patted the truck's hood. "This jalopy's seen me through a lot of hard times. One special lass, she is."

Whose blue paint job flakes off every time you brush up against her, Donovan thought.

The pick-up was likely the oldest vehicle in the parking lot, definitely the rustiest. Surely his uncle could afford something newer than the twenty-plus-year-old vehicle. Donovan shook his head. He needed to be fully present. It wasn't often he got to town, and he viewed these trips with a mix of excitement and fear. Being around someone else besides his uncle was taxing. If he'd just been allowed to go to school all these years, maybe he wouldn't feel so out of place.

The lessons had gone fine this morning. Donovan hadn't told his uncle about the weird boomerang stone and wasn't sure he should. It sounded bonkers.

Donovan drew in a steadying breath. He needed to get control of his anxiety. So far, his uncle hadn't noticed how much stress these trips caused him. At the same time, he couldn't deny his curiosity and the thrill of being around others.

They walked toward Abel's Grocery Mart, Donovan toting around seven cloth bags. He fetched a cart and stowed the bags underneath. With that, they shopped. His uncle got a couple fresh fruits and some lettuce heads. They still had plenty of garden tomatoes and loads of squash back home. They also grabbed pasta and rice and stocked up on chicken.

Donovan eyed the steaks. In the six years he'd stayed with his uncle, the man had never bought red meat, not even a burger from Jordan's

Snack Bar, a local fast food joint. Why? At this point, it felt a little awkward to ask.

As they pulled three gallons of milk from the display case, a store worker approached them. Donovan recognized the teen immediately as the one who had called him 'mountain boy.'

The teen scratched at a patch of brown whiskers frugally sprouting from his chin. Several red pimples sprinkled his cheeks and forehead. His thick brows were very close to merging into one impressive woolly caterpillar.

"Can I help you folks find anything?" He smiled.

Donovan didn't trust the boy. His words didn't ring true. Would his uncle see through the false sincerity?

"Thanks, but we're good." His uncle barely paid the young worker any heed. He strolled past him and retrieved two tubs of butter before yanking at the front of the cart to get Donovan moving again.

Their cart rolled over the teenager's sneaker, and the boy flinched. He served Donovan a scowl and just as quickly plastered an excessive grin across his face. "Happy to help. Have a grand day!" He glared at Donovan and made a fist.

Donovan mouthed an apology and surged forward to catch up with his uncle.

They selected a few frozen items, snagged an apple pie from the bakery, and topped off the cart with a variety of paper products.

There were a few self-checkouts open and only one lane with a cashier. Two people were in line there. His uncle got behind the other customers. Donovan had never seen him deviate from this and knew better than to ask. Two trips ago, he'd pestered his uncle to get in the self-checkout line and had to endure a lecture about practicing social graces the entire ride home.

They waited until the conveyor belt was half clear and then piled on their items.

The cashier was a pretty girl with blue eyes and lots of makeup caked on. Donovan knew her by nametag only—*Hello, My Name Is . . . Lydia.* She was always friendly and chatty to both.

Uncle Drexel slid a loaf of bread onto the belt and smiled at the cashier. "Salutations. Hope you're having a splendid day, young lass."

Donovan only mentally rolled his eyes; he didn't want Lydia to think him disrespectful of his elders. His uncle sometimes talked like he wasn't from this century. More like several centuries back, honestly.

"Nice to see you again, Mr. Strong." Her eyes darted to Donovan almost as fast as she scanned each item. "And hello to you too, Don-o-van."

He liked how she drew out his name. And the way she cocked her head at times caused the loose strands of brown hair that had escaped from her ponytail to pleasantly brush against her cheeks. Such tendrils were so appealing to him. He rushed out his one-word response. "Hi."

"Early storm coming tomorrow. Big temperature drop overnight. You two ready for snow?" she said.

Uncle Drexel smiled. "Winter and I have an agreement. She doesn't start until I pluck my last tomato from the garden."

"And have you?" She rang up all their cans and double-bagged them.

"Still about a dozen to go. Maybe another few days, a week even." He stroked his beard. "Then Mother Nature can blanket us in all the snow she wants."

"So you don't think it's going to snow?" she asked.

"Oh, in town? Sure. But it'll miss us this time."

Donovan smiled, not liking how his uncle lumped him in with his stubborn and bizarre forecast.

"Well, just the same, make sure you have shovels and some sand or rock salt. There's still a few left in our hardware aisle, at least there was an hour ago." She let out a sigh. "You guys live pretty far out, and I wouldn't want to hear you got yourselves stranded. That would be wicked bad."

"No more stranded than we already are," his uncle said, a far-off look on his face.

She punched the total button and dropped the paper towel bundle into their cart. "$207.86."

Uncle Drexel paid in cash, and they exchanged goodbyes.

Lydia waved and said to Donovan, "Stay safe. It's a pretty nasty blizzard coming. No tomatoes are going to stop this one." She patted Donovan's shoulder and scooted him on so she could greet the next person in line.

The clerk from the dairy aisle stared at Donovan as he left. The teen eyed him and Lydia. Clearly he'd seen their exchange and didn't like it. Was the cashier his girlfriend? No way. Lydia was a better judge of character than that.

They exited the store. Uncle Drexel looked up at the darkening clouds overhead and shivered at the slight cool breeze that struck them.

"Might be some truth to what she said. Snow is coming, indeed." He fished out a ten-dollar bill from his wallet and handed it to him. "Head back in and get two bags of gravel. I want to spread it on the steep part of the drive for added traction just in case." He smiled.

Grabbing the money, Donovan pushed the cart at his uncle. The man steered it toward the truck as Donovan tore off on his errand.

Having memorized the store layout long ago, he quickly located the aisle to find it was pretty empty. No more rock salt or sand, but still five bags of gravel and one shovel. A small older woman snatched up the last shovel and eyed the gravel. He approached, and she smiled warmly at him. "Would you be a dear and put two in my cart?"

"Sure thing." He stowed them on the bottom rack, and she thanked him profusely.

When he turned around to grab his own gravel, the stocker from earlier who had it in for him stood in front of the shelved gravel, his arms crossed.

"Uh, hi. I just need two bags of gravel. Could you scoot out of the way?" Donovan meekly waved his hand to the side, hoping the boy would cooperate.

The stocker squinted and wrinkled up his nose. "Don't flirt with Lydia."

"I wasn't." Donovan took a step back. Maybe he should just tell his uncle the gravel was sold out.

"You and your weird dad stroll into town like you own the place."

"We don't . . . and he's my uncle." Donovan shrank back and drew his arms up rather defensively.

The stocker noticed. His eyes widened. "You want to throw a punch?"

Donovan winced. "Not particularly."

The boy grinned, and not in a friendly way. He made a fist and held it up. "You come in and hit on my girl?"

Donovan replied, "Is she your girl? I mean, if I ask her, would she say you two are dating?" He didn't know why he was so determined to aggravate. He just couldn't believe the cashier would have anything to do with the creep.

"What? Well, not yet. I'm going to ask her soon. Just laying the groundwork." He scowled, almost as if bothered he'd opened up to Donovan. "Not that it's your business, hippie."

"I just need some gravel. I don't want any trouble."

The stocker looked around. No one else was in the aisle. He lurched forward and shoved Donovan hard enough to knock him down. He fell on his back and rolled left. Donovan stiffened, fearful.

The teen loomed over him. "I see you talk to her again and you're in for a world of hurt." He drew back his right hand and balled his fist.

Donovan gasped and sprawled on his back like an upturned beetle. Then he rolled to the left and peered fearfully up at the stocker.

Without warning, the gravel bags behind the stocker slid off the shelf and crashed to the floor. All three broke open, and bluish-white rocks spilled out. Only they didn't confine themselves to just covering the tiled floor.

Hundreds of tiny pebbles surged upward, forming a cresting wave that crashed down around Donovan's feet and then swept up his legs, arms, and torso, bouncing about in a frenzy before settling into a single layer that covered him to his neck like armor.

"What the heck?" The stocker staggered backward, slamming an elbow against the now empty shelf.

Relieved the rocks hadn't tried to blanket his face, Donovan blew out a breath. He closed his mouth just the same and swatted at his forearms, trying to knock free any of the makeshift armor. The stones stayed fixed in place. He stood, finding that the gravel didn't hamper his movements in the least. It shifted about at his joints to allow great freedom of motion. Donovan pinwheeled his arms, amazed that the stones were so cooperative.

"How are you doing that?" All color slipped from the stocker's face, and his hands trembled.

"I don't know," Donovan gasped. He shook his legs, trying to send the stones flying. His attacker's panic was infectious. His heart raced and his stomach was doing backflips. Now would be a terrible time to throw-up. *What's going on?*

The stocker staggered backward, fear and confusion vying for dominance in his eyes. He didn't say anything for a long time. Abruptly, he realized how stupid he must have looked to Donovan and regrouped by being angry. He pointed down the aisle. "Get out! You're a freak!"

Donovan clawed at the stones around his wrists, managing to pry one free and fling it to the ground. It skittered away, but then spun around and veered back toward him, assimilating itself around his right ankle.

What if the stones tightened? Could they crush him? He drew in a deep breath, suddenly worried that his chest hadn't swelled as much as it normally would. Were the rocks already constricting?

Donovan staggered down the aisle, afraid another customer would pop around the corner and see him. He couldn't just run out of the store wearing the gravel. Besides the fact that his appearance would freak everyone out, the minute he fled through the front entrance, he'd be technically shoplifting.

He didn't know what to do. He scraped his arms against a nearby metal shelf, hoping to knock any small part of the steadfast armor free. Not a single stone cooperated.

Suddenly, his uncle barked at him, "Donovan, settle yourself!"

Eerily calm, Uncle Drexel stalked down the aisle, sending Donovan and the stocker knowing glances.

"It won't come off!" Donovan said. His head throbbed, and he felt faint. This was just too much. Although the armor didn't cover his mouth, every breath was a struggle. Even short, quick inhales were a real undertaking. He'd only hyperventilated one other time, when he'd climbed too high in a pine and been struck with a surge of vertigo.

His uncle put a hand on Donovan's shoulder and issued a reassuring squeeze. "You can do this. Close your eyes. Think of something settling. A babbling brook, a gentle ocean breeze sending sand dancing in a spiral. Imagine yourself in the woods, the familiar comforting sounds all around you."

Drawing in a slow breath, he latched onto his encounter from two days ago of a fawn delicately prancing through short grasses. It had taken a tumble and looked up at him with its big eyes. Its mother had been at the edge of the field watching Donovan with suspicion.

He took in another breath, expelling it slowly but louder than he expected. Stones started to drop free, clattering to the floor. He resisted opening his eyes and returned to the memory of the fawn.

"You are strong, Donovan. You can tackle your magic."

Uncle Drexel's words sounded distant, but Donovan heard them loud and clear. *Magic?*

The fawn sprang to its feet and bopped a few steps closer, sniffing the air as it lazily batted its eyes.

More gravel fell away. He shook his limbs, sending even more free.

The stocker gasped.

Donovan opened his eyes. The last of the gravel hit the floor. The discarded stones formed a perfect, ankle-tall circle about as large as a hula hoop around him. His mind reeled. Stone armor that seemed to respond to his commands was crazy.

With a gentle touch, Uncle Drexel guided him out of the circle and to the end of the aisle. Looking back, he glared at the teen. "Not a word. Clean up this mess and get on with your day. Don't provoke my family again, you hear?"

The boy nodded and slowly picked up one of the busted bags. He didn't pry his eyes from Donovan's uncle as he dropped to his knees and started scooping the gravel into the torn packaging.

"I'm sorry, Uncle. I-I don't know what happened—"

His uncle smiled and winced. "You're a Strong, boy. It's in your blood. Time you got some answers, eh? Bet you have a million questions."

Donovan nodded as they drifted to the entrance and out to their truck. His mind reeled. His uncle had said 'magic.' *That's crazy!*

He looked back at the store, knowing something major had changed.

But was it for the better? He had a sneaky suspicion maybe not.

Chapter 3
A Faerie Family

Uncle Drexel didn't talk about the incident on the ride back. Once they returned home and stowed away their groceries, the man pulled out a chair from the dining room table and gestured for Donovan to sit.

His uncle slid a soda across the table and popped the top off his own. He took a long swig and smacked his lips in satisfaction, nodding his can at Donovan. "You're not human."

Donovan didn't reach for his drink. "What are you talking about?"

"Our family, we are Fae."

"Fae?"

"Faerie blood courses through every one of us. Your mother, your father, you, me."

He's looney, absolutely looney. "Like Tinkerbell? Yeah, sure . . . because we're tiny and have wings," he said, unable to keep the sarcasm from his voice.

Uncle Drexel unleashed a burp. "That takes a lot of magic. Doubt you can do that yet."

"Wait, what?"

"Shrink yourself and sprout wings. We glow when we perform that little trick. Your father and I used to hide from our parents when we were little, but they could always find us."

Donovan gave him an expectant look.

His uncle slammed his soda down on the table. "No, no, no. I won't demonstrate for you. It's been years, and I'm out of practice."

"I don't believe you." This had to be another lesson, an exercise in creative thinking. Would he make him write a story about Faeries?

"How do you explain the gravel sticking to you?" He paused, eyeing his nephew as if he could pinpoint some secret if he stared at him long enough. "And that's not the only time something weird happened with stone, is it?"

It freaked him out that his uncle suspected such, almost like he'd been spying on him. That didn't sound at all like Uncle Drexel. Maybe the man could sense when magic was being used nearby and had detected what Donovan had done this morning. Maybe he had some sort of magical radar sense. "I skipped a rock, and it came back to me like a boomerang. It shouldn't be able to do that."

"It didn't. You did it. You called it."

"I what?"

Uncle Drexel worried at his brow, pressing his fingers deep into his temples, almost as if he wanted to reach into his own head and scrub it clean of recent memories. "Oh, I knew this was coming, but I thought we'd have another year or two."

"What? Uncle, please. I don't have a clue what you're talking about."

He sighed and took another sip. "Of course. Let me illuminate. There are eight clans, each with a different magical affinity. Your father and I work fungus magic." He hooked the potted plant at the center of the table with a finger and dragged it between them. "Watch." He concentrated on the soil and waved his fingers a little too theatrically.

A trio of tiny mushrooms sprouted from the dirt. Their toadstools darkened, and green glowing speckles briefly flashed across their surfaces before the fungi halted their growth at about as tall as a thumb.

Donovan glanced out the kitchen window to their garden. "That's why we're always swimming in mushrooms!"

"Guilty. Good thing we both like them so much." His uncle smiled and pushed the plant back to the center of the table. The mushrooms didn't disappear back into the soil. Donovan gawked at the magical fungus. "So why can't I do that? Why is my magic with rocks?"

"You take after your mother. She worked stone." He pointed to the mushrooms. "Her affinity emerged first. Chances are, it will be your primary magic. Working with fungus . . .well, that will likely come in time."

"So my parents were different types of Faeries?" Donovan avoided most conversations regarding his parents, but this one couldn't be ignored. Any mention of them always left him feeling hollowed out. Surprisingly, this time he felt the opposite, as if some unseen energy filled him up. Was that his Faerie magic?

"Yes, and therein lies the issue. You, Donovan, are a hybrid. That's rare. The clans mostly keep to themselves. There's very little intermingling."

"Is it forbidden?" *Except Mom and Dad found each other, somehow.* It made Donovan proud that they defied their clans to have him.

"Not outright, but most clans shun one another . . . because of the prophecy."

"There's a prophecy? What is it?"

"Well, it's not entirely clear, but it basically threatens the end of all the Fae hold dear if the magic of a quartet of hybrids are brought together. It's why your parents left to live among the humans when they found out Klara was pregnant. There is one who hunts for hybrids like you."

Donovan felt ill. Something hunted him?

His uncle sensed his distress. "We hid you away, off the beaten path. Living among the humans kept you cloaked. At least until your magic kicked in. Other Fae can find you now."

"And that's bad?"

"It is. And you need one schooled in the ways of cold, unyielding rock, not fungus." He hung his head. "Your mother had a sister. She is much more equipped to shelter and protect you."

"I have an aunt? And she works stone?"

"Yes, and since that magic manifested first, she would be the best fit for training you." He scowled. "If you'd tossed mushrooms at that town bully, I would've been able to shepherd you to the next level." He scanned the room, looking sad. "Either way, we can't stay here." He stood and stared out the window at their garden, taking in every twisted branch and curled leaf.

Donovan didn't speak.

"Living among humans wasn't as bad as they said it would be. It's been time well spent. Your parents certainly saw merit in the species more than other Fae do." He looked at Donovan. "Keep your heart and mind open, always. Those were your parents' greatest strengths. They never wrote anyone off, not even a crusty old geezer like me who's made more mistakes than he can count."

"Uncle Drexel, when you take me to my aunt, will you stay with us?"

He dropped his head. "I'm afraid that wouldn't be wise. I'll get you to where you need to be and then take my leave. A little of you has rubbed off on me, try as I might not to allow it." He took in a shaky breath and sagged as if the weight of the world had finally caught up with him. "And that might serve to lure he who hunts away from you. The important thing is keeping you safe, nephew. You are my world, and I'd let great evil chase me down if it means saving you."

Donovan felt hollowed out once again. He knew his uncle didn't want to see how truly sad he felt, so he took in a hasty breath and put on a brave face. He hopped out of his chair and slapped his hands together.

"Where to next?"

"Stonebridge, your Aunt Esmel's haven. It's time for you to hide in plain sight, Donovan."

"What does that mean?"

He smiled. "You'll see. Nothing like diving into the deep end." His uncle clapped him in the back and steered him toward the storage room, which, among other things, held several suitcases and a rather large travel trunk. Since winding up with his uncle, they've never had reason to travel. Until now.

Chapter 4
Travel Preparation

Donovan stashed the last of his clothes in the third and final suitcase. He closed the luggage and heaved it onto his bed with the others.

Uncle Drexel entered his room with two plates holding a muffin each. He placed one on the nightstand, then leaned against Donovan's desk and took a huge bite from his own snack.

Donovan nodded toward the storage closet. "What about the trunk?"

"What about it?" He picked several crumbs from his beard and popped them in his mouth.

"Is that for my books and other belongings?"

"No, that holds something else." He smiled. "It is getting shipped off with you, but your aunt will decide when the time is right to open it."

Donovan so badly wanted to know what was inside. "Not even a little hint? Is it spells and a bunch of magic items?"

His uncle laughed. "Most Faeries don't rely on spells or items imbued with magic. Our connection is to natural energies. We have very little need for anything else."

"So all the clans are tied to something natural? What else is there besides rock and fungus?"

"Care to guess?"

"Do I have a choice?" Donovan already knew the answer.

"No, guess away."

Donovan thought for a moment. Faeries favored natural magic. He took a bite of his own muffin and spoke out of a full mouth, spraying a few crumbs onto his blanket. "Water?"

"Yes."

"Fire?"

He nodded.

Donovan named the other two elements. "Air and earth?"

"Yes, but now that you've exhausted the four elements, it'll be much harder."

He thought for a second. "Wood?"

"Not exactly. That's too limiting." Uncle Drexel took two small bites and looked at what little was left of his muffin with disappointment. He had a huge sweet tooth.

"Light and darkness?"

"No," his uncle said.

What else was left? "Spirit?"

"Oh, never that."

"Plants?"

"We refer to it as flora."

Remembering a recent biology lesson, Donovan said, "Then the last one has to be fauna."

"Correct."

He thought for a moment. "So what are my powers? Like, I guess I can make rocks fly in any direction, right?"

"Yes, but you'll be more able to handle smaller stones initially." Uncle Drexel chuckled. "No moving boulders or mountains anytime soon, and especially not here on Earth."

"So the Fae live elsewhere? Like another dimension or realm?"

"It's called Homeland, and it's a realm that exists side by side with this mortal plane. Some Fae live here on Earth, but not many. Our magic is less effective here."

"So when I get to Homeland, I'll be able to hurl boulders all about?" Donovan didn't even try to hide his excitement.

"Whoa, lad. Let's not get ahead of ourselves. It would be foolish to take you there, seeing as how that would make you far easier to hunt down."

"And who is this hunter of hybrids? You never said. Does he or she or it have a name?"

"The Twilight Monarch. A truly dark soul."

"And he needs four hybrids. Like I assume we all must be different combinations?"

"Yes."

"Does he have the others already?"

"No one knows. Perhaps he does. It could be that you are the last piece of his twisted puzzle, and that once he adds you to his collection, his infernal plan can proceed with great swiftness. All the more reason to keep you hidden."

"In plain sight?"

"Yes."

"And you're really not going to clear up what you mean by that?" He plopped the last of his muffin in his mouth.

"No."

"So that was armor I made with the gravel?"

"A crude set, yes."

Donovan wondered if he could fabricate weapons. "Can I make a rock sword?"

"No, a hammer would do if you could hold it together, but that degree of control is a long way off and likely not possible here."

Donovan suddenly felt the tops of his ears. "I don't have pointed ears. Or . . . do I?"

"You think your appearance is something different? That a glamour disguises you?"

"I don't know. I just don't think either of us looks like a Faerie."

Uncle Drexel sighed. "We are far more closely akin to humans compared to the other magical races." He tapped at the tops of his own ears. "We don't secretly have pointed ears, lad. We're not elves."

"So there are elves?"

"Yes, and goblins, and trolls, and dragons and what-not, but most reside in Homeland. It's really the Fae who insist on frequenting Earth. And since we look identical to them when we aren't in our shrunken state, we blend in far better than the rest. Can you imagine a dragon traipsing about on this plane? Or a giant? I do believe a cyclops came over recently but opted not to stay. That's the word, anyway." He shrugged. "I must confess I've really not kept up."

"How *do* you keep up? Crystal ball? Can you talk to my aunt through one of those?"

Uncle Drexel fished his phone out of his pocket. "No, through these modern wonders. Crystal ball . . . now, really? What do you take me for? Some wretched witch or warlock?" He took their plates and motioned for Donovan to follow him into the kitchen.

Donovan was the first to spot the change outside. He ran to the window. "Look, snow!"

"So it is." His uncle strolled over to join him. The snow was really coming down and in big, fat flakes. He shook his head. "Wasn't supposed to come so early. I don't like this."

"It's just snow."

"Made from water." He squinted at the frozen precipitation. "Could be nothing, but then again . . . it could be something." He slid the plates into the sink and closed the curtains before turning around and scooting Donovan toward the bathroom. "Shower time for you. We'll leave early tomorrow. I'll arrange a flight, and we'll be at your aunt's by late afternoon."

"We get to fly?"

"Yes, does that trouble you? Being so tied to stone, lifting you far from it might be taxing. We could drive if you'd rather not."

"No, I'd rather. I mean, I'd like to fly. I've never been on a plane before. I think it would be cool."

"Then scrub yourself mightily, young Donovan. We can't have you stinking up the cabin and upsetting the pilot."

Donovan laughed and raced to the bathroom. A few minutes later, he was shampooing his hair and singing a tune horribly off key. Tomorrow was going to be special. He could feel it in his bones. Yep, he was going to learn heaps of magic from his aunt and figure out how to get to Homeland and deal with this Twilight Monarch before the villain could sniff him out.

Donovan scrubbed away with the soap, thinking he could erase his magical scent and keep himself from being found.

Chapter 5
Blizzard Battle

They watched a little television and finished off the ice cream. Uncle Drexel tried to be sly when he periodically checked on the snow, which was now six inches deep. His concern was for more than the unfortunate tomatoes left stranded out in the cold on the vine.

He didn't explain his antsiness, and Donovan didn't feel like pressuring him. There was the sense that his uncle was drained from all he'd revealed and needed a breather. Perhaps Donovan would get more out of him on the plane ride. He wanted to know how flora and fauna magic worked. Did a hybrid Faerie versed in such control plants or animals? Could they transform into any animal they wanted? He scolded himself for thinking such. It's not like he could transform into stone . . . or a giant mushroom.

When his uncle went on his third bathroom trip—really another excuse to check on the snowfall—Donovan waltzed over to the plant on their kitchen table and tried to grow his own mushrooms. He failed miserably. In fact, the mushrooms his uncle had conjured almost seemed to shrink from him when he concentrated on trying to grow his own.

Around ten, Uncle Drexel insisted they head to bed. Donovan snuck a glance out his window to see the wind had picked up and the snow was being whipped about intensely.

Despite being so excited for the next day, Donovan went to sleep surprisingly fast.

* * *

A strong gust of wind rattled his window, waking Donovan. He bolted out of bed and pulled back the curtain to see the snow was now up to his windowsill. He rubbed his eyes, not believing it. That would mean it was close to three feet deep. His clock read a little past midnight. No way could a storm dump over two feet of snow in two hours.

A massive gust buffeted the house, vibrating the siding, especially the loose one above his window, which his uncle had been meaning to fix.

Donovan shivered. It was freezing. How was that possible? He flicked on his nightstand lamp, its meager light revealing he'd left behind some muffin crumbs on the stand. He swept them off. *So we still have power. Why is it cold then?*

He slid his thickest pair of sweatpants on and ducked into his fleece-lined hoodie. He doubled up on his socks and even toyed with racing out to the hall closet to fetch his gloves. But then a purple light bobbing near the front doors of their barn distracted him.

What the heck is that?

He leaned close to his window and wiped away the condensation.

The heavy snowfall made it almost impossible to see much other than the general outline of the old barn and the moving light. It lurked near the door handles for a second and then shot up and entered the structure through the open hayloft—another thing his uncle had been meaning to fix. The twin doors of the hayloft entryway were sitting on Uncle Drexel's workbench awaiting new hinges.

Donovan's curiosity was piqued. Was the purple light another Faerie? The Twilight Monarch? That didn't make much sense. If the big baddie were here, wouldn't he attack more directly?

He exited his room, slid on his boots, and donned a thick knit hat. He sank into his heavy winter coat and zipped it up snug as he tiptoed over to his uncle's closed bedroom door, thinking to enlist his help. When he heard the man's pronounced snoring, he lost his nerve. Uncle Drexel was extra cranky if you woke him before dawn.

He retreated to the front door. He'd investigate on his own. It was likely nothing. Although, he didn't really believe that; it was definitely out of the ordinary. None of the bulbs here gave off such a weird light.

He felt filled to the brim with energy. His magic making an appearance again? *Maybe so.* He patted his heart and directed his thoughts toward it. *You'll help me out, right? If it's something bad, you'll come to my rescue with a bunch of stones. In fact, there's an ample supply of gravel leading up to the barn. Feel free to use that if whatever's in the barn has teeth and means to use them . . . on me.*

Donovan felt foolish at his lengthy inner monologue. Uncle Drexel had recently had him do a writing assignment where he'd penned a villain's inner monologue. Had he done that because he knew his nephew would eventually have to face a villain of his own? Like getting him to know his enemy and how they thought?

Despite his apprehension, he opened the front door to be blasted by both wind and snow. Leaning forward, he charged into the waist-high drift, moving swiftly to close the door before any snow slipped inside.

The door clattered shut, and Donovan gulped in a hasty breath, suddenly nervous he'd made too much racket.

The wind tore at him, vengeful and determined to rip his coat free. His hat flew off and disappeared up and over the roof. He pulled his coat hood on and awkwardly tied it with his bulky gloves.

High-stepping through the snow proved a challenge. It came up to his thighs in places, and he kept having to pull his coat down to prevent the snow from creeping up and in around his waistband.

He waded through the white dunes, his boots sinking deep. The storm bombarded him with fat flakes, almost spinning him around twice from several strong gusts. The snow sticking to his cheeks melted even as it turned his face a rosy red.

Covering his eyes with one hand, he peered ahead between slightly separated fingers. That helped lessen the snow whipping at his eyes, but here and there it still got through. He blinked often and was soon teary-eyed.

Donovan stopped and looked back, estimating he was over halfway. It would be more work to turn around. With a heavy sigh, he soldiered on, lifting each plodding leg with a numbing steadiness.

Finally at the barn doors, he realized he couldn't swing either open without clearing away a ton of snow. Luckily, the left one always had some give, and he shoved it inward enough to squeeze through.

Once inside, the howl of the wind died down. The barn creaked and groaned, and some wind whistled through various large gaps in the wooden planks, but Donovan no longer felt battered from every direction. He pulled back his hood and trudged toward the ladder that led to the loft, almost flicking on the lights, but held off as he cursed himself for not bringing a flashlight. He waited a minute, allowing his eyes to adjust to the dark. The moonlight reflecting off the snow outside found its way in through numerous gaps, providing more light than would normally be the case.

It was surprisingly warm inside the barn, almost toasty. He thought about shedding his coat but knew the loft where he was heading was more exposed to the elements and wouldn't be this warm.

Looking up at the underside of the loft's floorboards, he was disappointed not to see any purple glow peeking through.

Donovan kicked his boots against the ladder's lowest rung to knock loose the clinging snow and started up. He opted to fling the trapdoor wide and surprise whatever was up there as opposed to propping it open only a sliver and scoping out the situation.

Fearing an ambush, Donovan shot up and out of the opening and scrambled to his feet. The trapdoor hit the floor behind him with a thud that echoed.

A foot of snow intruded on the loft near its elevated entrance, and the breeze forcing its way in almost knocked him back into the trapdoor opening. He scanned all about. With only a half dozen hay bales stacked off to the left, it took only seconds to determine he was alone. Donovan shuffled over to the bales and looked behind them to find nothing.

He made his way to the loft opening and peered outside. No purple light hovered in place anywhere that he could see. An inspection of the rafters turned up nothing either.

Looking down at his chest, Donovan addressed his magic aloud. "No one's here. Guess I imagined it."

The roof groaned, and a few shingles tore free and clattered across its length.

The temperature dropped behind him. His magic inside swelled. He detected it for sure this time. It was a welcome feeling, comforting. Of course, something was setting it off. Much like the bully and the gravel.

"You didn't," a voice from behind whispered.

He spun around to come face-to-face with the bearer of the purple light.

Only the figure didn't hold some lantern torch that gave off the unique light. The person backlit by the storm, visible through the open loft entrance, *was* the source of the light.

She was slightly taller than him and wore blue jeans and a yellow crop top. Not at all dressed for the weather, but she didn't act cold. Her long blond hair flew all about as she stared at him with narrowed eyes, her irises an icy blue. The purple glow came from her hands, which she held toward him as if about to dive at his chest and skewer him with her slender fingers.

"Umm . . ." He couldn't move.

The girl smiled. She wasn't a local. Of course she wasn't.

"Are you Fae?" he asked, noticing that his breath came out in white gusts.

She nodded. "Like you, a hybrid." The girl furrowed her brow and lowered her hands, their glow subsiding slightly.

"Are you okay?"

She rubbed at her temples as if trying to vanquish a massive headache. "Not really. He's . . . not happy . . . with me."

"Who? My uncle?"

Letting out a gasp, she doubled over. The purple glow flared.

"Are you . . ."

She clenched her teeth and took in several sharp breaths. "My boss isn't happy. I'm not being a good little puppet." Her expression softened. "But I couldn't do it. He wanted me to take your loved one from you. I stood over his bed and almost did. Just freeze the moisture in his lungs. He nudged me, but I refused."

Donovan gasped. "Uncle?"

She smirked. "I didn't. I raced out here to fight him off, but—" She fell to her knees and slapped at the floorboards. "He's really got his hooks in me now. You have to deal with me before I lose control."

"I don't know what you want."

She squeezed her eyes shut as tears slipped out. "Knock me out . . . or he gets you, too. He just needs you and one other."

"I don't understand."

She screamed and then sobbed. "Of course you don't, but you have to. He just snatched me up. He's not as in control with me as he is with Ithor. I don't know why he didn't just send him after you. That snake would do his bidding even without being masterminded."

"You're not making sense."

Biting her lip, she wiped the tears streaking down her cheeks as she slowly stood. Her voice deepened. "Foolish child. You have no say."

It was clear her boss spoke through her now, only Donovan didn't know if he was being addressed or the girl was being scolded. He stumbled backward. "Wait!"

He focused on the gravel leading to the barn. If he could summon it and wrap himself in armor again, she couldn't hurt him, right?

She shook her head, and the wind whipped about in the loft with renewed fury. Her voice was hers again. "Knock. Me. Out. Now."

Suddenly, the gravel he'd been trying to summon shot into the loft, only it didn't funnel in his direction. Instead, it veered toward the girl, specifically her head.

No, wait! I wasn't thinking that. Don't! He flung his hands up as if he could scatter the gravel with such a gesture.

The stones pelted the back of her head. She whirled around and threw up her hands. They glowed a bright purple, and two icicles formed in her hands. She knocked aside the gravel with her weapons. Surprisingly, neither broke. How solid could she make ice anyway?

"I'm sorry," he said, feebly willing the gravel to fall to the ground. *Go away! Stop hurting her.*

The stones didn't listen. Several slipped past her whirling blades and battered her forehead.

She howled, and the gusts picked up even more. One blast threw Donovan into the hay bales, almost knocking the wind from his lungs.

Her expression twisted into a grimace, and her eyes glowed purple. "The passion from both of you, such a delight."

The bad guy was in charge again.

With malice, the girl stalked toward him. His gravel littered the floor, not a single stone airborne. He didn't have the heart to hurt her. He sniffled and cringed.

Awarding him a sickly grin, the girl held up her icicles. She concentrated on the blades, drawing them together and fusing the ice into a larger mass that she shaped into a hollow globe with an opening underneath. It resembled an astronaut's helmet.

"I need you alive. The same can't be said for your uncle. He's a loose end." The girl chuckled and dropped the helmet on Donovan. It sealed around his neck and immediately fogged up from his heavy breathing.

She intended to deprive him of oxygen. Trying to slow his breathing failed because his body refused to cooperate. He took in several more panicked breaths before starting to feel lightheaded.

The girl registered as a blur. As he fought to stay conscious, another figure emerged from the trapdoor and barrelled toward them. The girl spun around and squawked.

Her attacker had to be his uncle, but the fogged helmet made it hard to tell for sure. The man looked to be the same size as Uncle Drexel.

Spots appeared in his vision, splotchy and threatening to crowd out his sight. He closed his eyes and then immediately opened them. He needed to stay awake. His chest hurt. No, not his chest. His lungs, they burned. He tried to suck in a breath, but nothing entered his throat.

He pawed at the globe and watched the blurry figures wrestling. The larger one held some sort of long flat object, a pipe or board, maybe? They hit the girl in the side of the head as she crumpled to the ground.

The icy globe atop his head melted away, instantly becoming liquid and soaking his shoulders. He shivered as he gulped in a flurry of breaths. The spots dancing about in his field of view dissipated, and he struggled to his feet.

"Take deep breaths, lad." His uncle threw the board to the floor and helped him to his feet. Uncle Drexel hugged him tight and almost smothered Donovan with his beard.

Donovan sputtered and slipped free from the jungle of straggly facial hair and smiled at his protector. "Is she okay?"

Uncle Drexel grinned. "Should be, but we can't wait around to find out. I'll take her inside and tie her up." He inspected her scant clothing. "If we leave her here, she'll freeze."

"But she can control snow, so she has water magic, right? She wasn't cold earlier."

"Yes, she's the hybrid with an affinity for water." He looked up at the roof.

Donovan registered that the wind had all but stopped.

"And air, I wager. A striking combination." Uncle Drexel lifted her up and cradled her gently. He nodded to the ladder. "You go first. Get inside and get ready to leave." With a forgiving tenderness, his uncle looked at the bruise coloring the side of her head. "We've maybe bought only minutes, hours if we're lucky."

With that, he shooed Donovan out of the barn, and they made ready their escape. Donovan felt sorry for the girl. He didn't even know her name but was certain she wasn't bad. She was being controlled by the Twilight Monarch, made to do his bidding.

He frowned as he marched into the garage and shoved his luggage into the bed of the pick-up truck, noting the trunk had already been loaded.

Uncle Drexel bolted into the garage, waving his keys. "Time to fly. You ready?"

Donovan nodded.

They climbed into the cab. His uncle fired up the engine and triggered the garage door to open. He shoved it into second gear, and they shot forward and plowed into the snow.

The faceoff in the barn greatly bothered Donovan.. The girl didn't deserve what had happened to her. She was just a pawn. Donovan fumed. He hated bullies. He hated the idea of someone forcing anyone to obey.

He so wanted to stop this Twilight Monarch, whoever he was.

Chapter 6
Up in the Air

They powered through the snow, getting stuck only twice. Both times, they had to get out and rock the truck to free it. At the end of their long driveway, the snow was nonexistent.

Both looked back at their home, marveling at just how localized the storm had been.

Donovan's uncle nodded at the wide-open road ahead. "We're not out of the woods yet. Did you learn anything from her? I came in at the end, but from what little I caught, she was trying to assert herself. That's impressive."

As they careened down the windy road at an alarming speed—Uncle Drexel was normally a stickler regarding the speed limit—Donovan filled him in on what she'd said.

His uncle merged onto the interstate and adjusted his rear-view mirror. "So he's got two already, the girl and someone named Ithor. Sounds like she's a feisty one, resisting him for now. I suspect when we next encounter her, he'll have her suitably muzzled. You can't depend on her to show you mercy, Donovan."

"But isn't she a victim?"

"She is, but she's dangerous. Promise me you won't underestimate her. You can't trust her as long as he has his claws in her."

"I won't. Will we have to wait for our flight? Won't she catch up to us?" He imagined the girl arriving at the airport and dropping another storm on the runways.

"It's a charter. After I tied up the girl, I called a good friend of the family and alerted her we're coming. She grumbled, but she'll be fine. It's about an hour away. Rest if you can, okay?"

Donovan situated his coat so the hood was a pillow. Thankfully, it was mostly dry from earlier. He closed his eyes and let the reliable shudders and shakes of the old truck while him to sleep.

* * *

Their pilot turned out to be a chatty and friendly woman named Bonnie Reynolds. She ran them through a preflight checklist, ribbing Uncle Drexel at every opportunity. It was clear they had known each other for some time and the woman liked him.

She handed his uncle a matching blue baseball cap from under her seat. Her cap had the single word 'Experienced' stitched in gold, while his said 'Always a Rookie.'

Reluctantly, Uncle Drexel took the cap and tugged it down over his messy hair with care.

"So, heading out to the island again, are ya? Going to wreck Esmel's weekend by showing up, you know that, right?" She smiled. "Sort of the busy part of her decade right now."

"Woman is expecting us. She'll be fine." He spoke gruffly, almost endearingly so.

Suddenly awash with emotion, Donovan stared at him. This man, who had been by his side since his parents' deaths, was about to leave him. So what if he couldn't show him exactly how to work stone. Donovan wasn't ready. He still needed his uncle.

Bonnie checked in with the tower and taxied out onto the lone runway of the small airfield. With only two small hangars, a supply shed, and a stubby control tower that stretched its definition somewhat, the airport was quaint.

Fascinated, Donovan watched Bonnie nose the joystick forward. He was somewhat familiar with the controls, having played video games and even tried a flight simulator on the computer. Not that he'd been any good. If the goal was to crash every time, then he was the guy.

He caught himself holding his breath as the plane picked up speed. He stared out the side window.

Uncle Drexel peered back at him then pointed to the nose of the plane. "Look out the front. Less motion sickness later."

He did. Suddenly, the plane lifted free of the runway and bobbed ever so slightly. His stomach did several loop-de-loops, and he was thankful for dinner having been so much earlier. On a full stomach, he might've lost his lunch. Well, dinner, rather. He chuckled and then swayed as the plane banked left.

A few minutes later, they were above the clouds and cruising with very little turbulence.

Bonnie looked back at him and smiled. "You're doing good for a first-timer."

"He's earning his sea legs for sure." His uncle grinned and laughed. "Although, maybe it should be air legs. Nah, doesn't have the same ring to it."

She looked over at him. "Us humans and our idioms. Took you forever to figure them out, Drexel."

"Well, I was sort of forced to when you bandied them about so much."

"Wait, she knows?" Donovan said.

"That you're Fae?" Bonnie said. "That magic exists? Sure do. Who do you think put up with Drexel all those years he was in exile?"

Exile?

Uncle Drexel shot her a harsh look. "He doesn't know about that little chapter in my life." He sent him a forlorn glance. "And I'm not ready to share it right now. We have enough on our plate already."

Donovan nodded slowly back.

Bonnie glanced at his uncle. "You paid in paper money. I appreciate that. None of that Faerie coin that goes up in smoke a day later."

"Hey, that was a joke. I made good on my debt to you after." He laughed. "The look on your face when it poofed away was worth it."

"And was the black eye I gave you worth it, too?" She waved a fist playfully at him.

"Definitely."

Donovan wasn't stupid. He could tell there was sincere respect between the pair. They were being playful, flirty. Which sort of surprised him. Had they dated in the past? Was that even allowed? He knew now was not the time to ask. Although, he had the feeling Bonnie wouldn't have a problem opening up about it, while his uncle definitely would.

"He's bringing me to my aunt to hide in plain sight. Do you know what he means by that?"

She laughed. "I do, but he must have his reasons for holding out on you. With the Fae, you can't rush them into sharing if they don't want to."

Donovan frowned. He was getting nowhere. A different approach might unearth more details. "So if the hybrid we just ran into controls air and water and I control stone and fungus, what do the other two work with?"

"I don't say this with any sort of certainty, but my guess would be flora is with fauna and fire with earth." Uncle Drexel wagged a finger at Donovan. "And we don't *control* anything. We're attuned to the magic. If you go around thinking you're in charge, the magic might just leave you high and dry."

His uncle definitely talked from experience.

"Pride goes before the fall," Bonnie said, both cryptically and matter-of-factly.

"Woman, stop teasing the boy. I said I wasn't sharing that."

She banked right and dropped them slightly.

"And none of your showing off. I certainly don't have the stomach for stunts, and Donovan isn't faring so well as it is." He nodded at his nephew.

Donovan knew what he was getting at. His own stomach was tied in knots, and he was suddenly very sweaty. Panic surged, coming out of nowhere. He subjected his armrests to a lethal grip. "I don't understand. Why do I feel so bad?" He leaned forward, finding that eased his stomach ache.

"It's what happens to those who wield stone or earth." His uncle nodded to the ground below. "Being so removed can be vexing. Just take slow breaths and work through some of the meditation techniques I taught you. It'll subside."

"I'll get us a little closer, but just a few hundred feet or so. Not going to clip her on any trees tonight." She patted the dashboard with affection and dropped them back into the clouds as Donovan regulated his breathing and tried to clear his thoughts of worry.

His unease and nausea lessened, and he felt his magic flare ever so slightly. He fixed on it in his chest and tried to think of it as a flame that needed more oxygen to burn brighter. How was he supposed to do that? What stoked magic? Being open and receptive, maybe?

Donovan tried to reach out with his mind to the terrain below. He couldn't see much as it was still so dark, but a slight connection pulled at him like gravity was giving him a handshake or pat on the back just to let him know it was still there.

"Um, he's glowing," Bonnie said. "Thought you folks only did that when you went *tiny*."

Uncle Drexel gaped. "We do. This is . . . unexpected."

Donovan gawked at his hands. His palms emitted a faint red glow. He clamped them together, afraid beams of destruction would shoot out if he left them exposed. The glow didn't fade, and now the backs of both hands glowed. He sucked in a quick breath. "What do I do?"

His uncle put a hand to Donovan's chest and whispered, "Breathe. Slow and steady. Settle yourself. This is nothing bad. It just means your connection to the magic is strong. It's impressive, really. I wouldn't expect anything like this here. If we were back in Homeland, this would make some sense."

Donovan tried to calm himself, but his uncle's lengthy answer was upsetting. Why was the magic seeping out of him here on Earth? Was it too much for him to handle?

Bonnie said, "You got this, Donovan. You're a Strong. Your father had these flare-ups the few times he flew with me. You can manage them. The magic isn't going to rip free of you."

Easy for her to say. Although, knowing his dad had wrestled with the same issue helped. And the fact that she knew him also put him more at ease.

She met his gaze and smiled. "You have his brown eyes. He was a real charmer. Always having me lug that trunk around to so many godforsaken places and filling it with such weird things."

"Did you know Mom?"

"Oh, yes. Wouldn't set foot in the air. She preferred to stay grounded. Your father worked fungus, but he seemed just as out of sorts off the ground as any adept with stone or earth."

Sadness swept over his uncle's face. "I didn't know that. He never told me. I mean, I knew you two took to the air here and there, but he didn't share anything about glow-ups."

Bonnie squeezed his uncle's knee. "It's okay. Your brother had a way of leaving his mark with all of us. He takes after you. His big heart can't help but want to share his magic." She nodded at Donovan. "And it appears his son is the same. That's nice."

Uncle Drexel removed his hand from Donovan's chest and dropped it atop her gloved fingers, squeezing them ever so slightly. He eyed Donovan's hands. "Looking much better."

Donovan checked out his palms. The glow was gone. He flexed his fingers and slid his gloves back on. No reason to tempt fate.

Bonnie tapped at a gauge and eyed the clock. "Got about an hour before Donovan *drops* in with his aunt." She snickered and flicked on a small radio. Classic Rock flooded the cabin. Both grownups sang along to "American Pie" as Donovan wondered about his father and the trunk. What mysteries had he socked away for him? First chance he got, he was determined to pry the blasted thing open and see for himself.

Chapter 7
Rod Lobster

Despite it being the middle of the night, his aunt's island was visible, in large part due to the faint red glow radiated by the stones littering its numerous beaches. Donovan stared down at the small island as they circled it yet again. Even in the dark, he could make out most of its terrain. Two sizable mountains with a valley between them, all covered by a variety of hardwoods and evergreens. There was a very large clearing but nothing that he considered a long enough stretch to be called a runway.

"Where do we land?" he asked.

"The stones don't normally light up," his uncle said. "That's your aunt showing off. Of course, her magic is enhanced by her locale. She settled near a worn spot."

"What's that?"

"A place where the wall between realms is thin. Magic from Homeland can get through more easily here, and so she has more access to it. Her stone fireworks every July are quite the spectacle if you like encouraging such a show-off."

Bonnie said, "Where is he? Big guy should be here already." She scanned the skies instead of the land below.

Donovan looked out across the ocean. His uncle had told them they were far off the coast of Maine. He couldn't see the mainland. Was his aunt's place on any maps? His gaze wandered to the two buildings on the island, a large mansion and a small barn painted yellow.

"Again, where do we land?" he asked.

"We don't." Uncle Drexel unbuckled and slid into the back, pulling the suitcases out and stacking them in the empty seat next to Donovan. He eyed the trunk. "That'll go last."

"Wait, we're not landing?"

"Nope." His uncle smiled, enjoying Donovan's alarm.

"Parachuting? I've never jumped out of a plane before." Donovan looked around. Neither were handing him any skydiving gear.

"You're jumping, but you won't need a parachute. Roderick will take care of you." Uncle Drexel looked out the side window.

Bonnie pointed out the window to the left. "And there he is now. Better late than never."

A dark blue lobster flew beside the plane, matching their speed and altitude. The crustacean was huge, easily four times the size of any lobster Donovan had ever seen. A flying lobster? How? The thing had no wings but coasted alongside them just the same.

"What *is* that? Fae?"

"*Who* is that? Be mindful. He's sensitive about his situation." His uncle chuckled. "And not Fae at all. Better to let him tell you his story. He likes to flap his gums." He reached for the door handle. "He's going to bring you down safe and sound."

"Wait!" Donovan cried in alarm. "Are you sure? H-how?"

His uncle slid open the door and tossed the first suitcase toward the lobster. The luggage sailed through the air and slid into place a few feet above Roderick as if locked by an unseen force.

"Some sort of magic tractor beam?" Donovan yelled.

With the door open, the engine noise was quite loud, not to mention the howling wind. Donovan strained to listen, shivering at how much the temperature in the cabin had dropped.

"Something like that." Uncle Drexel raised his voice. "He can handle a lot. I've seen him cruise around with three passengers in tow. He's bragged of ferrying more." He flung the other two suitcases. Both tagged along with the creature just below them. Its long antennae tapped at the luggage as if confirming it was there.

"Nice meeting you, Donovan!" Bonnie shouted over the roaring winds, offering him a salute. "It's not as crazy as it looks."

"Seriously? Because it looks a whole lot crazy." Donovan tensed as his uncle unbuckled him and pulled him up to a hunched standing position.

"You got this. Roderick won't screw up. He owes your aunt too much to deliver damaged goods." He pointed to just ahead of the soaring lobster. "Jump slightly forward and high, and you should fall right into his magical field."

"Should?"

"Will, I meant *will*. I've done this many times. It's actually quite a thrill. Now go." He shoved Donovan forward.

The wind seemed to pick up outside, and he could barely make out his uncle's additional words of encouragement. At least he *hoped* they were encouraging.

He clenched his hands and leapt. The air swept him back, and an unseen force grabbed hold and stopped him from flying past the plane and the lobster's tail.

Donovan sucked in a breath and stared up at the lobster. Unlike his luggage, he was flying along below the beast, his claws looking huge up close.

Uncle Drexcl threw the trunk out next. It settled into a patch of airspace to the lobster's left and above Donovan.

The plane banked right and flew away from the island.

Donovan waved and then made eye contact with the lobster. Staring at the creature's eyes was unnerving.

"Hello, I'm Donovan. Nice to meet you, Rod."

Roderick's gaping mouth opened like a zipper, revealing rows of teeth. His voice was gruff and deep. "I am Rod to my friends. You and I are not that, so address me as Roderick P. Lobster until such time I deem us more than just forced acquaintances. Let's land first and then exchange pleasantries. According to your aunt, you and I are going to be spending far too much time together, something I'm not relishing particularly."

The lobster pointed his head in the direction of the mansion, and they plunged toward the island.

Despite the ground rushing up to them rather fast, he wasn't afraid. The magic the lobster had him wrapped in was thick and strong. Even if they crashed, he sensed the magic would cushion the impact. At the most, he might stumble away with a few scrapes and bruises. *This is scary, but way cool.*

The lobster slowed their descent at the last possible moment, and they set down just scant feet from the house's wide porch steps.

Roderick deposited the luggage and trunk on the porch, using his magic to smoothly nudge Donovan's belongings between the porch roof and the beautiful wrought iron handrail.

The lobster floated a few feet off the ground, his swiveling eyes slightly higher than Donovan's. This close, it was easier to see the lobster's true coloring was more of a bluish-green. While most people thought lobsters were red, Donovan knew those found in the deep sea were dark blue, with those off the Maine coast being a blackish green.

"Are you like a magic lobster?"

"Nothing of the sort." Roderick crossed his front claws, coming off rather indignant.

The mansion's double doors swung open, and a plump, short woman with fiery red, shoulder-length hair surfed out atop a board made of hundreds of red and blue stones. She zoomed down the steps and hopped off the board, waving a dismissive hand at her ride. The stones separated and dropped to the ground, crowding together to form four mosaic stepping stones.

"Rod's currently a lobster. A setback that should work itself out soon." She had a thick accent, not quite Irish.

Keeping his claws crossed, the lobster issued a rather creaky harumph. "So you say, but I see no evidence that the curse will be going away anytime soon."

"That's some stinkin' thinkin', Roddy. You have to have faith." She winked at Donovan. "In the meantime, you're in charge of safekeeping my nephew. With the Convocation just a day away, I am simply too distracted to keep tabs on him."

"Um." What was that? Sounded religious.

His aunt waddled over, stowing her hands behind her back as she looked him up and down. She was a head shorter than him, so definitely under five feet. *She looks more like a Faerie than anyone else so far. Where are her wings?* He almost cracked a smile at the thought.

She crinkled her nose and winked, her many creases letting him know she was significantly older than Drexel, so his mom's much older sister. "I'm Aunt Esmel. It's wonderful to finally meet you. You've got your father's eyes and your mum's hair. So handsome."

"Thanks. Nice to meet you. I wish I'd known about you before." He extended his hand.

His aunt took it, shook vigorously, and then drew him close for a hug. She squeezed him tight, like she was trying to empty out the stubborn holdout in a tube of toothpaste. "Such skin and bones. Leave it to Drexel to have you so malnourished. Probably fed you mushrooms at every meal, didn't he?"

"Well, lots of things from our garden, actually." Maybe he could ask her why his uncle never ate red meat.

"Well, listen. Let's get you settled in, and I can give you a tour tomorrow morning. I can squeeze in thirty minutes or so to get you up to speed with this place, and then Roddy can spend the rest of the day with you."

"I simply can't wait," the lobster said drily and floated off toward the yellow barn. As he approached the large closed doors, he uncrossed his claws long enough to wave them about as if conducting an orchestra. The barn doors swung open, and the lobster disappeared within.

Donovan watched the doors swing shut.

"He seems . . ." Donovan didn't quite know what to say next.

"Like a lot. Ah, he's a good egg. Made some poor choices early on, crossed a fellow warlock he really shouldn't have and wound up here all hardened on the outside. Happy to have him. He'll get himself sorted out. In the meantime, he's quite handy and dependable to a fault. I'm sure he'll fill you in on his exact circumstances tomorrow. He just loves a captive audience." She grabbed his hand and pulled him up the steps. "Now come. I need my beauty rest. And from the looks of you, so do you. Having your life turned upside down tends to leave one rather haggard, doesn't it?"

He nodded and allowed her to lead him inside. Exhausted both mentally and physically, getting some shuteye would be smart.

A small check-in desk sat to the right, taking up half of the foyer. Hanging on the wall behind the desk was a metal sign cut in the shape of a serpentine dragon, an elaborate greeting etched along its length in loopy cursive: Welcome to the Sleeping Dragon.

He tensed, fearful the island might be crawling with scaly firebreathers.

Aunt Esmel caught his apprehension. "No worries. Just a fanciful name. There hasn't been dreadful snoring from any giant cranky reptiles on this island in years."

He paused. It sure sounded like sarcasm.

His aunt grinned and tugged at his hand. "Come now. Just messing with you."

She guided him up two flights of stairs and to a small pink attic door. "All the other rooms are booked. Any other week and you'd have your pick of the place. But this being the only bed and breakfast on the island, we're all filled up with guests this week. The Convocation, you know."

"Actually, I don't. What is—"

Bells rang downstairs. Donovan couldn't recall hearing them when they'd entered the house.

The noise snapped his aunt to attention. She looked down the stairs rather fretfully as she whipped open the door and shoved him inside. "Not now. I have to check someone in. Been expecting her, and she doesn't like to be kept waiting. The last thing I need is to set off her fiery temper. The wards on this place are strong, but she burns rather hot when miffed. I'm not feeling like testing their limits right now."

With that, she blew him a kiss and raced down the steps, moving surprisingly fast for someone so small and old.

Donovan found the light switch to the left of the door and flicked it upward. A single bulb hanging from a rafter lit up ahead. He waded past several stacks of storage boxes—all leaning this way and that so precariously that any jostling would topple them with ease—until he reached the bulb, where he found a small cot wedged under a window that looked like a half moon.

Before climbing under the covers, he swept a stuffed moose off the bedding and fluffed the lone pillow. He drew up the dark red blanket and settled in. His eyes closed almost immediately, and while he normally slept without any lights, he was too tired to get up and turn it off. Plus, he wasn't sure he could find his way back to the cot in the dark. He rolled on his stomach and burrowed his nose in the pillow, surprised that the bedding smelled fresh and not musty in the least.

Tomorrow was when the real magic would happen, he was certain of that. Tomorrow he'd get some answers and find out what he needed to know to deal with this Twilight Monarch fellow. He clung to his confidence as he drifted off. Tomorrow would be . . . spectacular.

Chapter 8
Convocation Education

The rain came down in sheets. From the porch, Donovan watched the puddles grow. Roderick hovered next to him, his long antennae sticking out past the porch roof. Streams of water ran down each, leaking onto his eyes. How could the lobster stand it? Not that he could wipe at his eyes with his huge claws.

"Dark clouds, dark times. Never ignore omens, child."

Before he could respond, Aunt Esmel shoved the screen door open and emerged from the house. She popped a pastry into her mouth and offered one to Donovan. He'd already had three of the delicious treats inside. He waved the additional helping off.

She shrugged and scarfed it up in two quick bites. "Suit yourself." His aunt swatted away the crumbs from her hands and wiped at her gray sweatpants. "I've got just enough time before Miss High-and-Light-Everything-on-Fire marches down to grumble about our sparse breakfast offerings."

"Wait, um, what about the rain?"

The lobster snickered.

"What about it? Not a concern." She stepped off the porch. The second she was exposed to the rainwater, the red and blue stones that formed three of the four stepping stones from last night darted into the air and crowded together to make a thick umbrella over her head. It happened so fast that not a single drop landed on her person. "Your turn."

Smiling back at Donovan, she gestured to the last cobbled-together stepping stone. The gravel quivered and leapt about. His aunt was prodding it with her own magic, priming it for him.

"What?"

"Forge your own shield, Donovan." She hopped off the steps, ignoring how her boots sank slightly in the mud.

Donovan concentrated on the stones. The red ones were more hyperactive, hopping about and threatening to lose themselves in the depths of the nearby puddles. *Not so fast, boys.* He cast out his right hand

and waved his fingers as if registering the heat radiating from a stovetop.

The lobster snorted.

Ignoring the judgy outburst, Donovan concentrated on his magic, picturing it rushing forth from his chest and scooping up the gravel.

The stones lifted free of the mud and sailed toward him. He ducked and urged them to slip higher. Some mud dripped off the rocks, splattering his jacket and landing one or two drops on his right ear. He wiped clean the mud and coaxed the unruly stones into more or less an umbrella shape. Only his was upturned like a big bowl. That wouldn't do. He pictured it filling with water and collapsing on their tour, drenching him.

Aunt Esmel nodded her approval. "A decent effort." She raised a hand and tapped twice on the nearest red stone in his umbrella. The whole assembly inverted, mirroring the correct orientation of her own handiwork.

He sighed and stepped off the porch.

Immediately, his gravel shield sprang leaks. Not many, but here and there random raindrops pelted him. He concentrated, making it more watertight. That did the trick, mostly. Just a few got through, whereas an inspection of his aunt's revealed hers was structurally sound. *I'll get there*, he thought.

She darted toward a stone path to the left that wound its way up a gentle slope just past the barn.

The lobster didn't accompany them.

Aunt Esmel blew out a breath. "Not a fan of water. He sees it as a necessary evil. It's a good thing his curse didn't make him a complete lobster, otherwise he'd have to stay submerged 24/7. Sure, he has twenty pairs of gills all over him, but they work just fine out of water as they do in. One good thing about his curse, eh?" She waved at Donovan to quicken his pace.

They ambled downhill and into a heavily wooded stretch, mostly pines. A glance back revealed only the roof of the bed and breakfast was still visible. Needles blanketed the forest floor, reducing the amount of exposed mud. As soon as they were under the interlocking branches of the conifers, the downpour besieging them diminished. Both still maintained their umbrellas. Donovan found he didn't have to concentrate too much on his magic. Once built, the shield overhead held together with very little supervision on his part. He bet his aunt would be impressed to know this. Not that he was going to toot his own horn. As nice as she was, he doubted she appreciated a braggart.

"What's the Convocation?"

"We'll get to that. Let's talk about you and your family. We have some peace and quiet on our walk for a good while, let's really dig into your plight."

"Okay, so we're Fae."

"And you just accept that?"

"Well, a lot has happened in the last day that I can't really ignore."

"Yes, magic has a way of being stubborn like that." She smiled. "So lots of upheaval for you right now."

"Yes."

Yellow and gray morel mushrooms carpeted the base of a thick pine ahead and to their left. Uncle Drexel had made sure Donovan could identify every type of fungus as part of his schooling. Now he knew why. What exactly could he do with mushrooms?

His aunt noted his attention. "Your father's gift. Your uncle says that hasn't manifested yet, just your affinity for stones."

"Yeah."

They continued apace in silence.

"Your mother would've liked this island."

"Did either of them visit? How long have you lived here?"

"No, that wouldn't have been wise. They were hiding you. And I've been here close to sixty years. I'm a steward of this worn spot."

"Uncle Drexel called it that, too."

"I'll get to that in due time. Let's stay focused on you. What went through your head when you squared off with your fellow hybrid? That must've been unsettling."

"It was, but she's not the enemy. She's being used." He felt sorry for the girl.

"She is. I'm surprised you survived the encounter. It's unlike him to send out one who isn't fully under his influence. You were very fortunate. I don't think he'll make that mistake again."

"The Twilight Monarch?"

"Yes."

"What does he want hybrids for? Some sort of prophecy?"

She stared at him and then looked as if she were reciting a well-practiced speech. "Yes, four that are eight shall converge and merge the realms wrought asunder, birthing a great dark magic to be controlled by he who shepherds the hybrids." She frowned. "Prophecies are such dusty, unreliable things, dispelled and unraveled by the strong and unswerving."

"So I can undo it, make it not happen?"

"Not as you are right now. Never confuse raw pluck for courage. You must build yourself up, shore up your magic and your ties to others. That's why you'll stay with me for a short period."

"How long will that be?"

"As long as it takes. Less if he finds you here."

He shuddered, and his stone umbrella wobbled. "What's stopping him? I mean, he found me almost as soon as magic came my way."

"Well, the hiding-in-plain-sight deal Drexel mentioned. It's not wise to bring you over to Homeland where his magic is strong. He'd unearth you in no time. And your fresh magic is a beacon among humans now. So you need to be here among the many drawn to this place." She smiled. "It's actually perfect timing. Synchronicity is another way to bring down a prophecy."

"I don't understand."

The trees thinned, and they stepped into the clearing he'd seen from the plane, only it wasn't empty.

The rain stopped. His aunt waved a hand, and her stone umbrella collapsed, dropping to the ground without hitting her. The gravel rolled together, forming one large stepping stone. She pointed to his umbrella. "Rain's done with us."

He severed his magic from the stones, imploring each rock to avoid him. Sadly, they dropped on his head and shoulders, making little effort to avoid his person. "Ouch."

Aunt Esmel laughed.

His gravel didn't come together as a unified shape. It scattered among the grasses.

Arranged in a circle were eight large archways built from stacked stone. Two were made from huge slabs, while the others consisted of fist-sized rocks heaped atop one another. All the stones were either gray, white, or streaked with both colors.

That's not right. The looming structures had been missing from the clearing last night. He was quite positive they hadn't been there before.

His aunt noted his surprise. "Didn't see them here when you first spied this clearing, did you?"

"No."

"A Faerie glamour to hide this from the humans. Since you spent so much time among them, the magic influenced what you saw from high above last night." She stomped her feet. "Now that you're touching the ground, you're more connected to the magic in this place and can see the gates."

"What are they?"

"You're looking at doorways to Homeland, specifically to the respective territories of each clan."

She walked over to the nearest one. A variety of toadstools littered its upper half, growing out of every crevice. Donovan scrutinized the next two archways. One was covered by flowering vines, its lower half lost amid roots that were thick enough to belong to some great tree, only there was none such towering over the clearing. Ice coated the adjacent archway, and the structure straddled a large puddle of the clearest water.

He raced over to the next gate. It had the biggest gaps between the stones, and wind whipped through each. He placed a hand over one crevice only to have it buffeted by a sharp blast of air.

Further along, he spotted paw prints and fossilized remains on and in the flat stones that made up the largest of the archways. An elephant could easily ride through the opening, whereas all the rest were smaller by half.

Being covered in soot, there was no mistaking the fire archway.

He completed the circle by touring the last two gates, stone and earth. The one he had an affinity for was hewn from the smoothest stones, as if they'd been snatched from the bed of a mighty river.

The earthen gate looked as if many small hands had slapped clay and mud over the rocky framework and let it bake in the sun. Very little rock poked through.

How many came over to the island? With this many gates, it could be dozens, maybe even hundreds in short order. He imagined armies of Fae marching out of the gateways.

Her bed and breakfast didn't seem that big. He hadn't explored it other than to find a bathroom this morning and to walk through the first floor to get to the kitchen. He assumed maybe the second and third floors might have five or six bedrooms between them. It wouldn't take much to fill it. "Do you get a lot of visitors?"

"Once every ten years when the Convocation is held here. Other than that, on occasion a brave soul turns up who is curious to visit the mortal realm."

"Okay, so what is it exactly? A religious ritual?"

No. All Fae see this plane as neutral ground," she said. "Every ten years, each of the clans sends an emissary. During the Convocation, treaties and trade are worked out. Disputes are resolved and relationships are strengthened. That's the idea, but sometimes clans don't come to an agreement or compromise and leave with slight bitterness." She closed her eyes. "That hasn't happened for a long time. I've overseen three Convocations in my lifetime. All ended amicably and without any bloodshed."

She was being guarded. He pressed her further, "But you're worried about this one?"

"I am. While it makes sense to bring you here during the Convocation, what do we do after? With all eight emissaries in attendance for the next week, their magic will allow you to blend in. Three are already underfoot. We missed them this morning, but you'll run into them in due course." She worried at her lip with a forefinger. "I just fear the Twilight Monarch will somehow still zero in and disrupt the Convocation. Most clans are terrified of the Prophecy. They would like nothing better than to have any and all hybrids cease to exist. For that reason, you must not reveal your dual affinities. Just work stone in their presence, especially the fire ambassador."

He nodded. "I will."

Suddenly, the water gateway lit up, the stones glowing green as blue and white energy coalesced inside the arch. Seconds later, a tall pale man in flowing brown robes stepped through, his bare feet splashing in the puddle before he stepped among the knee-high grasses. His glasses were tiny ovals that sat low on his large nose. A thick head of black hair was gathered in a neat ponytail in the back. Despite his hair being so ample and dark, he was old, possibly pushing a hundred based on the layered-upon wrinkles. He spotted Aunt Esmel and waved, drawing attention to the many rings that weighed down his fingers.

She waltzed over to him, laying extra thick on the wit and charm. "Grandl, they sent you yet again? Seems to me your council would find you well beyond the age of any sort of usefulness."

He laughed heartily. His voice thundered, surprisingly strong considering his age. "This will be my last. I brought along the next generation to fill my boots." He turned to eye the gateway. "Fellow is a lively one. You'll appreciate him."

Suddenly, a winged Faerie no taller than a hand flew out of the churning gate. Being his first encounter with a Fae in their smaller guise, Donovan delighted in watching the younger water emissary fly past both grown-ups and buzz around Donovan's head. Flecked with gold veins, his translucent wings discharged a spray of water with each flap. The boy's curly brown hair was held barely in check by a headband.

He zoomed about, talking a mile a minute in a high-pitched voice that bordered on comical. "Salutations, fellow sprout. I am Frayson. Are you also a fledgling here to learn the ways of the Convocation?"

Donovan nodded slowly.

Grandl stormed over and swatted at his young charge. "Spruce yourself up. No one likes a dazzler. You waste your magic winging all about. It is not so plentiful here on Earth as I told you before we left Homeland."

Frayson laughed and soared high into the sky. No sooner was he past the treetops than he suddenly expanded. His arms and limbs ballooned up first, followed by his torso, while his head swelled last as his wings disappeared into his shoulder blades. He dropped like a stone.

Luckily, Grandl shot his arms upward, sending a wave of water seemingly cobbled together from thin air at the fledgling. The spout slowed him down, and he landed with a splash in a mud puddle. The boy hopped to his feet, shook his boots, and smoothed out his blue pants and tunic as he wagged his soaking wet hair to dry it.

Frayson bowed to both of them and dropped a small, wrapped box in Aunt Esmel's hand. "A gift for our host. It's a delicacy crafted by the finest cook from my enclave. Enjoy."

The package wobbled, and Donovan saw one side of it swell and contract as if something were worming around inside.

"Many thanks, young steward." She nodded to him and immediately returned her attention to Grandl. "Your usual room has been prepared."

"And it's well away from my former lapse in judgment?" He looked nervously around as if about to be attacked.

"Yes, she's well away from you. Let's hope she is equally keen on preventing sparks flying between you two. What you ever saw in that hothead is beyond me."

"Beyond my older and wiser self." He looked at Frayson. "We are quite foolish when so young and naive, aren't we?"

Aunt Esmel pointed to the woods we had just exited and addressed the older representative. "You know the way. Egon has prepared some lovely pastries. If you hurry, you might catch a batch fresh from the oven."

Grandl shooed Frayson along, sharing at length with his young charge the delicious experience they were about to embark on.

Aunt Esmel checked her phone. It amazed Donovan that she got service this far off the coast. "I'm expecting Flora in just a few minutes. Very shy people. How about you head back and get with Roddy? Rain should be gone by now. It really only came down because Grandl was arriving. Weather gets a little wonky when he comes upon the scene. Now that he's here, it'll be stable and predictable. It was just the sudden surge of his brand of magic that triggered it."

"Okay, but aren't you supposed to train me?"

"What do you think the umbrella lesson was? You passed with flying colors. I'll get with you after lunch. Be sure to introduce yourself to Egon and get in his good graces. He's a mite bashful, but you'll understand once you meet him. Best cook in the hemisphere, though. It's worth putting up with his quirks when he whips up such fine food."

"Got it." He turned to leave.

"Let Roddy know I need him to drop you off at the North Beach at one sharp. Very important training there."

Donovan stepped back into the woods. Most would be lost, but he'd always had an innate sense of direction when it came to nature. He wound his way through the thick pines, passing the morel mushrooms from earlier and spotting a few other varieties of fungus, including two that were quite poisonous and not normally found in such cold climates.

Maybe magic was involved. For such a small island, it sure had plenty of surprises. He wanted to know about Roderick's curse. It sounded like it wouldn't take much to get the lobster to open up. That would be one mystery solved. Feeling a sense of purpose, Donovan quickened his pace, eager to interrogate the warlock if it came to that, but he didn't really think it would.

Chapter 9
Tempers Flare

Once back at The Sleeping Dragon, Donovan found the lobster no longer on the wraparound porch and both barn doors closed. With the downpour long gone and it now being a sunny day, he could take in more details of the mansion. The red shutters stood in sharp contrast to the cream-colored siding that wrapped the exterior above the first floor's dark red brickwork. Had his aunt used her magic to float each brick into place? Would stone magic even work on the construction material?

His aunt's home was an imposing structure. He didn't know what made it Victorian exactly, but that was the vibe it gave off. His uncle could probably identify numerous architectural specifics that made it Victorian, but Donovan classified most old homes as such. He always thought of any home that could be confused for a haunted house as that style, not that the bed and breakfast was scary. If anything, it exuded a welcoming air.

The fourth-floor attic he'd slept in last night looked so high up. He located its moon window, catching that two small stone gargoyles faced the ocean atop the twin turrets of the home. Above the front door was a small balcony on the third floor. If he ever needed to escape from the attic, he could slide down the roof to access that overlook.

Why am I thinking of escape? That's weird.

Donovan turned his attention to the barn. It leaned to the right and threatened to fall over if a stray sea breeze looked at it funny. Its yellow coat of paint peeled here and there, exposing patches of the previous coat, a gaudy sea green. He toyed with approaching the lobster's quarters and listening to see if Roderick was inside but opted to check out the grounds instead.

Realizing he hadn't toured the nearby beach, Donovan took the narrow path toward the water. After cresting dunes that were more rocks than sand, he came across an ancient dock that stretched out into a small cove. He knew the lobster wasn't taking a dip as his aunt had been adamant the warlock didn't like getting wet. He strolled onto the wooden pier, walking its length in under a minute. The handrails on either side were rough, so he kept his hands clear of them for fear of receiving a splinter. Moored at the pier's end, a small motorboat rocked in the water.

Oddly, there was a wooden sign nailed to the last span of the right handrail. Anyone stepping onto the pier from the ladder that led to the boat would see it first. In black paint was scrawled: Faeries Don't Exist! In smaller red lettering was a second statement: Enjoy your stay at The Sleeping Dragon!

Why the sign? Unless his aunt let non-Faerie guests visit and she was trying to squash any curiosity they might have. If the Convocation was only once every ten years, she might open the place to humans the rest of the time. *But then why the disclaimer about the Fae?* He made a note to ask her about the sign.

Donovan scanned the waves and the cloudless sky. The earlier dark storm clouds were long gone. They'd fled rather quickly, which made it all the more believable that the rain had been tied to the water emissaries' arrival.

He dashed back to the rocky beach and skipped several stones in the choppy water, trying to get one to boomerang back to him. But his magic seemed to have retreated for the morning. Maybe that was why his next lesson was this afternoon. His aunt knew he needed to cool it with the magic and recharge.

Donovan walked back to the bed and breakfast. If he didn't come across Roderick outside, he'd go see if he could find the cook Egon. It seemed important to his aunt that he meet the man.

The right barn door hanging open greeted him when he crested the last rocky dune. The lobster's voice rang out within. "Back away!"

Donovan raced into the barn to find a literal inferno.

A tall thin woman dressed in black stood amid a tornado of flames, its uppermost reaches licking at the rafters overhead. Thankfully, there was no hay to be found, but the wood already looked blackened. It wouldn't be much longer before it caught fire.

Clearly frightened of the heat coming from the Faerie, Roderick cowered in a corner.

With her hands on her hips, the woman was chewing out the lobster. "And just why was she not here to break bread with me this morn?" There was a slight echo to her voice, which was rather smooth despite her angry volume. "You'll cook even faster in your current state, warlock."

"Um, excuse me?" Donovan said, not even sure he knew why he spoke up.

The woman whirled around, sending a wave of heat Donovan's way. Despite it feeling like the very air was igniting his eyebrows, he didn't flinch. His uncle would've been proud of how he stood his ground.

Of course, Donovan was unsure if his expression betrayed the true terror he felt. Something about how the fiery Fae looked him up and down made him think he'd telegraphed just how spooked he was.

"And who are you, grubby little child?" Her long black hair spiraled upward, the center of the fiery cyclone.

"Donovan Strong, fair lady." He glanced at Roderick. Being polite might save both their hides. *No one needs to be parboiled today.*

The lobster floated out of the corner and situated himself behind Donovan, resting the tip of a claw on the boy's shoulder. "Esmel's nephew," he announced to the Faerie. "A sad turn of events. The poor boy lost both his parents and was away with his uncle for a time. Little orphan's staying with his aunt now. He needs our support, don't you think?"

"Same bloodline as Esmel, of course. Sadly, your mother never had the honor of meeting me."

She curtsied, and her flames dwindled until they were just a flickering crown. Her hair settled to her shoulders as her expression softened. Above, the rafters smoldered but none looked on fire.

Employing exquisite grace, the Faerie dropped to one knee and bowed her head. "Lady Reena at your service. I'm sorry you had to see me like that. My clan's emotions can really flare up. We feel everything so deeply. I was merely asking the warlock here if he knew when Esmel might attend to me this morn. I was also about to inquire as to whether any other emissaries had arrived."

"Three guests overnight including yourself. My aunt is at the gateways, greeting some recent arrivals. She should be along shortly."

"Did she say whether Grandl would be attending?" She raised an eyebrow.

Staring out the barn door opening, Donovan said, "He's around here somewhere. I just met him and his fellow emissary." The water representative had a history with her.

She asked, "He brought another with him? Who?"

"A fledgling. A boy that's his replacement," Donovan replied. "This is going to be his last Convocation."

Reena paused, looking briefly sad as she absorbed what he'd said. "I would like to catch up with him."

"Well, I'm sure you will." Not that Grandl seemed too fond of her. Then again, who knew? How grown-ups acted when they liked each other tended to be confusing. Donovan knew people caught up in romance sent a lot of mixed signals to one another. He hoped to never worry about that. Falling for a girl seemed way too complicated, even more than adapting to finding out magic existed in the world.

Reena rose and marched past them. "Please display discretion. There's no reason your aunt needs to know about my little tantrum. I'm afraid traveling between realms can do that to one. It's positively draining. I'll be down at the water's edge if anyone inquires as to my whereabouts."

"Nice to meet you, kind lady." Donovan waved.

She looked over her shoulder at him. "And you too, young Strong. You are gracious and a delight. So sorry about your parents."

He didn't respond beyond just a slight nod of acknowledgment. Both he and Roderick watched the Fae until she disappeared behind the first rocky dune.

The lobster tapped Donovan's head with an antenna. "Many thanks. Reena is so volatile. She's consistently inconsistent. I really worried she was going to do something drastic."

"Like make you the catch of the day?"

The warlock laughed. "You have a sharp tongue for one so little and pale."

"Aunt Esmel wants me to meet Egon and then hang with you. She said to take me to the North Beach at one."

"Oh she did, did she? That blasted woman has my whole day planned out for me, does she? Well, I just don't know about that. I mean, I had plans."

Donovan remembered Roderick enjoyed hearing himself talk about his favorite subject: himself. "I really would like to hear about your former life as a warlock. When do you think your curse will run its course?"

The lobster sailed out of the barn, scooting Donovan ahead with the nudge of a claw. "We can absolutely delve into that. You pop inside and meet the cook, and then we'll talk at length. It's a remarkable turn of events that deserves a delightful setting. Tell me, has your aunt shown you the island's waterfall? It's just a wonderful spot for one to engage in contemplation or revelation."

"Nope." Donovan raced onto the porch. The lobster stayed put, not even mounting the front steps. "You coming?"

The lobster frowned, which was a ridiculously complex expression that almost made Donovan guffaw. "I'm afraid my armored girth is just too much for the narrow confines of your aunt's hamlet. One day, I'll walk its halls again. You go on. Egon'll be in the kitchen. Good fellow never leaves it, actually. Has a cot there and everything. He's one dedicated chef."

It pleased Donovan that the lobster didn't seem as cranky as before. Seeing as the crustacean was assigned to be his would-be guardian, he'd try to stay on the warlock's good side.

It had been just him and his uncle for so long. He was meeting so many new people, three emissaries so far and counting. He was positive the rest would be just as memorable.

Despite the dire circumstances this new world of magic threatened, he couldn't help but fairly skip down the hall. Something had shifted in Donovan. There was nothing routine about his life now.

Chapter 10
Unseen Cooking

Despite feeling like he was intruding, Donovan pushed through the swinging saloon doors to enter the kitchen. He'd only been in the butler's pantry and the dining room earlier.

The kitchen was huge. And, sadly, empty. No one was washing dishes in the spacious farmhouse sink. No cooking was happening on the gas stove. Nobody was peering into the large refrigerator. On a long prep counter, several onions sat by a cutting board next to a large knife, awaiting their sliced fate.

"Hello?" Donovan peeked around a corner to stare into a cavernous pantry, its shelves filled to the brim with every imaginable canned or boxed ingredient.

Abruptly, a door on the black upper cabinets swung open. Donovan saw the open window next to the door and reasoned a strong gust to be the culprit. He made his way over and was about to close the door when a glass baking dish slid itself off a shelf and floated to the counter with the onions and the cutting board.

A few seconds later, the cabinet door slammed shut and whistling erupted in the kitchen.

While Donovan didn't recognize the tune, he could pinpoint it came from over by the onions. He approached the area cautiously. Was the whistling coming from a radio?

Suddenly, an onion hopped onto the cutting board and spun about as if positioning itself to be chopped. The knife lifted into the air as the whistling swelled.

The blade cut the onion in half. One section wobbled while the other slid about and flipped over. The knife sliced up the onion into sticks and then into perfectly diced portions.

Magic? Donovan looked around, expecting to see a wizard or Fae dancing their hands about and controlling the knife from a distance. He was still the only occupant of the kitchen.

"Hello?"

The knife twirled about, and the whistling stopped. A gruff voice rumbled through the space. "Oh, hello. You're the Strong boy, Esmel's nephew. Pleased to meet you. I'm Egon." The knife swept up and outward as if saluting him before going back to cutting up the other onion half. "Sorry about your parents. Your uncle is a good man. I'm sure he's been good company over the years and has prepared you for this magical milestone."

"Um, hi. Where are you?" It sounded like the voice was right next to the onions. Donovan moved closer.

"Invisibility spell."

The knife cut up the other two onions, and Donovan could tell from how it moved that the utensil was being held by unseen hands. A door under the counter opened, and a bowl hopped out and dropped onto the counter. The diced onions lifted into the air as if cupped by large hands and then fell into the bowl.

Heavy footsteps headed away. A second later, the sink ran, and the water splashed about as if someone were washing their hands. The towel hanging on a rod next to the open window flew into the air and slipped all around before tucking itself back in place.

The footsteps marked the return of the invisible Egon.

"Invisible! Are you Fae or human?"

"Neither. I'm coming in for a handshake."

Suddenly, the sensation of a meaty hand clasping Donovan's and vigorously shaking it caused him to tense. Egon's hands were huge and rough. Donovan slipped his own hand free as soon as the shaking ended and massaged each tenderized finger. "You've got quite a grip."

"You think so? My fellow trolls don't see it that way. Truth be told, I'm the runt of the litter. Not much in the muscle department."

"Why are you invisible?" Was the troll hideously disfigured and ashamed of his appearance? Did his aunt make the troll stay unseen so her human guests didn't freak out?

"Well, because of the curse."

"What?" Was Donovan the only one on the island *not* cursed? It was beginning to feel that way.

"I have gorgon magic draped over my purple hide. If anyone caught a glimpse of me, they'd quickly become statuary."

"Oh, I'm so sorry."

"Not your fault, Donovan. I was a fool to set foot in that awful palace. I knew what I was getting into. I'm extremely grateful your aunt came along all those years ago and saw enough in me to take a chance. She paid for this industrial-strength invisibility spell so I could find my true calling. She also funded my culinary training. I owe her, which is why I toil away on this mortal island, feeding all who frequent the place."

"Can you get rid of the gorgon magic?"

"Maybe. Not so far, and Esmel's given it quite a go. It's not that bad. At least I don't have to look at myself in the mirror each morning to bear witness that I no longer have a swimmer's body. I've put on a few pounds over the years. And Roderick keeps me supplied with proper invisible garments. I tried running around in visible clothes, but that spooked what few mortal guests we've had. So I make do with wardrobe that can be a challenge to keep track of when it's not being worn."

He remembered the advice to keep the troll on his good side. "My aunt says you're an amazing cook. I loved the pastries this morning."

"Did you? I thought maybe I'd used a little too much lemon curd. They weren't too acidic?" The troll's voice lessened, indicating he was on the move.

"Nope. The perfect amount of acid." Donovan smiled at where he thought the troll had wound up, inside the pantry. He realized he was looking in the wrong spot when he caught a skillet lifting itself free from the hanging pot rack above the stove and lightly placing itself on a burner. A knob on the front of the stove twisted right, and a blue flame leapt into action under the pan.

"You sound like you know your way around a kitchen." Seconds later, the pan was oiled and the onions dropped in. The troll moved back over to Donovan after salting the caramelizing onions.

"My uncle was a good cook. He taught me some things. I'd love to learn more."

The troll's voice lifted. "Really? Would you care to learn under me? I've always wanted to shape a young chef's mind. Would you like to help out sometime?"

"I would. Is that okay with you?"

The troll could barely contain his excitement. He sounded positively elated. "Absolutely, but I must honor your aunt's time with you. She made it quite clear why you're here. I'm so sorry you've been dealt such a cruel hand. All of us will help you through your many trials to come. The Twilight Monarch will not get his filthy hands on you." A pull drawer opened next to Donovan, and an oversized spatula hopped out and waved itself about rather menacingly.

"Thanks," Donovan said. "I'm going to go hang out with Roderick for the morning and have a magic lesson with my aunt this afternoon. Maybe I could help you with dinner."

"Yes, yes. That would be lovely."

The troll scooted past him. Donovan felt what he thought might be a long tail knock into him as he watched the fridge open.

Egon retrieved a large brown sack from a shelf, along with a bright red thermos. He handed both to Donovan. "I knew you might need something on the go. I hope you like roast beef. And I hope it's okay I added just a squirt of truffle oil to the top bun of your sandwich."

Donovan smiled. "That sounds yummy." He took the bag and thermos and headed toward the saloon doors. "See you later, chef."

"A pleasure meeting you, Donovan. So well mannered and so open minded with food." The chef resumed whistling. In addition, Donovan heard him tapping what sounded like clawed feet on the tiled floor.

Donovan lingered. While he couldn't see the troll, he suspected Egon was smiling from ear to ear . . . or horn to horn. He really didn't have a clue what to visualize, as he didn't know the first thing about a troll's appearance. Perhaps his aunt had some sort of field guide that contained pictures of all the magical species. He was curious what the chef looked like.

He joined Roderick outside, and they set off to explore the island. Their first stop: the much-touted waterfall.

Chapter 11
Aquatic Dodger

Roderick floated toward the cave opening. "The isle of Stonebridge is a spelunker's delight. Under our feet are miles of tunnels and caverns, most excavated by magical hands."

Judging from the gaping cave opening, it had to be something large. Donovan found himself gripped with excitement. "Dragons? Giants?"

"No, trolls." The lobster spun around in the air and tilted his head toward the boy. The warlock's antennae almost struck Donovan's head. "Excellent burrowers with an unparalleled work ethic. Then again, they have their fancy arcane gauntlets that really allow them to tear into any material. And they needed them here. This island, in case you didn't notice, is quite rocky."

"Did they leave any of these magic gloves behind?" He started inspecting the crevices all around, hoping to discover the aforementioned magical accessories.

"No, they wouldn't leave behind something so valuable."

It dawned on Donovan why the island had so many rocky beaches. "The stones they removed here wound up on the beaches?"

"Yes, and care to reason out why the name Stonebridge and why your aunt made this her home?"

"Because it's a worn spot and allows her more access to magic. It's acting like a link or bridge to Homeland. And the stone part is because she picked it to have access to so much stone magic."

"Very good, but the island picked her."

He wanted to ask how an island could pick a person but didn't have a chance. Roderick changed topics.

"I know I promised to tell you about the origins of my curse, and I will, but let's deal with the waterfall first. There's a theory I'd like to test about you." Roderick drifted into the cave. Donovan followed.

The entrance sloped steeply, narrowing into a tunnel no wider than a foot or so. Roderick twisted sideways to enter the passage. "It's a little tight here but opens up soon enough."

Donovan scooted through. *Definitely not tunneled by dragons.* No way could the great beasts squeeze by such a bottleneck. Unless, of course, real dragons were tiny. He remembered something about small dragons called wyverns. Playing video games helped in this situation. Maybe the makers of his favorite RPG, *Goblin Cauldron*, had a magical member on their design team, a transplant from Homeland that wove real facts about the various magical species!

Their progress slowed as the tunnel veered left, cutting off any light from the opening. But they weren't plunged into darkness because the lobster's claws lit up, glowing a bright yellow. While the passage had grown steadily wider, the reduced lighting still made for slower going. The lobster stayed slightly ahead of him, and the light cast didn't reveal all the pitfalls. Donovan tripped twice on several rough crags. Creeping lines of glowing moss or lichen on the walls aided the warlock's bright claws.

Donovan said, "So you can fly and make your claws glow. Seems like you can do quite a bit with magic."

The lobster shrugged. "I can manipulate some magic in this form. Not nearly as powerful as if I were back in my real body, though."

They wound through the tunnels. Three times they came upon forks, and each time they went left. Donovan paid attention to this in case he got separated from his guide, not that he could do much if he found himself alone in the dark. Still, he liked to think he could slowly crawl his way back out if he needed to. His uncle had taken him to several local caves back home and made him practice getting out with just a little candle. Once, he'd taken too long and had the candle burn down to nothing. He'd made his way through the last hundred feet by touch. Donovan rubbed at the knuckle scar he'd earned on his left hand from the effort. This could be another instance of his uncle preparing him for this. Perhaps Uncle Drexel figured he'd be called on to traverse underground.

The passageway widened even more, allowing him to hear the growing rumble of moving water ahead. They entered a large cavern, the walls of which glowed a faint green. Donovan inspected a patch of the radiant coating. "Bioluminescence?"

"Yes, no need for magic here." The light from the lobster's claws faded away.

Within the echoing chamber, the sound of falling water was deafening. Ahead lay its source. A waterfall towered over them, easily a hundred feet tall. The water plunged downward as wide as a pair of closing theater curtains. Here and there, rock outcroppings jutted out to interrupt the flow. Donovan peered at each small platform, imagining his game character of Orik the thief using his stealth and dexterity talents to bound from outcropping to outcropping as he climbed to the top of the waterfall. Only the path would strand anyone halfway up as the protrusions ended around that height.

The top of the waterfall glowed a brighter green than the rest of the cavern. Donovan pointed to that spot. "Any treasure awaiting us up there?"

Roderick snorted. "No. Why would you think that? Treasure is best stored in a much drier place." The warlock drifted over to the water's edge.

Noting the basin the waterfall emptied into was shallow and led off into a side tunnel, Donovan asked, "Where does it go?"

"I never checked, but I assume somewhere outside eventually." The lobster floated over the pool only an arm's reach away from the sheet of water crashing into the basin. The waters foamed white.

"What do you want me to do? See if I can swim in it?"

"What I have in mind does require you wading into the water."

Donovan kicked off his shoes and removed his socks, depositing both on the shore. He rolled up his pants and waded in, tensing at how cold the water was. That made sense. They were underground, away from any warmth sunlight could offer. "If the test is to see how long I can last in this freezing cold bath, the answer's not terribly long." He shivered and hugged himself.

"No, not that." He drifted closer to Donovan. "Some who wield stone magic can affect water."

"What do you mean?" He glanced down. "Would love it if I could make it warm up! Can I do that?"

"No, that's not what I meant at all. Let me say my piece." Roderick huffed. "Stone can cleave or redirect water. It's rare. Your aunt can't do it. I don't know if your mother could. I believe you might be one who can do such."

"Why?" The mention of his mom dealt an icier blow than stepping in the freezing water. He shivered.

"Since you have a connection to fungus through your father, it might also enhance your stone abilities. Fungus is so interwoven with water. Frankly, I'm surprised your parents found each other. It's much more likely for those adept with fungus to forge a water connection."

He fought the sadness that rose within him. The lobster needed to stop mentioning his parents. Donovan was glad for the poor lighting. At least Roderick wouldn't spot the glistening tears he wiped from his eyes.

"What should I try?"

"Step under the waterfall, but project your magic upward and part the waters assailing you."

"Shouldn't I be doing this with my aunt?"

The lobster's tone wavered. "Well, let's keep this endeavor our little secret. She doesn't need to know."

This bothered Donovan. "Why are you so keen on keeping this hush-hush?"

"Time is ticking. Let's be on with this." Refusing to meet his gaze, the lobster strummed the air with his tiny walking legs.

Donovan waded through the water. Just short of the waterfall, he winced. The mist it sent flying was bitterly cold. He wiped at his cheeks, slinging the gathering moisture aside.

"If you do it right, not a single drop will soak you." Roderick slid closer, clacking his claws together in anticipation.

Sucking in a steadying breath, Donovan focused on the spot where he'd drawn forth his magic before—his heart. He located it by how warm it was. The magic was comforting. He drew it out, closing his eyes and imagining the energy arranging itself overhead much like the umbrella of gravel from earlier. Stones underfoot jostled against his shins, causing him to peek at what was happening. The many rocks in the pool lifted out of the water and hovered in a circle around his waist.

"Forming those into a shield will not do the trick like it did before," the lobster called. "The water about to assail you will knock all that away. You must take your magic and see yourself as contained within a boulder, one staunchly anchored to withstand the onslaught. You must harden both within and without, forging an armor of the essence of what it means to be a stone. Be impervious, be steady and unyielding." He added, "If you like, you can imagine your father's magic. I know that hasn't manifested yet, but picture your dad lending his spirit of support. His fungus magic may just help solidify what you need."

Donovan balled his fists and concentrated. He envisioned one of the large gray boulders found at the shore of his uncle's lake, settling himself into the middle of it. His body tingled at the thought, goosebumps racing up and down his arms. He swept his fists high and marched forward.

His magic cleaved the water, diverting it away from him. He stood in a hollowed-out space that caused the water to swerve away and form an impressive arch overhead. Not a drop struck him. Even the water he stood in swept clear of his knees and feet. Donovan gasped when he watched the wet spots on his pants dissipate, the droplets expelled from the clothing.

"Maintain your control. You're doing excellent." The lobster spoke reassuringly.

Donovan studied the water pummeling his barricade. It was frightening and impressive at the same time. He shored up his magic, pushing away any doubts. He was doing it! He was parting the waters! Could he do that for rivers, oceans, and seas? The scene of Moses parting the Red Sea swirled into the forefront of his thoughts. Maybe Moses was one of the Fae!

"I think you've proven you can do it quite handily. Step out and draw the magic back in. Be careful to gather it up and not let any slip free. Sometimes with magic of this magnitude, fragments of it can break loose. We don't want any of your formidable self leaking out. For one, your aunt might detect the runaway magic and nose into our business."

Being asked to sneak around didn't sit well with him. But he also didn't want to disappoint Aunt Esmel. Best to keep this under wraps. He walked free of the waterfall and back onto dry land. The waters of the pool swirled about but steered clear of his path as he did so.

Next, he corralled the magic and funneled it into his chest, sending the energy calming vibes. *Stay snug. Be at peace. Rest up for the next time I need you, little guy.* He knew he was being silly personifying the magic, but it helped him deal with the sheer outlandishness of what was happening to him. Treating it like a pet made wielding magic less frightening.

He spun about to see the waterfall no longer diverged. If anything, the water seemed to strike where he'd stood in defiance with even more force. Letting his imagination get the better of him, he entertained the idea that the water was angry. He mouthed an apology to the waterfall and gave Roderick an expectant look.

"You promised to share about your curse?"

"That I did. And do please keep what just transpired quiet. I'm very impressed by your abilities. They will come in quite handy down the road . . . in your quest to defeat evil and what not."

As much as Roderick tried to make it sound like this new aspect of his magic would help Donovan, he sensed the warlock looked at it as how it could benefit the lobster.

They exited the cavern and found a fallen log for Donovan to sit on. The lobster settled into his tale with gusto.

Chapter 12
Worst Cursed

A very animated Roderick shared his curse. Every appendage flailed all about, especially his large claws. Several times Donovan had to duck to avoid being hit.

"I have been afflicted by the worst curse. No one else has had to endure as much as I have. In the history of agonies and injustices, my plight rises to the top. You will see just how horribly I've been wronged. More importantly, you will witness how I have adjusted and thrived, facing down my fate with courage, bravery, and valor."

"Aren't those all the same thing?" Donovan suspected two things—the warlock had a flair for the dramatic, and he was being so over-the-top to make him forget about the little secret between them.

"Yes, well, it's the repetition which gooses up the drama that's required to properly report my dire circumstances and how I overcame said circumstances."

So in the warlock's mind, a thesaurus would be the most dramatic and emotionally intense read out there. Donovan tried to resist commenting further.

"I've been imprisoned in this fool creature for nigh fifty years."

Oh, you know it's serious when nigh is stuck in there, Donovan thought, keenly aware he was likely being internally sarcastic as some form of protest for being forced to keep his aunt in the dark.

"It happened when I stumbled across the Twilight Monarch in the Whispering Marshes of Daedylon."

"You've actually faced him?" Donovan perked up. Anything he could learn about the evil he might face sooner or later was helpful.

"Yes, may I continue?"

Donovan nodded.

"He was a foul individual. I was there testing myself against the gossip magic of the marsh. I had come quite prepared to shield myself from the pestering secrets the whispers used to lure lesser individuals to their deaths amid their viny embraces."

"Wait, marshes eat people in Homeland?"

"*This* particular marsh only. Not all marshes in Homeland are so treacherous."

"And you entered it willingly?" Donovan knew he was letting his snark slip into his responses, but he couldn't help himself. The wizard's demeanor invited doubt.

"Yes, I was testing my limits. Being much younger, I needed to hone my magic, so I put myself in ordeals that would do just that. I was certain I knew the risks and could overcome them. I had scrolls to combat the gossip."

Because scrolls are the first defense against gossip. Donovan did a poor job hiding how he rolled his eyes. "So you came ready to fight off their gossip magic?" That didn't sound so dangerous.

"Yes, and I was doing just fine. The underhanded vines and grasses thought they had me mired in some juicy news about the Queen, but my silence spell was working beautifully. I did not fall prey to their twisty utterances."

"How does the Twilight Monarch figure into this?"

"Purely an accident. He had chased a hybrid into the marshes and was dealing with freeing it from the muck along with negating the gossip magic that was slowly getting its clutches in him."

"So you freed the hybrid and left the bad guy to his fate?"

"No, sadly, I thought I was freeing the hybrid, but the Twilight Monarch had cast an illusion spell. His reputation was well known, and he realized I would not save him outright. He cast his appearance on the hybrid and the hybrid's on his."

"So you freed the wrong one?"

"Regrettably, yes. Once clear of the marsh, he dropped his illusion and ordered me to go back in to extract the hybrid he'd been hunting down. I refused."

"And he didn't like hearing 'no'?"

"Yes, so I cost him a hybrid."

"Why couldn't you go back in?"

"Well, I'd severely underestimated the marsh. My scrolls barely worked, and I would certainly fall to the insidious whispers if I tried so soon." He drew in a long breath. "He was furious, ranting how this particular hybrid had been hard to come by and would set him back tremendously. Back then, most didn't know what he'd planned. It's only recently that his intentions have been exposed."

"What happened?"

"He was so outraged that he summoned the lowliest creature nearby and shoved me within."

"A lobster?"

"Yes, a lobster."

"What did he do to your body?"

"He sent it far away, taunting me that I would never find it in a million years." The warlock waved his claws furiously.

"Wow. I'm so sorry."

Roderick slumped slightly, dropping down almost a foot so that his claws touched the log. "Yes, and he was true to his word. I have never found him or my body again. I don't even know where to begin looking, but your aunt has promised me she can locate it."

"Did you run into her soon after?"

"No, I wandered about for many a year, my magic barely a sputter in this blasted crustacean's form. Slowly, I gathered my wits and some magic, finding I was the most clear headed and well-armed magically when I'd visit a worn spot. It was at one of these, this one, that I met your Aunt Esmel and she pledged to help me."

"How long has that been?"

"Almost ten years. It's proving a challenge, but I believe she is close. If anything, the fact that the Twilight Monarch is on the hunt for more hybrids again might lead us to him and my rightful body."

"I hope she can help you."

"As do I." The lobster paused and then cocked his head back to the cave. "Please don't bother your aunt with what you did in the waterfall. She's got enough on her plate with the Convocation and keeping all her guests happy and peaceful."

"But shouldn't she know what I can do?"

"Well, yes, and she might try such eventually, but she told me I was to be your guardian and to not teach you magic. She's a little uptight about that."

Donovan was torn. Why did his aunt entrust the lobster with protecting him but not train him in the ways of his magic? It should be a plus to have a warlock assist in his schooling.

"I'll keep quiet." *For now.* The warlock was up to something. Donovan didn't quite trust him but knew that to run to his aunt this time might mean he would never figure out the warlock's agenda. He just couldn't tell if the man was bad or just desperate. Either one could signal trouble, but for right now it was easier to stay quiet.

"Thank you. Let me take you back. Maybe we could each snag some rest before I have to fly you all the way out to North Beach."

They left, Donovan's mind racing a mile a minute.

Chapter 13
Horseshoe-Crabbing Around

Upon returning to his aunt's bed and breakfast, Donovan met another emissary. The Fae was kneeling on the roof of the house, surrounded by seagulls, stroking their feathers and talking to them. With the man being so high up, Donovan couldn't hear what he was saying, but from his gentle expression it had to be something soothing.

When the emissary spotted Roderick and Donovan waltzing out of the woods, he leapt from the roof and floated gently to the ground as his winged audience dispersed.

"The nephew."

The Fae touched down and executed a deep bow. He wore a simple unbuttoned, white shirt and dark-blue trousers. Barefoot, he approached, not minding the rocky terrain in the least. His chest and neck were covered in tattoos depicting a variety of animals. Donovan identified a bear, racoon, ram, scorpion, eagle, and octopus amid unknown creatures that had to be native to Homeland. The eagle tattoo had glowed slightly as he'd descended. On solid ground, it faded to match the dark ink of all the rest. Clearly, this was the Fauna emissary.

"I am Knord. Your aunt says this is your first Convocation, that you weren't even a gleam in your parents' eyes for the last one. Ah, to be so young and innocent again."

"Donovan Strong. Nice to meet you." He extended his hand, and Knord shook it with confidence.

The Fae was bald. In fact, Donovan couldn't spot any hair on him, not even eyebrows. His skin was pale and his eyes a bleached-out yellow. An albino?

"The eyes of this island tell me you were exploring the caves." He tipped his head at the gulls soaring off. "I trust the warlock is good company?"

Roderick nodded at the emissary and floated into his barn, closing the doors behind him with a nudge of his magic.

"He's an acquired taste, but a noble lost soul." Knord smiled as he clamped down affectionately on Donovan's upper arm and led him toward the cove. "Let's chat by the shore and see what fun the tide sends us."

"Um, well, I was going to rest up."

"A nap when the day has barely begun? Nonsense. Nothing works up an appetite better than an adventure." He winked and rolled up his right sleeve, exposing several tattoos of aquatic life—a fish, a shark, and some sort of winged eel that looked related to a dragon.

Knord made him leave his bagged lunch and thermos on the steps before they departed.

They crested the first dune, and Knord sucked in an exaggerated breath through his nose. "Oh, how I missed the distinctive quality of the sea air of your land!" He patted Donovan's head. "I was being shown to my room last night when your aunt received word of your impending arrival. She was all out of sorts, a rarity to witness with her. She was scant on the details of your sudden decision to attend but referenced how your uncle, who you normally stayed with, had taken ill. I hope the fellow will be okay."

"Not much can keep Uncle Drexel down." Donovan liked how he went along with the lie but didn't confirm or deny it.

"Well, this gathering will be rather eye-opening. Is it true you've never been to Homeland, that you were raised here on Earth?"

"Yes." He didn't know what to add.

"That's so unexpected. I'm sure your family has its reasons. Might your parents be research-minded and love digging into the history of humankind? I've known a few Fae so inclined."

Not wanting to talk about his parents, he simply nodded.

"You're not one for conversation. I would swear you have an affinity with Flora, judging from your shyness."

"It's Stone."

"Oh, they can be somewhat stoic as well. But one so young should never have such allegiance to being distant. You simply must display more spirit, child. That's what the recklessness of youth is for." They stepped onto the beach, and the Fae emissary snapped his fingers and scanned the waves. "I think a suitable diversion would loosen you up. Let me see what's out there and ready to lend us an adventure."

Knord dashed across the gravel and plunged into the water, swimming until the incoming waves swelled up to his neck. He sniffed about, dunking underwater several times as if searching the ocean for something.

The tattooed Fae surfaced and grinned at Donovan. "I found a lovely diversion. Just one sec, Donovan the Reserved."

He really was curious what this strange Fae was doing. Knord was quirky and gave off the fun uncle vibe that Donovan knew of, not from his own relatives but from the colorful ones he'd seen on television.

The Fauna emissary emerged closer to shore and trudged through a breaking wave, lugging two black-shelled creatures under his arms. Horseshoe crabs! Only these were huge, twice the size of any he'd seen on the various animal programs he watched. This was his first time seeing them in the flesh.

Knord fell from the weight of the creatures. He staggered to his feet and marched forward until he stood in front of Donovan. After gently placing each crab on the beach, he warbled at the pair.

They didn't reply but did orient themselves so their tails pointed at the dunes as if having heard a command.

Knord grinned. "They've agreed to be our steeds."

"What do you mean?"

The emissary stepped atop the larger of the two, situating his feet almost at the edge of its armored body. He nodded at the tail. "I ask that you not step on their telson. It's rather painful for them and you."

As soon as the Fae named the crabs' tails, Donovan recalled a few more facts. "They use it to flip themselves over if they ever get thrown on their backs. And they can't sting with it."

"You are well-learned in the natural world. I commend you—but do make sure to experience the riches your realm has to offer, young Strong." He nodded for Donovan to step onto his ride.

Donovan removed his shoes but opted to keep his socks on; he wasn't looking forward to feeling the armored creature underfoot and worried it might be slimy.

He didn't slip off the horseshoe crab. In fact, as soon as his feet came in contact with its shell, they were stuck fast. He couldn't pry them free and suspected magic at work.

"I can impart the balance of a winged rock eel to both of us, but it's still going to be a little topsy-turvy. Bend at the knees and keep your arms out. You might take a nosedive here or there, but luckily the ocean can be a highly forgiving playground." The winged eel tattoo glowed.

Donovan attempted to mirror Knord's crouching stance.

The horseshoe crabs took off, streaking across the receding water at a diagonal.

Donovan wobbled but didn't fall off. He leaned forward as they gained speed. Their rides veered right and plowed into an approaching wave. Rather than sink, the creatures skimmed the water and curved left to ride the wave. It was a little like surfing in the shallows, although they were zooming far faster than the crab's little legs could move, so Donovan knew magic aided their velocity.

"Try directing it. Put more weight on the side you want to go." Knord demonstrated, coaxing his steed to curve left and coast along a stretch of receding water. Just when he was about to strike a dry patch, he maneuvered so he headed back into the waves.

Donovan gave it a try. Applying pressure to the left caused them to swerve suddenly and slam hard into a tall wave. This sent him flying off his ride and tumbling end over end inside the breaking wave. He popped to the surface to spy the horseshoe crab not abandoning him but heading his way. He grabbed hold of it and pulled himself to his feet. It was shaky, but the Fae magic again aided his balance, enabling him to stay aboard.

After riding two more gentler waves, Donovan then steered ashore, drawing up next to Knord, who had taken a knee and was petting his crab. The creature's many legs underneath quivered and thrashed, excited at the attention. The emissary gently rapped its plating and sent it on its way.

Donovan stepped off his steed and was about to pat it on top when the crab just dove underwater and fled.

"Don't take it personally. They have limited attention spans. You did well."

"Thanks. That was fun."

"Yes, it was. And now I'm hungry. I am so eager to dine on one of Egon's whimsical salads. He's a master with vegetables."

The Fauna emissary being a vegetarian made perfect sense. He did wonder if that meant the Flora representative only ate meat. Did the two clans get along?

His aunt called at them from one of the closer dunes. "Nephew, I have an errand for you to run." She waved at him to hustle over.

Knord placed his hands together as if about to pray and bowed in his direction. "Another time, young one. We shall have fun again before the Convocation is upon us?"

Donovan nodded and thanked him for arranging the ride.

He scooped up his sneakers and attempted to race across the stony beach. About halfway across, he stopped and put on his shoes. The uneven gravel was just too painful without footwear. His clothes were waterlogged, and he knew he needed to change before they chafed him in all the wrong places.

His aunt was of the same mind. "Next time, put on proper swimwear. No more of this plunging into the ocean fully dressed. March back and change."

"I didn't know Knord would have us crab surfing."

"Always expect a wild time with that one, Nephew. He doesn't disappoint." She smiled and waved at the emissary, who had waded back into the water and was aiming to dive under. Knord waved before submerging.

Thinking the emissary might surface, Donovan lingered. After a full minute, his aunt grew tired of waiting and prodded him to move along.

I guess he'll get himself that salad later, Donovan thought.

Chapter 14
Spying Petals

Donovan emerged from the house with fresh clothes, light brown shorts and a blue T-shirt depicting a scene from *Goblin Cauldron*. It felt so much better to not be trudging around completely soaked to the bone. It was an unseasonably warm day. Come to think of it, the ocean hadn't been as cold as it should be. Magic?

His aunt stood on the porch and pointed to the woods. "You know the way. Your uncle always bragged what a strong tracker you are. I'm just asking you to be there to welcome the next two emissaries. They'll arrive together because Stone and Earth have always been such united clans."

"Why aren't you going?"

A woman shouted from inside the bed and breakfast, and a male voice barked back at her. When the woman responded again, Donovan thought he recognized her voice as being the Fire emissary's.

His aunt rolled her eyes. "Reena and Grandl have taken their feud to the next level. I'm afraid I really need to step in."

He hadn't heard anything out of them on his way up and down from his attic room. Maybe they'd been civil up until then. How did his aunt know they were about to lose it before they'd actually lost it? She probably had amazing intuition like his uncle. Uncle Drexel was always good at anticipating trouble and smothering it before things got out of hand. Aunt Esmel must be equally talented if she was counted on to host the Convocation once every decade.

Frayson burst out the front entrance, almost knocking the screen door off its hinges. "Lady Esmel, we need your mediation expertise. It's not going so great inside."

His aunt stared at Donovan and pointed to the woods. "Go." She rushed inside.

Frayson held open the door and smiled sheepishly at him before the young emissary fled within as well.

Donovan grabbed his bagged lunch and thermos and took off into the woods. On his way, he pulled out the food Egon had prepared for him. It was close enough to lunch, and he was starving. He tore into the roast beef sandwich and was immediately salivating. It was so flavorful, and the bread soft and airy. The crisp lettuce and tomatoes worked perfectly with the light mustard and Swiss cheese. And while he'd never had truffle oil before, he found its earthy tang offered just the nicest finishing touch. Having grown up eating his share of mushrooms, it lent a familiar flavor to the sandwich.

He chugged the water in the thermos, then balled up the paper bag and tucked it deep in a front pocket. Quickening his pace, he made good time and arrived at the clearing a little out of breath but far faster than before.

The gates all stood inactive. He waited outside the circle, between the earth and stone archways, which were right next to each other.

This was all so unbelievable. He hadn't had much time to process how drastically his life had changed. One minute, he was living on the outskirts of a small town, feeling like an outcast. And the next, he was hitching rides with flying lobsters, meeting all kinds of different fellow Faeries, and coming to grips with a much larger world than what little he'd been exposed to since his parents had drowned.

He tried to remember if either of them had ever displayed any magical talents. He couldn't recall seeing his mom manipulate stone or his father sculpt fungus. Neither had his uncle ever performed anything remotely magical around Donovan. They'd done an excellent job of keeping him in the dark. Not that he resented them for it. He felt barely qualified to deal with all the magic at the age of fourteen let alone if they'd thrown him into this fantastic world any younger.

What was he truly going to do? The more Fae he met, the more he felt overwhelmed. And he had to worry about some evil Faerie determined to snatch up all the hybrids like him? The Twilight Monarch already had two and was halfway to his goal. How could Donovan explore his magical abilities and grow strong enough to face such evil? And he wasn't so sure that hiding in plain sight among so many magical beings was the wisest strategy. If any knew of his parents, they'd quickly come to the conclusion he was a hybrid. Had his aunt and uncle thought of that? Were all the emissaries ignorant of his family other than Aunt Esmel? Maybe so.

His growing paranoia didn't sit well with him. He needed to calm down and trust that the grown-ups in his life—who had lived with and managed magic for far longer than he had—knew best. Still, didn't most fantasy stories with young heroes always paint the adults in their life as clueless or simply obstacles? He really didn't see either of his living relatives that way.

Faeries Don't Exist! How easy would his life be if the sign on the pier were true? Then again, he wouldn't *exist* if his parents hadn't. He didn't want to wish magic away. He liked it too much to want it stripped from the world. Maybe he just needed to take things slow, soak in every new mind-boggling experience one at a time.

Although, judging by how quickly they were whisking his way, even that approach wasn't easy. Already, he'd dealt with magical gateways, a woman on fire, an invisible troll chef, a fauna Fae who could connect with any animal he saw fit, and whoever was about to come through the gates in the next few minutes. He'd met four emissaries so far: two water, one fire, and a fauna. The bed and breakfast would soon be quite crowded.

He studied the gateways, urging one or both to light up. Almost in response to his appeal, the opening in the Stone gate sprang to life, filling with spiraling currents of red and gray energy, like when one swirls two flavors of ice cream in a bowl.

A tiny girl in a blue dress exited and set foot in the clearing. She turned around to gaze into the swirling magicks and spotted him. She smiled and waved.

"Hello," he said.

A yellow rectangle about the size of a small flatscreen television materialized to his left, and what Donovan spoke aloud appeared in elaborate cursive in black ink.

She moved her hands about, which he registered as sign language. Not knowing any signs, he had no idea if she was using their version or one native to Homeland. Either way, a yellow rectangle blinked into existence to her right, and words etched in black appeared, taking up three lines: *Greetings. I am Lut. Where is Lady Esmel? Are you her employee or apprentice?*

"Her nephew. I'm visiting." The words changed on his caption box. *Impressive magic.*

She continued to sign, and her own box offered up her reply: *I am the stone emissary. It is nice to meet another of our clan. Has your magic emerged recently?*

"Yes. I'm still getting used to it." He didn't want to share that he'd thought himself human up until two days ago. That would make her suspicious. "I'm Donovan Strong. I lost my parents a while back."

She nodded and signed more somberly: *My thoughts be with you. I hope the pain isn't still wearing heavily.*

The Earth archway activated, and a tall, tan Fae with alert blue eyes and a curly head of brown hair stepped through. He wore simple brown pants and a matching shirt with metal clasps instead of buttons that ended halfway down. Several large pouches hung from his blue belt. He carried a bow with a quiver of arrows slung over one shoulder.

He darted over and hugged the girl as he signed to Lut at a surprisingly quick pace, his rushed words appearing in a yellow rectangle that managed to keep up with him. Then he scampered to Donovan's side, springing off the base of his archway onto Lut's solid gate with an acrobat's grace, or how Donovan's *Goblin Cauldron* game character parkoured through the narrow alleys of the coastal city of Grimseer.

The Earth emissary smiled at Donovan and landed with a flourish, his boots making nary a sound amid the swaying grasses.

So stealthy.

"Amad of the Wandering People. You are a young one. What clan do you represent?" He spoke even faster, and the spell that projected his words kept up just fine.

"Stone, but I'm not an emissary. Lady Esmel is my aunt. I'm with her."

"Ah, yes. Family bonds. Lovely to have you here. This Convocation is only my second. I may carry myself with the light steps of youth, but I'm almost your aunt's age. Positively ancient, but those of us tied to earth magic hide our many years so well, yes?"

Donovan nodded. His caption box didn't respond. He guessed it only displayed sign gestures and anything spoken.

Lut drew up next to them and placed a hand on Amad's shoulder more to settle him than anything else. She smiled and signed: *Forgive him. He is addled and twitchy because he's been lost in a desert for quite some time. We're probably the first people he's spoken to in months.*

"Yes, my pilgrimage. So you did receive my messenger detailing that I would be hard to reach for a time. I thought not hearing from you might mean you were upset at me."

She shook her head. Her hands worked overtime: *Not at all. I know your clan lives a whimsical existence and that the one thing you take seriously is the frequent Walks of Solitude. Did this trek put you closer to your trickster god?*

74

"Indeed. Can you not see my swift sureness has returned? I'm no longer weak and weary. My recovery is complete from my time trapped with the Ghost Traders." Amad seemed to register something upsetting out of the corner of his eye. In response, he bounded to the top of the Fauna archway, nocked an arrow in his bow, and spun around. He fired off a shot and hit a vibrant red flower nestled at the base of a small tree, splitting the plant in two. "Why would Aunt Esmel let such a foul thing grow so close to this hallowed ground? Does she not recognize a Scrutiny Rose? Someone is taking note of this Convocation's comings and goings."

Lut looked upset. Her dismay came out in how sharply she gestured: *That is worrisome. Could it be the work of the flora clan?*

Amad vaulted over to the split flower and uprooted it. Holding the plant high, he glared at its pale roots and shook his head. "No, that seems too obvious. But whoever placed this here might be trying to throw us off the scent. I don't think flora is to blame." He looked at Donovan. "Has their emissary already arrived?"

He nodded. "Just before you. And . . ." Donovan thought back to his first trip to the clearing, recreating his meeting with the water emissaries.

"And what? Spit it out." The earth emissary raced over as he tucked the flower into a side pouch. He made sure none of the plant hung out.

"I don't remember seeing the flower here the first time."

Lut signed: *We should bring this to your aunt.*

"We very much will." Amad looked back at the gates. "Are we the last to arrive?"

Donovan again nodded. He hadn't met flora or the two others besides fire who had arrived overnight. Those would be air and fungus.

"Then let's be off." He reached out to get their attention. "But we should keep this to just the three of us and your aunt, agreed?" He stared longer at Donovan than he did Lut, probably because he was an unknown. Donovan could tell that these two were close, that their history was complicated. Had there been a spark between them like Grandl and Reena?

He nodded. Lut did the same. They entered the woods, Amad soon making a game of trying to bound from rock to rock or stump to stump to avoid touching any pine needles. He fared well until they reached the section of the woods filled with evergreens. At that point, he rambled on about his feats of agility he executed in escaping some sort of many-legged terrors who called the Canyons of Sorrow home. Donovan so wanted to ask why the Fae would ever willingly enter such a named place but held his tongue. He rather enjoyed the spirit the earth emissary brought to the conversation.

Donovan wondered what it meant that a Scrutiny Rose had been found. Had the Twilight Monarch planted it? Or had someone here done it and was working for the villain?

With every new stone he turned over, more presented themselves, all eager to be unturned and their secrets brought to light. Donovan kicked at a patch of gravel, pleased with the metaphor.

Chapter 15
Thoroughly Trapped

When they arrived at the bed and breakfast, Reena was sitting on the porch, studying a scroll that floated in front of her. Nothing appeared engulfed in flames, which was a relief. The fire emissary looked withdrawn, but not upset. She gave Donovan and the new arrivals a begrudging nod.

Grandl and Frayson were nowhere to be found. Donovan wondered about their disagreement but knew not to ask Reena.

A stout bald man with dark skin and a trim white beard stretched as he walked toward the beach. His robes were a light orange with yellow fringe at the ends of his billowy long sleeves. He wore sandals that didn't touch the ground. As he walked past them, a stiff breeze struck, but just as quickly was gone once he was clear of their path. The Fae, obviously the air representative, who Donovan hadn't yet met, gave Lut a knowing smile and signed as well as spoke his greeting. A caption box formed directly overhead and danced like a rowdy flag from the winds he seemed to generate around him.

"Fair, Lut. Always a pleasure. I see the boisterous Amad is at your heels. My clan is eager to renegotiate our fishing rights treaty with you. It's time to lift the embargo on hunting nail sharks." He raised a frosty eyebrow to spur agreement.

Lut signed: *Not the day for business. Tomorrow will be here before we know it.*

"Very good. Of course, ever the one to honor protocol. I appreciate your professionalism." He looked at Donovan and tipped an invisible hat his way. In response, a targeted jet of air shot at him from the emissary's direction, causing Donovan's shirt to flop about and almost bat him in the face. "Fare thee well, nephew to Esmel. She speaks favorably of your respectful demeanor. I suspect you will enjoy listening to our dealings and not be inclined to interject in any fashion."

He nodded as the dark-skinned Fae disappeared over a dune. Donovan turned to his companions. "Does Sir Blowhard have a name?"

Amad laughed and then replied, "Lymol. He's a lot of bluster. Don't let him steal your wind. Speak up if you have something insightful to share. In fact, you should be the one to deliver the espionage news to your fine aunt." He nodded at Lut to elicit her approval of his plan.

She tipped her head and walked up the steps, disappearing inside.

"Where's she going?" Donovan asked.

"To get Lady Esmel and likely to pester Egon with her dietary expectations. She's quite the picky eater."

"Are all in her clan deaf?"

Amad frowned and shook his head. "No, and be glad you didn't ask that to her face. Quite insulting."

"I'm sorry. This is all so new to me."

"Yes, you said you've been limited in your experiences, but surely your family let you read up on Homeland and even take a scrying tour?"

"Um, yeah, sure." He hated that he lied but was embarrassed his parents had kept him in the dark. They'd only been trying to shield him. Being told one might be mired in a horrible prophecy isn't an easy conversation to strike up with a child.

"And you've encountered a deaf human before, yes?"

He actually hadn't but didn't want to admit such. "Of course. I'm sorry. I didn't mean to offend."

"No worries. Just treat her nice. Lut is special to me."

Donovan gave a weak salute.

The stone emissary exited the house with Aunt Esmel, who gave him an expectant look and said, "Lut shared you have some sensitive information about your diet?"

Reena glanced at him out of the corner of her eye.

Smart. Lut hadn't wanted to raise suspicion. "Yes, it's a little embarrassing. Mind if we talk about it discreetly?"

Amad headed toward the house. "Lut and I shall settle into our rooms. I trust our clothing arrived ahead of time in our wardrobes?"

"Yes, your garb is all accounted for and no worse for wear after being shuttled between dimensions." Aunt Esmel walked to the barn. "Let's discuss with Roderick. I'm sure he'd love to know the story behind why shellfish upsets your sensitive tummy." She smiled.

Reena snickered and went back to studying her scroll.

Donovan closed the barn doors behind them.

Roderick floated next to his aunt, clearly upset. "Must we? I caught a few vibrations of your conversation. Just not sure I need to hear how seafood makes the boy gassy."

Aunt Esmel lowered her voice. "Not to worry. That's not our true topic. Donovan, along with Lut and Amad, discovered something disturbing. The stone emissary didn't spell it out because there were other eyes and ears all around us and her translation magic broadcasts everything she says. I'm sure it's more than just Donovan's dietary peculiarities."

"Then let's get on with it." The lobster tapped his walking feet expectantly.

"Amad spotted a Scrutiny Rose growing at the gateways," Donovan said.

Aunt Esmel reacted with slight shock. "Really? Do you have it with you?"

"No, he shot it and stuffed it in one of his pouches. They were both really bothered and wanted to limit who knew about it." He avoided making eye contact with the lobster as he wasn't sold on the warlock's honorable intentions.

"This is troubling." The warlock floated lower, allowing his tail to touch the ground.

"Is it the work of the Twilight Monarch?" Donovan asked.

"Likely. I've never had such a breach of security on the island before." His aunt rubbed at her brow. "We have to assume that the rose transmitted your two appearances and that he knows you're here."

"So do I have to leave?"

"There's a bit of a snag with doing that," she said.

"Meaning?" Donovan asked.

"Well, I'll have to take credit for this little snafu. I assisted your aunt in establishing some extra security for this Convocation. The spell I wove locks the island down once all emissaries have arrived. No one can come and go until the Convocation ends."

"But that's good. I mean, if he's not here yet. Is he here yet? Do you know?" Donovan resorted to lots of questions when he was anxious, both out loud and in his head.

"Well, yes." Aunt Esmel raised a finger. "There's that possibility. But there's also the chance he saw you when I brought you out to the gateways this morning and is already here."

Donovan slumped against a wooden post. "Do you have a spell that lets you know who's here on the island?" He imagined the map on a video game with icons showing everyone and their location on the island.

"That would be a wise one to cast, but I really can't muster that much magic. And to do such now would take longer than the Convocation runs." Roderick stroked a claw through the space below his mouth.

Donovan wondered if the warlock had a beard when he was human. The gesture made him think he did.

"What do we do? Do we tell everyone to be on the lookout?" Donovan glanced through the gap between the doors. Reena still sat on the porch, out of earshot.

His aunt said, "No, because someone planted that rose. Anyone could be working with him."

"Well, not Lut and Amad," Donovan offered. "They arrived after the rose was already here."

"Very astute," Roderick said.

"What should we do?" Donovan asked.

"Go about our normal routine. We can't let anyone know we suspect anything. That means Roderick will need to shadow you whenever you leave the bed and breakfast."

"What about in the house?" Donovan said.

"Well, either myself or Lut or Amad could be enlisted in safeguarding you. I'd even say Egon could be brought in on this, but no one else. One of the emissaries is working with the Twilight Monarch. We need to flush them out somehow."

"And we need to hope we're prepared for when the base villain makes his move. I fear we are lacking there." The warlock appeared genuinely rattled, which was not a pleasant look on a lobster. His antennae were quite aflutter, and he squirmed this way and that in mid-air.

Aunt Esmel scolded him. "Get ahold of yourself, Roddy. We can't let our apprehension show."

"Yes, you're right. I'm just not at all pleased about our circumstances. I don't think I'm ready to confront the villain and demand he reveal where he's stowed away my body."

Aunt Esmel looked at him as if she were surprised.

"I told your nephew all about my connection to him. We have a mutual adversary, which means our goals align."

Such a strange way of putting it, Donovan thought. It didn't instill him with confidence that the lobster cared about his fate one bit. If it meant finding out how to be put back in his rightful body, the warlock came across as a little desperate. Could Donovan truly count on him? "We're on the same team, right?"

"Of course. That's what I said. We are bound in our identical goals. We shall prevail. Evil will not win out, not on our watch." The warlock seemed to be rallying a bit too much.

Donovan was about to call him out when his aunt shook her head at him.

She seemed weary of their back and forth and waved at Donovan as she flung open one of the doors. "Come, come. Off to North Beach for some important training. You two are allies. Please act like such."

Chapter 16
Casting the Last Stone

Aunt Esmel didn't let the warlock tag along. She checked in with her guests and then met Donovan on the back porch.

His aunt pointed to a small trail that led into the woods, which was the opposite direction of the gateways. They entered, and Donovan soon found this section of forest to be much denser. He had to watch out for far more branches and exposed roots than on their earlier treks.

Once deep among the tall hardwoods, his aunt spoke in a hushed tone. "So you've met all the emissaries except for Flora and Fungus."

He nodded and batted at an insect buzzing around his ears.

"Princess Ny, the flora representative, is not a suspect. Her people are far too timid, and they have a history with the Twilight Monarch. Their territory borders his stomping grounds in the Alldeep Mountains. They would like nothing more than to see him gone from Homeland."

"What about my dad's clan?"

"Slim chance, but it might be better if you tell me your thoughts. You have a fresher take on them since I know all the emissaries except for Grandl's protégé. And Frayson doesn't seem to be sneaky enough to align with someone so vile."

Donovan thought for a second, long enough to stop paying attention and whack his forehead on a low-hanging branch. He rubbed at the scrape and hoped it wouldn't bleed.

"Let me get you started. What are your thoughts about Reena?"

"She's got a temper and feels wronged by Grandl. I don't think she'd team up with a bad guy. She's all about drama, but it *has* to be about her. If she were in cahoots with the Twilight Monarch, that would rob her of the spotlight."

"Very observant." She smiled. "I can see your uncle's influence on you. Drexel spoke highly of how intuitive you are. Reena is an obvious choice. We shouldn't rule her out, but I think she's too selfish to work for another like you stated."

He appreciated how his aunt was letting him take the lead. Uncle Drexel often used the same approach with his lessons.

"So what about Knord? I hear you got to hang out with him." She started up a steep slope littered with pebbles.

"He took me to the beach, and we rode horseshoe crabs. It was a lot of fun."

"And why do you think he spent so much time with you?" She squinted ahead and took a sudden right, not happy with a thick patch of thorns she'd spotted in their path.

"Well, he was dead set on getting me to come out of my shell. He advocated I be adventurous. I don't think he's working with the bad guy."

"But what if he took the time to bond so you wouldn't dare suspect him? What if he was feeling you out, seeing just how much he could get away with? Have you thought that perhaps encouraging you to be a thrillseeker might play into his plan?"

"How so?"

"He's gauging if you might be drawn into his plot just because you are thirsty for something different. That's how I'd do it if I was trying to manipulate a boy whose uncle kept him locked up tight and away from much contact all these years."

Donovan slipped and slid down the slope, annoyed it was gravel that had proven to make their route more treacherous. "Maybe I should add *you* to the list of suspects."

She laughed. "Not a bad idea, but that would require a great deal of expertise to either mimic my appearance or take me over. I don't think this Twilight Monarch has that much power. Yet."

"He's only got two hybrids, and one seemed not fully under his control."

"Yes, well, please don't count that one as an ally. I'm sure he'll be confidently pulling her strings when next we face her."

"I don't understand this prophecy. What's he going to get out of it? How does having four hybrids help him?"

"I wish I could tell you more, but prophecies tend to be cryptic, and this one is quite old, much of its specifics lost. I can only speculate that it will give him massive amounts of dark magic."

"It sure would be nice if there was a prophecy revealing how I need to go about saving the day."

His aunt laughed. "Would that magic was so easy."

"Why do you have that sign on the dock? The one that says Faeries don't exist?"

"We have human guests and contractors on the island from time to time. The sign is infused with a spell that hides any magic happenings to the mere mortal. I just thought it would be funny to state the obvious."

She crested the hill and concentrated on the gravel still causing Donovan so much difficulty. The stones seemed to cling to each other and not slide about as much. He looked ahead to see she'd maneuvered several clusters of rocks together to create a dozen handholds and footholds.

Latching onto one just above his head, he tested its give. It held fast, and he worked his way forward until he'd made short work of the rest of his climb. He stood and brushed off some of the debris clinging to his clothes. "Thank you."

"I should've had you do it. It's good practice." She put her hands on her hips. "As for relying on someone else to script your fate, just don't. What will get us out of this is trusting in ourselves and others. The Twilight Monarch knows that. He's clever and wants us to doubt those around us."

"But you just made me suspicious of nearly everyone!"

"Now, now. It was merely a mental exercise. Don't go thinking I want you to see enemies around every corner. At the most, there's one person on Stonebridge who's a traitor. We just have to be cautious." She fairly jogged down the hill, which was mostly grass on this side.

They crossed a small stream, which made Donovan wonder if it was where the water underground flowed into, but he was so turned around he couldn't be sure. They'd been so caught up in conversation that he hadn't kept track of their progress. He felt that maybe they were too far away from the waterfall for it to be connected to the stream. He was about to ask his aunt when she waved at him to get his attention.

"Donovan, eyes forward." She stabbed a finger at the next small hill.

A massive boulder rolled toward them. It knocked over a small pine and skewed left, bouncing high when it hit a rock outcropping.

"Is this a test?" he asked.

"Not my doing. Let's move." She grabbed him by the collar and yanked right.

They scrambled up the hill. Thankfully, there was very little gravel to slow their progress.

The boulder hit a stump and bounced even higher and away.

"It's really off course. We're safe." He let out a sigh.

In mid-air, the boulder changed direction. When it crashed to the ground, it was back on track to steamroll over them.

"Wait, how'd—"

"Magic. Hurry! We have to get higher, let gravity help us."

They shot forward, rushing uphill with surprising swiftness.

The boulder struck a tall oak, went airborne again, and veered even more on course to hit them.

Ahead, the slope was littered with large, flat stones. With how steep their ascent was becoming, Donovan was positive they'd slip and slide all about.

His aunt tripped, slamming her chin into the ground. She shot back up and pointed to the field of stones. "Pick a decent-sized one and concentrate on it. Vault onto that rock and prod it to fly you forward."

Donovan doubted he could coax that much magic out of any stone.

The boulder thundered toward them. If they had any hopes of getting above it and letting gravity work its magic, they needed a miracle.

"We can do this, Donovan. You are your mother's son, and she would eat that boulder for breakfast."

Donovan honed in on a gray flat slab, one that would make a fitting stepping stone in a rock garden. He concentrated and rallied his magic to race forth. There was no sign it had, but he felt he'd accomplished something. He leapt into the rocks and landed on the stone in question after three scrambling strides.

The winds whipped all about, buffeting them.

His aunt landed on a surfboard-sized stone, and it catapulted her uphill, sticking to her shoes as she flew high.

He demanded the slab he'd mounted do the same. He felt it surge forward and fling him hard. His ride also stuck to his shoes, propelling him uphill. Like how he'd ridden the crab, the magic underfoot seemed to also spread up and all over him, aiding in keeping him balanced and in place.

The boulder slammed into the rocks to his left, but it didn't bounce high again. It rolled past them, seemingly losing its magical support.

The winds died down in that instant, too.

Donovan dropped to the ground, leaping off his perch and urging his legs to match his speed so he wouldn't take a nosedive into the gravel. He staggered and almost did a split but managed not to plow headfirst into the ground.

Aunt Esmel raced over and lifted him from his crouching position. They watched the boulder roll end over end until it hit a solid pine and stopped.

"Stone magic?" Donovan whipped his head about, searching the woods for the culprit. The only other on the island tied to such magic was Lut. Had they misjudged her?

"No, it only changed direction in the air."

"And it got really windy." He knew who to look for now—the hybrid who'd attacked his uncle's place.

His aunt also surveyed the woods. After both completed several three-sixties, they relaxed and took in ragged breaths.

"So we know at least one of his hybrids is here." Donovan thought he spotted movement to their right and slightly upslope.

She dusted herself off and plodded forward. "Then it's imperative I see what you're working with today."

"So we're still having a lesson after that?"

"She's long gone, Donovan. I'd rather we test you than have the enemy do so."

* * *

They arrived at North Beach with no further incidents. He'd wanted to snoop around and see if they could find the girl, but his aunt had refused.

The beach held more stones than the shore by the bed and breakfast. Nothing as large as the boulder that had almost flattened them, but a lot that were close.

Aunt Esmel walked over to the most impressive gathering of rocks and climbed the tallest. She sat atop it, crossing her legs and staring at him expectantly. "Whenever you're ready."

He looked around. "What do you want me to do?"

"For starters, let's not have me limit you. Explore, see what you can unearth."

From the uneven terrain, he picked up a blue stone the size of his fist. Donovan hefted the projectile, deciding it was slightly heavier than a softball.

He imagined his mind drilling into the center of the rock before pulling back his arm and hurling the stone at the base of where his aunt sat. His magic headed away from him, his link to it unspooling as if leaving a contrail behind the rock.

Donovan didn't have a great arm. A normal throw would maybe make it halfway to his target. Thanks to his magic, it kept going. If only his aim had been improved as well. The throw was much higher than he'd been going for. In fact, it was sailing toward his aunt.

Panic-stricken, he felt his magical connection to the projectile unravel. Sadly, the rock remained in line to smack into his aunt. As fast as lightning, he reached out with his mind and reasserted himself. He implored the magic to alter its direction, to imitate the trajectory of his boomerang stone from a few days ago.

The stone changed direction. And while it didn't sweep all the way around and return to him, it safely missed Aunt Esmel and arced over the waves, landing in the water what seemed like a whole football field away.

"Whoa! I'm so sorry." He rushed over to her.

Unfazed, she smiled and rested her hands on her knees, her pose looking very meditative. "Nothing to be ashamed of. You boosted its speed and distance and managed to correct it. That's impressive."

"Really?"

"Yes, really." She wagged a finger at him. "And know that the stones here are much more volatile than anywhere else on the island."

"Why?" He inspected the beach, suddenly fearing the rocks would rear up and fall on them, possessed by a magic with a mind of its own.

"These rocks, as well as those used to construct the gateways, were brought over from Homeland. They are supercharged with magic."

"Wow." He pulled his feet closer, suddenly feeling bad for stepping on the stones despite knowing they didn't have feelings.

"Show the magic respect, and your affinity with stone will grow exponentially. I think we should try something else." She climbed off her perch and patted it. "Try to lift this."

"What?" Donovan gawked. "That's like Stonehenge big."

"Yes, and I'm not expecting you to juggle it about. Just manage to raise it off the ground a few inches."

"But . . ."

"If all you do is work small, you won't strive for anything more. Lifting a heavy load several times strengthens your affinity much like an athlete develops muscle."

Donovan huffed, hoping his lack of confidence wasn't showing on his face.

"Sit in front of it, close your eyes, and employ what Drexel taught you about meditating."

He sat, crossed his legs, and stared at the boulder. *Okay, Mister Far-Too-Massive, let's go.*

Studying the wear and tear on the dull gray surface prompted him to imagine the tides wearing it down. He cataloged all its grooves and jagged edges. The stone was brown with veins of white and bluish gray. In *Goblin Gauntlet*, red rocks could be exploded with the right spell from the skill tree.

"None of these 'special' rocks explode on you?" he asked.

She laughed. "By the Eighth Seal, of course not. Where would you get such a notion?"

He was embarrassed to say. Instead, he closed his eyes and reconstructed the stone before him in his head. He pictured it as it was and also as a skeletal digital framework, playfully attributing weak points to it. This spurred another question. "I can't analyze a rock and identify its weak spots and then karate chop it and split it down the middle?"

"Not yet. That's much more advanced. Just try to lift it. Brute force is required. You don't need much finesse." His aunt sounded irritated.

Returning the mental image of the stone to mirror what it looked like for real, he erased the imaginary stress points and the lined framework.

Donovan imagined the magic as a pair of large hands sliding underneath the boulder. He clenched his teeth and furrowed his brow, suddenly aware he was sweating. A bead of perspiration raced down his cheek and slid into his mouth from the side. It was quite salty.

His senses were somehow heightened. That was likely expected. He had no desire to ask and have his aunt huff her answer back at him. The magic originated in his chest yet again and grew as he followed the beat of his quickening heart.

So brute strength, raw muscle. Magic, you are mine.

The energy swelling in his chest contracted, almost as if it was annoyed by his thought.

Okay, you're not mine. I don't own you. We're a team. You help me, and we get stronger together. He felt silly thinking of it as a person.

The magic expanded, somehow more vibrant and pumped.

The hands image returned, and he slid them forward, dropping both into the gravel and sand. The magic encountered no resistance. This made him smile. Working with the stone enlivened him. He felt energized.

Donovan brought the hands up, lifting the stone with them. It tilted forward, and one magic hand shot out to stop it from dropping on his head. He hadn't told it to rescue him. It had been instinct.

Thank you.

The magic held the stone so it was horizontally parallel to the beach. He didn't think he could return it to being upright.

"That's amazing, but do be careful." Worry colored his aunt's advice.

He opened one eye to see what might be stressing her.

The stone loomed overhead, half its length hanging directly above him with only clearance of about a foot between them.

He sucked in a quick breath. The stone dipped a few inches and wobbled. Adamantly, he engaged his magic, instilling in it the importance of keeping the stone from dropping and crushing him. *Please, I don't want to wind up a pancake today.*

The stone bobbed upward as if suddenly more buoyant.

He opened both eyes. There was no way he could manage enough magic to get it back to a standing position, and he was also not confident he could make it drift left or right to clear his airspace.

Instead, Donovan maintained his magical connection as he slowly put himself in a crawling position. He crept to the right. Feeling confident he was in the clear, he let go of the magic, drawing it inside of himself.

It snapped back into his chest.

The large stone crashed to the ground, sending smaller rocks shooting out. Several hit his shins as he stood and skedaddled a few more feet back.

His aunt clapped with gusto. "That was extraordinary! You manipulated the magic with such expertise. So impressed!"

Wiping sweat from his brow and cheeks, he blew out a breath. "Thanks. It was something."

His muscles quivered. It felt like he'd just run a marathon. Everything was jittery and ached. "Am I supposed to feel so tired?"

"That's normal." She grabbed him by the elbow. "Steady. How about you catch your breath, and we head back in a few minutes? I think a little rest has been well earned."

"I hear you." He squinted at her. "And I see you." His vision blurred, and his aunt multiplied. "Two of you, to be exact."

"You're such a goof. Just sit down and take some deep breaths." She dabbed the sweat he'd missed from his brow. "You did good. Your mother would be so proud."

He grinned. Or at least he thought he did. It was so hard to tell, what with the general back and forth battle between numbness and achiness raging throughout his body.

Chapter 17
View Askew

When Donovan and his aunt returned to the Sleeping Dragon, she went off to attend to her guests and put Roderick in charge of Donovan's well-being for the afternoon.

The lobster insisted they continue their tour of the island. "If you're attacked," Roderick said, "it's better to be away from the emissaries."

The warlock snatched him into the air with his magic, and soon they were zooming above the forest. They passed over the gateway clearing. Donovan searched for new Scrutiny Roses but didn't spot any.

The lobster flew up the side of the largest mountain to where the trees gave way to rock. The only path up from this point on was a narrow route that didn't look very safe. The lobster bowed his head at the zig-zaggy trail. "Your aunt carved that many years ago. It took a lot of time. She doesn't visit here anymore."

Despite being high up, it was still warm. "Why is the air and the ocean so warm?" Donovan asked. "It should be cold."

"Another warlock's doing. Once the gateways were built, the one who minded this island before your aunt had a warlock use a blanket spell to keep it perpetually warm. Sadly, that means no snow on this divine peak." The lobster set them on the mountaintop, a flat expanse that wasn't very large. Maybe just enough room for a small house. It wasn't much to look at.

"What's here you wanted me to see?"

"Something hidden." The lobster motioned for Donovan to walk toward a slight rise.

He made it four steps before his foot bashed into something invisible. Fearing he'd kicked the cook, he said, "I'm so sorry. Is that you, Egon?" What was the troll doing up here? Gathering some rare ingredients that could only be found at this altitude?

Roderick laughed, and Egon didn't respond.

Donovan extended his hands and felt a curved stone wall before him. He glared at the warlock. "Okay, so what's here?"

"Not Egon, obviously." The lobster chuckled.

Donovan walked sideways, maintaining contact with the wall and getting a sense of its overall shape. It curved and kept going. He paced around it until he was back to where he started. "So a building?"

"A watchtower. It goes up a couple hundred feet."

"I didn't feel any doors or windows." He glanced upward, wishing the tower to materialize.

"It has a door that only appears by request. And sometimes not even then. The spirit inhabiting the tower is rather fickle."

"Someone lives in it?"

"No, the tower *is* a someone. It's a living being of sorts," Roderick said.

Donovan gaped at the empty space, trying to imagine what the tower looked like.

"Ask it if you can come inside." Roderick couldn't hide the amusement in his voice, as if he knew Donovan would have difficulties with the spirit.

After taking in a confidence-building breath, he declared, "Greetings, kind tower. My friend and I would love to see your finely etched walls. Can you also give us a door so we can enter?"

The wind picked up, but nothing else happened.

The lobster eyed him expectantly, then indicated to try again with a nod.

"I'm new to Stonebridge and would love to take in the breathtaking view."

"Oh, it's *breathtaking*, but you won't see this piddly isle if you make it up my stairs." The voice was deep and husky and seemed to come from on high.

"Would you show us your walls . . . and door, please?" Donovan asked.

"What's in it for me? No one simply visits to just ask how everything's going anymore."

"Um . . ."

Roderick doubled over, suppressing a belly laugh.

"Well, I've never met a talking tower. I'm new to this magic stuff."

"How can that be? You have Fae blood coursing through you."

"Well, I've been here on Earth all this time and only recently learned I was from Homeland."

"You mean you've never set foot there? Never seen its glorious sunsets?"

"No." Donovan wasn't sure he was getting anywhere with this tower.

Suddenly, stacked stones appeared before him, blinking into existence from the bottom upward.

The tower revealed itself. All the rocks making up the structure were red. There was no roof that he could see, which made him think there was an open overlook. To his left, a wide wooden door shimmered into existence. Donovan reached for its wrought iron door knob.

The entire tower disappeared.

Donovan yanked his hand back.

"Now, I'll let you up," the deep voice boomed. "You can see what you can see, but then you have to tell me something interesting about this miserable planet. And it'd better be fascinating. I don't get out at all and would love to know more. Lady Esmel used to visit more often and tell me tales of what the humans were up to."

The tower along with the door reappeared.

"I can. I will." He reached for the knob.

"Impressive." Roderick said. "Gregor usually gives folks more of a runaround. He must like you, or at least find you tolerable. I really need to ask him what he sees in you, but I'm unable to join you. I'll remain vigilant down here."

The tower responded, "That's okay. There is one other already here. She'd rather have this place to herself, but I'd think she'd be okay with you."

Roderick looked suddenly bothered.

"Is the person in the tower the hybrid who's just flung a boulder at me and my aunt?" Donovan asked.

"She is one of the emissaries." The tower didn't elaborate.

Donovan sighed in relief. The lobster also relaxed.

The door opened inward on its own, and Donovan stepped inside to find a spiral staircase lit by torches mounted on the wall every ten feet. He raced up it until he started to lose his breath. He slowed and wondered how many steps were left. Was he even halfway?

"Pace yourself. Let's get to know each other better before you summit and then I lose you to the delightful vista. I'm Gregor the watchtower."

"I'm Donovan Strong. Lady Esmel is my aunt."

"A delight. I'm glad you hail from that bloodline." The tower's tone was pleasant, sounding like each line was being read from a poem.

Ignoring his aching muscles, Donovan kept plodding upward. "Are you cursed to be a tower?"

"Heavens no. I'm a spirit. I lived a full life in Homeland, and this is how I chose to spend my afterlife."

"As a tower on Earth?"

"It is a dignified career choice. And, frankly, dragons don't have much to look forward to in the Great Beyond."

"You were a dragon?"

"I still am, but my fire-breathing days are over. The only flames I control now are the ones lighting your way." The torch ahead flared brighter as the one behind dimmed. Donovan had been so fixated on ascending the tower that he'd paid little attention to its lighting.

"Wow."

"And what clan do you hail from?"

"I can work stone." His answer was partially true.

"Well, I have a special appreciation for your people. It's their handiwork that built my sound structure."

The stairs should've ended by now. "Why be a tower?"

"You'll see why when you reach the top. You're almost there."

Donovan sped up and soon passed the last torch. Blinking in sudden daylight, he emerged onto an overlook with a four-foot high parapet. A woman with green hair and green tattoos of vines running up and down her bare arms sat leaning against the short wall. Her dress was a reddish brown with clumps of moss arranged in a checkerboard pattern. A fringe of roots as long as fingers dangled from its hem, thrashing about as if a living thing.

"You're the flora representative," he said. "I'm Donovan."

She looked at him with large green eyes and nodded. Her green hair was all tight curls and trailed down her back to her waist. Sandals woven from tree roots exposed her long toenails, giving her a feral appearance. "Princess Ny. Welcome to Stonebridge, young Donovan."

She wasn't as old as the others, maybe late twenties, but then again, he wasn't sure how old the Fae got. His aunt and uncle were obviously older than they looked.

"Ny is good company," the tower's voice rumbled. "This is her third Convocation. She always visits more often than the others and keeps me current on my old stomping grounds."

As Ny went to stand, Donovan leaned over and took her hand, intending to help. Their fingers brushed up against each other, generating what felt like static electricity. The princess snatched her hand back.

"What happened?" Donovan gasped, mortified. "I'm sorry!"

The tower said, "She doesn't like contact. None from her clan do. It's nothing personal." Gregor struck a consoling tone.

Donovan's aunt had mentioned how shy many of the Flora were. "I'm sorry. I didn't mean to offend."

Ny stared at him as she dropped her hands slowly to her sides. "No one forewarned you. There was no malice in your courtesy."

Her tattoo ink shuddered as if wanting to leap off her skin. Ny concentrated on her tattoos as if willing them to stay put.

"It is fine." She turned her back on him and nodded at the view. "Take it all in, Donovan."

The land spread out before them wasn't the island. He rubbed at his eyes and gawked all about until he'd exposed his open mouth to the four corners of the world. All he could see was land in all directions, no ocean whatsoever. "But . . . we're on an island!"

"Here on Earth, yes—but I look out at Homeland. This is the realm of magic and mystery."

"What? How?" Donovan examined a large swath of snow-covered land. His eyes roved past the numerous mountain ranges, dipping into lush valleys crowded with forests, lakes, and waterways. He spotted a smoking volcano far to the left. Sprinkled across the terrain were various castles and homes, many looking like cottages. There were villages, and, if he squinted, he could see people coming and going in the streets and along roads that roamed throughout the land. Farms were everywhere.

And the air was filled with activity. He spotted numerous birds, several people flying about, and one yellow-scaled dragon that plunged from a cloud and dropped onto an open meadow to snatch up what looked like a furry turtle.

"This is Homeland. Watchtowers were erected at several worn spots so those stationed on Earth could easily check in with their world. My tower looks out over the stone and fungus territory."

At the mention of the two clans, Donovan became aware how one of the villages seemed built from fungus. As he stayed focused on that spot, the view zoomed in, affording him a closer look at the hustle and bustle on the streets. He gasped.

Gregor said, "Yes, you can zoom in even more if you fix your gaze. I see the hamlet of Yord fascinates you. A noble people, if a little too anxious about betrayals in their past. They see conspiracies everywhere and have maintained their distance with the other clans, especially Stone."

So his parents falling for each other probably hadn't gone over very well. Donovan watched the trading happening in the town's center. A bazaar made of numerous stands was the busiest section. One vendor looked to be selling canoes fashioned from oversized mushrooms whose caps had been emptied out.

When he looked away, the view returned to normal, leaving him a little dizzy.

"Don't try to zoom in too much. It's quite taxing if you're new to it." Gregor sounded concerned.

"Thanks." To take a break from the view, he eyed the opening that led to the stairs. "So watchtowers look out at Homeland."

"They can if possessed by a spirit. My essence acts as an anchor, a connection to the other realm. If this were just made of stone, the island would be what you see. If I was evicted from my refuge, that would be all you could view. Your aunt came here often just after her sister passed. I helped her feel connected to something. She nearly gave up on her duty, almost fled back to Homeland, but she saw that her life's work was important. She is a strong woman."

Mom. Why did so many he met keep bringing up his parents?

The tower spoke even more quietly. "I'm sorry, Donovan. In my haste, I forgot. It was insensitive of me to bring up your mother." He paused. "Your aunt thinks the world of her family, of you. She's determined to make sure you have a happy life. I know that from our many discussions."

Princess Ny stiffened and looked upset. She glared at the staircase. "Trouble."

"What?" He could tell she was nervous about something.

"I'm an empath. Your friend below is frightened. Something lurks with ill intent." She writhed and grabbed at her right knee as if someone had skewered it. "He needs us. He cannot dispatch her alone."

"Who? Roderick? Can you see the warlock through your connection with the plants outside?"

The flora emissary locked eyes with him. "One who wishes you and yours harm. I can't really glimpse your companion, but I can sense his magic which I'm familiar with. Come, Donovan Strong. We must leap into the fray." She bounded down the stairs, taking the steps three at a time.

Due to constantly knocking his shoulder against the stairwell whenever he tried to match her speed, Donovan struggled to keep up.

They emerged outside surprisingly fast. Somehow, it felt like there were fewer steps than on the way up.

Gregor's support echoed like thunder as they spilled out of the watchtower. "Be steadfast and brave, young Strong."

Chapter 18
Tumbling Down

The air and water hybrid flung an ice javelin at Roderick. The lobster swatted it aside with a claw. His enemy glared at Donovan, growing even more riled up by his arrival.

Donovan raced over to the warlock. Ny joined them. There was nothing to hide behind except for the tower. Donovan spotted the narrow path, their only escape route.

"And here is Donovan now," the hybrid snapped with fiercely glowing eyes. "My boss is keen to meet you."

"Can you fly us out of here?" he asked the lobster.

Roderick glanced at Ny. "She's small enough. I can manage you both, but with our attacker's mastery of the air, we'd be at the hybrid's mercy."

The hybrid said, "Come along quietly, and no one need get hurt."

Donovan had no clue what to do. Flying away didn't make sense. And neither did trying to rush down the path. She could easily blow them off that precarious route. And none of the rocks underfoot were small enough. The mountaintop seemed like one big stone. No help there. None of it was getting flung at their attacker.

Two more ice javelins shot their way. Both crashed into the tower stones, hitting high and away. Was she deliberately missing? Like before, was she not completely a willing slave of the Twilight Monarch?

Deciding to test her allegiance, he stepped forward, hands out. "Look, you don't want to do this."

She grinned, exposing her teeth with menace. "Oh, you think I don't want to do this? You think I'll cave and fight off his magic?"

"He doesn't care about any of us. We're just a means to an end." Donovan recalled how his uncle used that line a lot. "We're more than just slaves to some prophecy."

The girl hesitated, but her expression didn't soften.

"Let us go. Come with us, and we can free you somehow." Donovan wished he knew more of what was going on. His promises sounded so vague.

Her voice deepened, and she seemed to have more presence in her bearing. Her boss was talking through her. "You're just a child. You're nothing. Your hybrid magic, however, is what I need. Simply let me snatch you and the other up and suck you dry. The magic might let you walk away untouched."

Ny seemed to be concentrating on the hybrid. Her tattoos juddered and quaked on her skin. She risked a look at Donovan. "Her name is Joven. She is still in there, just so very battered and scattered."

Donovan didn't know what that meant. He made a fist. "Let Joven go!"

"You do not order me around! Your magic is mine for the taking!" The air around Joven wavered, and the clouds darkened. It began to rain hard.

He toyed with shielding himself by imagining a boulder like he had with the waterfall, but before he could, the wind picked up. It whipped at them—especially Ny and Roderick, who were blasted off the mountaintop.

Ny screamed and dropped away. The lobster tumbled on his back but flipped over and zoomed free of the narrow wind tunnel attack. He flew downward and shouted, "I'll save the princess, fear not!"

Donovan took a step forward. The rain was now a deluge. It struck so hard it stung. If a downpour could bruise, this would be it.

Gregor said, "Use me, Fae. Drop my stones on the villain."

"What? No!" He could barely hear the tower. Joven looked far enough away that she likely hadn't heard Gregor's outburst.

Joven lashed out as if pitching sidearm. A funnel of water shot past Donovan and struck the tower. If it had hit him, he'd be over the edge as well.

"You must. Knock the maiden unconscious, and the villain will abandon her. His tether to her is not reinforced enough."

"How can you know that?" The gust swatted his legs out from under him, sending him on his back. He gasped for air as he sprang to his feet.

"I can read spiritual energy. There are two within her. Joven is still strong, while the other is growing in influence but isn't fully anchored. Knocking her out will let you subdue her and maybe evict the other."

"But what about you? If there's no tower, what happens to your spirit?"

"I can stay a while longer and lose some of myself or head on to the Great Beyond. Donovan, let me give aid. It would be an honor to help you along on your hero's journey."

Joven hurled axes of snow at him now. One smacked into his side, knocking him back. Thankfully, it didn't slice into him. Being made of snow meant the blade had heft but was quite dull.

"I don't know . . ."

"Topple me!" Gregor howled.

Donovan cringed. He stared at Joven. *Please say you didn't hear that.*

She increased the rain and wind, glaring at him with glee. The angry Fae seemed too caught up in attacking to be bothered with their exchange. Plus, she was at the center of the most intense winds.

Despite the rain coming down in sheets, Donovan spotted Roderick flying overhead with the princess in tow. He waved at the pair, uncertain if the warlock would take a run at their attacker or steer clear. There wasn't much room on the mountaintop for all of them. Princess Ny slipped free of the lobster's magic, dropped back onto the plateau, and charged at the hybrid.

An axe struck the princess in the head. She fell to the ground, unconscious. Joven grinned and sent a sustained wind at the girl, pushing her body slowly toward the edge. Donovan almost rushed over but froze when he witnessed the roots hanging from her dress and those making up her sandals extend and dig into every available crack, stopping her from being forced off the mountain.

A snow axe smacked his shoulder hard, sending him spinning into the tower. He gripped at the stones and concentrated, hoping she hadn't overheard their plan. He had to act fast. There wasn't much room, which made it more likely the tower would fall in the right direction to take out the hybrid.

Best not to try and shove it over with a push from the top. Many nights of playing *Jenga* with Uncle Drexel had taught him the tower needed to be destabilized. Plucking out a few stones at its base should do the trick.

He dodged several more axes while keeping a hand on the tower. His magic spread down that arm and into the rocky terrain his fingers grazed. Pulling the gravel all out at the same time was key. If he did it individually, she'd figure out his scheme.

Donovan glanced over at the Flora emissary. Her roots were even more thoroughly anchored. Her inert body was still being buffeted by the Joven, so at least her focus wasn't on him.

He yelled at the hybrid, "Even napping, she's not going anywhere!"

Joven fumed and directed more of her magic at unmooring the girl.

Just stay distracted for a few more seconds. She didn't seem suspicious. He never once looked at the stones he touched. Thankfully, his magic rarely announced itself with any sort of glow. He was glad for that. Being not so showy might pay off here.

His magic now inhabited a total of fourteen stones. That had to be enough. *A sudden jerk to the left, please.*

He squinted and envisioned the stones rocketing free. Every last one flew at Joven. That hadn't been intended but was probably a good strategy. She'd think he was attacking her.

Joven scowled and easily dodged the projectiles, mostly because Donovan's control of them was lacking. None sailed at her very fast, but hopefully he'd done the trick. She even leapt onto one and springboarded off it, executing a flip and landing in a crouch.

Once the stony volley was beyond the edge, he retracted his magic, and all fourteen plummeted out of view.

Donovan peered back at the tower as it shuddered and began to topple. He leapt right and scampered over to Ny, placing himself atop her to offer some protection.

It all happened so fast. The tower landed hard on Joven, kicking up a cloud of choking dust and making the ground shake. Donovan covered his mouth and coughed out what felt like half a lung.

The wind and rain died immediately.

The watchtower was a line of rubble, the twisted metal of its staircase poking out like the exposed spine of some great fallen beast.

"Gregor?" Donovan looked around as if he might see the shimmering residue of the spirit as a hazy outline of magic energy.

Princess Ny struggled and slid out from under him. She took in the devastation and grinned. "Good work."

"Thanks. You okay?" He awkwardly stood and brushed himself off.

She rose as the roots of her footwear and dress unhooked themselves. "I'm fine."

Gregor's voice filled the air. "You are quite powerful, young Fae."

The motes of dust had mostly settled, allowing a much-improved view of the sky. Where the tower had stood, the curled length of a winged serpent faded into view, glowing a bright red. It looked like someone had constructed a dragon from Christmas lights.

"Gregor!" Donovan blurted out.

A nest of horns occupied the top of the dragon's head. His wings unfolded to display just how massive they were. Gregor's tail ended in a spiked ball. His forearms were long and slender, in contrast to his thick hind legs. Every part of him was hazy, transparent.

The dragon looked at them with wide eyes. "I could stay, help you out."

"But if you linger, you said it would be bad." Donovan couldn't believe he was talking to a dragon, an insubstantial one, but still.

"Yes, my mind fragments the longer I'm not moored to anything, but I think I can muster a day or two before I have to depart. Would you like my help?" He dropped his head toward them.

Donovan wondered what exactly the spirit could do.

Almost as if Gregor could read his mind, the dragon said, "I can produce a lovely plume of flame here and there, but I can't physically affect anything."

"So the flame would just be for show?"

"No, it would be hot and burn, but if I tried to stop an attacker with my tail or claws, it would be for naught."

"I could use any help." He grinned.

"Then I will stay as long as I can."

Suddenly realizing no one had checked on Joven, Donovan approached the rubble where he thought she had wound up. It took seconds to spot her leg jutting out from under several stones. He dropped to one knee and carefully removed key rubble to expose her upper half and reveal several cuts mostly on her face, but nothing nasty. Her chest rose and fell slowly.

"Who is she?" Ny asked.

Deciding to be truthful with the emissary, he shared everything that had happened to him, being as brief as he could mostly out of fear Joven was playing possum and would bolt to her feet and attack any second.

When he was done, she studied his face. Did she believe him?

"When we touched, I sensed something was different about you. It felt like two pools of magic were trying to dwell within you at the same time."

"All my parents' fault." He smiled sheepishly.

Ny paused, looking as if she were going to hold back a crucial detail. That indecision lasted for just a few seconds. "There was also something else . . . with your memories, but now is not the time." She nodded at Joven. "We need to deal with her."

"What do we do?" he asked.

"Take her to your aunt and bind her with magic. Either the warlock or one of the emissaries could do it." She removed several rocks from atop Joven's legs.

"I will follow you back but stay out of view until needed." The dragon disappeared except for his glowing red eyes. A second later, they winked out too. "I'm still here," he informed them.

Roderick lifted Joven into the air with his magic. "I will take her to your aunt. My magic is rather weakened. I can't transport all of you. I assume the princess can get you both back, since she had no trouble climbing?"

Princess Ny nodded.

"If I can find your aunt, the two of us will be in the barn working the binding spell." He glanced at his cargo. "Let's hope she stays knocked out."

The lobster floated off with his passenger. When they were over the woods and Joven hadn't attacked, Donovan relaxed slightly.

Ny stood at the edge, sticking close to the line of debris as she looked down. "Sad to have lost such a wonderful spot." She stared at the space the dragon spirit had last occupied. "I so enjoyed our talks. I hope you will give the Great Beyond a chance, Gregor."

"I will try," the invisible dragon spirit replied.

He walked over to the edge. Going down, especially without the handholds, wouldn't be easy.

His anxiety must've been obvious as Ny laughed. "Worry not, Donovan." She held her hands out and concentrated. From the edge of the woods, long green vines scurried across the ground and up the side of the mountain, forming a ladder whose rungs looked rather flimsy. He couldn't escape the notion that, in effect, they would be descending a vertical rope bridge.

She waved downward. "You first."

He stepped onto the first rung, unnerved by how much give it had. He was five rungs down before he realized he'd been holding his breath and nervously gulped in several lungfuls.

Chapter 19

Ink Makes You Think

No sooner were Donovan and Ny on solid ground than the vine ladder retracted and disappeared into the forest. He eyed the flora emissary with respect. So far, each clan's representative had shown him powerful magic. And all he could do was toss rocks about or knock them over. His aunt needed to show him something impressive with stone magic.

Princess Ny stared at him.

Probably wondering why the Twilight Monarch needs me, of all people.

It certainly didn't feel like his meager magic was on par with everyone else's. Joven could make a localized blizzard, throw water-based weapons about, and apparently summon tornadoes. She could work both her affinities. He had yet to try his hand at fungus. It's possible the villain would discard him once Donovan proved unable to do much of anything.

In an effort to feel less conspicuous, Donovan said, "Do you get along with the fauna emissary, Knord?"

She entered the woods. As soon as she stepped from bare rock into lush vegetation, she eased into a smile. "Of course. We're one of the few clans who do."

"So all the other tribes don't like each other? Is this Convocation a lot of arguing?"

"There is an uneasy truce between all the clans. Fire and water do get along, not that Reena and Grandl behave, but they're the exception."

"Why don't the clans play nice? Was there some big war?"

"It's complicated but comes down to territorial disputes, magical overreach, and, yes, a rather nasty war called the Sundering where dark magic tore the clans apart. Those at the Convocation won't like knowing the Twilight Monarch is trying to enact such a horrible prophecy. No one wants to see the return of dark magic. It nearly ended Homeland the first time."

"I don't know any of this. My parents didn't tell me my magical heritage."

"Are you sure?"

Despite the urgency to get back, their progress slowed. Donovan sensed the time for getting answers was now. "What do you mean?"

She looked away. "Earlier when I felt the duality of your magic within, I also sensed something unusual. Some of your memories were closed off."

"I don't understand."

"Because someone erected a magical barrier, keeping a section of your experiences hidden to you. Do you know how your parents died?"

Donovan felt tears welling up. He tensed. "I don't want to talk about it."

"That might just be the magic influencing you. It's fairly elaborate. Someone wants to keep you from a part of your past. Perhaps you've been to Homeland and something happened." She hesitated, then spoke in a low tone. "Do you have a complete picture of how your parents died?"

Donovan was angry and feared he would lash out at Ny. He drew in a slow breath. It didn't help. "Can you unblock it?"

"I can try, but is now the time?" She looked around, nervous.

He stopped and widened his stance. "Please."

She cupped his cheeks with her hands. The intricate vine tattoos on her arms wiggled and stretched, extending themselves up and along her fingers and onto his skin. His cheeks went numb as the ink raced across his face.

He raised a hand, but she brushed it away. "Don't interfere."

While unable to see his own face, where the ink traveled went cold and numb like having ice water splashed and running down his face. He shivered.

Ny grimaced and dropped her hands away. The numbness disappeared.

As she took two steps back, warmth and sensation returned to the affected skin. The ink on her fingers retreated to her forearms as she also shivered.

"What? I don't feel any different."

"I couldn't take it down, but I did sense which type of Fae magic erected it."

"Which one?" he asked.

"Stone."

The only people he knew that worked stone magic were Lut and his aunt. "My aunt did this to me?"

"I don't know. Possibly, but please calm down. I didn't mean to bring strife to your world."

Donovan charged forward. "It's a little late for that."

* * *

Storming up the porch steps, he shouted for his aunt.

She raced out, quite angry. "What's gotten into you?" Aunt Esmel spotted the princess and nodded. "I see you've met another emissary." She looked about. "Wait, where's the warlock?"

Donovan had a whole rant prepared, but her question threw him off. "What do you mean? He's not back already? With Joven the hybrid girl who attacked us?"

His aunt came down the stairs, guiding them away from the open front door. "Let's quiet down. I've gotten everyone settled. Egon's prepared an early dinner, and most are chewing away and catching up with one another."

Donovan quickly filled her in on what happened at the watchtower, omitting where Ny revealed he had memories blocked off. He was still upset, but knew he'd need to confront his aunt soon.

Aunt Esmel looked around, especially in the sky. "So that means Gregor is with you?"

"Right here, fine Lady Esmel." Two red eyes appeared, floating in midair. The dragon didn't reveal the rest of his spirit form. The eyes just as quickly disappeared.

He paused. Maybe the dragon had been with them when Ny had tried to unlock his memories. He didn't think so as they'd wound their way through the thick of the woods. The dragon must've been higher. "He flew here." Donovan hated how simple and obvious his statement was. "Because it's too tight for him in the trees."

"Yes, it is. Being a spirit, I could slip through them, but it does cause discomfort. I flew high to avoid that." His voice deepened. "You two certainly took your time getting here. I beat you easily. Did you run into trouble?"

"Nope, none." Donovan avoided looking at Ny, who also shook her head.

His aunt approached him and clamped a hand onto his shoulder. "You sure? You look upset."

"Just annoyed." He squirmed out of her grasp. "Where's Roderick? Do you think Joven woke up and blasted him out of the air?"

"Yes, we'll need to check that out. Get a quick bite and meet me here in five minutes. Ask Lut and Amad to come with you." She glanced over at Ny. "The princess looks like she needs to recharge, yes?" She raised an eyebrow at the flora emissary.

Ny nodded and trudged up the steps.

"And you have me. I'll be your eyes above," Gregor announced.

Donovan stole inside, passing the princess, who seemed deflated. Both walked down the main hall. She parted ways and went up the stairs rather than enter the dining room.

"Where are you going?" he asked.

"Egon knows I take my meals in my room. I'm sure he has a lovely entrée already at my bedside. Being social wears on me. The price of being an empath. Attending the Convocation will be hard enough. Breaking bread with such a disquieting group after what we went through together would not be good." She stopped and lowered her head to be seen. "And go easy on your aunt. She's not the villain here. If she walled off your memories, she likely had a good reason."

Donovan nodded slowly.

That satisfied the flora emissary, and she fled up the stairs.

Upon entering the large dining room, it dawned on him that he'd yet to eat in the regal setting, having taken breakfast more on the run in the breakfast nook around the corner. A dozen high-back chairs ringed a long table of rich purple wood. Donovan wondered if it had been brought over from Homeland, as he'd never seen such a wood color. All the emissaries seemed to be there, making it a bit of sensory overload. It became apparent why the princess shunned meals here.

Reena sat at one end of the long table, while Grandl and Frayson were situated all the way on the opposite end. The two exchanged glances when the other wasn't looking. The water emissary in training asked a million questions of his mentor.

"Are you sure we can get the earth clan to see our side of the bridge dispute?" Frayson said.

"Lymol will give us a sincere audience. Do not be put off by his haughty nature." Grandl stole a look at the fire emissary, watching her conjure up a flame to dance in her palm and warm a piece of meat.

The emissary who'd been the subject of their conversation was down near Reena, absorbed in hearing himself talk. The fire emissary, who he was chatting up, wasn't giving him her full attention.

Lymol floated instead of occupying one of the chairs. He seemed oblivious that someone wouldn't hang on his every word. Being so far away, Donovan couldn't hear what was so all-fire important. Lymol also woofed down his meal with great relish, speaking with his mouth full half the time.

Knord sat the closest to where Donovan entered and tipped his head at him. The fauna emissary inspected each forkful of salad that he drew to his lips, commenting extensively on the 'lovely dressing' and praising the troll for his attention to detail.

A large platter holding a roasted chicken floated into the room and slid onto the table. The cook responded to the praise. "You are too kind." His deep, discorporate voice echoed in the large room.

Lut and Amad sat across from Knord. They waved at Donovan and motioned for him to take the empty seat next to Amad.

A man with long black hair and beady eyes stared at Donovan. His plate was loaded down with mushrooms in a heavy brown sauce. He stroked his braided beard and nodded at Donovan even as he scowled, seemingly put off by the boy entering and interrupting their meal.

Amad noticed the man's grumpy demeanor and tossed a roll at him. "Ease up, Brin. That's Esmel's nephew. A fine boy."

Brin snorted and went back to eating his mushrooms.

Here was someone from his father's clan. And the Fae wasn't exactly pleasant. Donovan cringed. The emissary smelled like he hadn't bathed in a month.

Donovan ran over to Lut and Amad and spoke in a whisper. "I need you outside. Lost lobster."

Amad stiffened as he held up another roll, ready to pelt Brin again. "Then off we go." He leapt over the table and landed in the hall, managing to toss the roll at Brin during his impressive vault.

With much more discretion, Lut excused herself, standing up, tucking in her seat, and taking the long way around, stopping to thank Egon for the meal. The yellow caption hanging over her head filled with kind words: *You toiled so much for our meal today. Thank you for such an excellent taste experience. My favorite was the fried knock rays.*

Well, at least it had to be the troll, as she spoke to the space next to a stack of gravity-defying dirty dishes that were making their way back to the kitchen.

The floating plates zoomed over to Donovan, and he felt the troll's breath sweep across his face. It was pleasantly herbal, likely basil. "Sorry I fixed this meal without you. Your aunt insisted I move up dinner to distract this unruly bunch. Maybe later you can come by and we can whip up a special dessert together, yes?"

"I'd like that."

The plates dropped onto the table next to Brin, who squinted at them with disgust. Several rolls lifted off a serving dish in front of the fungus emissary. Brin flinched, thinking it was Amad sending another round his way. When the airborne bread sailed past him, he relaxed.

Donovan felt the troll grab his hands and pry them open into a cupped position. The rolls dropped into the boy's hands.

"Take some of these," the troll said. Seconds later, two apples floated over and were deposited next to the rolls. "And these. I'll save some of the casserole I made specially for you to try later."

"Thank you, Egon. You're my favorite troll, ever."

Something about how he replied made him think that the invisible troll was likely blushing. "You are so thoughtful, but I also know I'm the only one of my people you've run into. I'm no one special." The troll picked up the dirty dishes and bumped Donovan toward the hall with his hips.

Lut and Amad joined him, and they marched to the front door.

Once out of view of the diners, Lut fired up her magical captions: *So what's really going on?*

Donovan kept his response quiet. "A lot."

Chapter 20

Lobster Roll

After briefing Lut and Amad on everything, Donovan set off with them into the woods along with Gregor and his aunt, who took the lead. The dragon declared he could track their progress and would join them when they reached any large breaks in the trees.

"How does one lose such a big fella like Roderick?" Amad said in jest.

Ignoring the earth emissary's joke, Aunt Esmel said, "And neither you nor Ny saw evidence of a dust-up on your way back?"

"We weren't really paying attention." *Because I was so upset at you for blocking off my memories.*

"That's not wise. She's attacked you twice now. You should've expected she'd awaken and try to harm the warlock." Aunt Esmel's scowl was almost as disturbing as his uncle's rankled expressions.

"Sorry." He kicked at a stone, sending it bouncing away.

She stopped and eyed a steep slope to their left. "We have to assume that if one of his hybrids is here, then the other is as well. And the Twilight Monarch, too." She must've spotted something worth investigating as she headed that way.

They followed.

The ground was all torn up and pitted, the grass flattened in spots. It looked like their backyard after he'd spent the whole afternoon sliding down on a large appliance box that his parents had turned into a sled. His dad had been mildly annoyed that their fun had messed up the lawn so extensively. His mom had joked it was all his winter weight he'd put on that had caused the most damage.

Donovan stole a glance at his aunt. *There's a memory I can remember.* So maybe Ny was wrong about the magical block.

"Something big rolled down here," Aunt Esmel said.

"The lobster?" Donovan asked.

"Likely. Some of these bigger divots might be from his huge claws swatting at his attacker or trying to stop his plunge." Amad stroked the dirt as if personally wounded by the disturbed terrain. He might very well be since he was attuned to earthen magic.

Aunt Esmel scanned the woods, moving suddenly toward a section to the right. She snagged a hanging broken branch and pointed into the forest. "Down here."

They followed, navigating the rather steep slope with care. More earth was disturbed along with snapped branches and vines, painting a picture of the path the lobster likely tumbled.

His aunt nodded at several scorched spots on the trees. "She had help. I can't imagine it was Reena. She's been at the house all afternoon."

"The other hybrid?" Donovan asked.

She nodded.

Donovan looked up through the trees, wondering if Gregor flew overhead. Wouldn't he have seen the flames? Maybe not. This was slightly off course from his own path back. The dragon probably had been too focused on their trek.

Amad drew up next to him. "The warlock is a hearty fellow. He'll be fine."

They reached a rock outcropping and peered over the sheer drop. About thirty feet below, the lobster lay on his back, not moving.

His aunt summoned a large rock, jumped onto it, and floated easily down to Roderick. Lut did the same but gathered up multiple stones to fashion her ride.

Donovan expected Amad to construct a dirt slide or disc, but the emissary situated himself so he could climb down the side of the steep rock formation. He looked up at Donovan. "Care to race?"

Instead of crafting a stone ride, he swept over the edge and started mapping his way down. This was more of what he was used to. Uncle Drexel had them rock climbing all the time. He identified the best route, jammed his left foot into a large crevice, and started down.

Amad cried foul. "Hey, I didn't say go!" He scrambled downward, catching up with ease.

The pair made short work of their descent and reached solid ground together.

They approached the lobster. His aunt and Lut were already by Roderick's head, in deep discussion.

Lut's caption box was angled for his aunt to see, which made it hard to read from Donovan's perspective. He craned his neck to make out the words: *He's breathing, but a fall like this . . . he's bound to have a concussion. How can we even tell?*

The lobster's front running leg on the left was missing. Torn off by Joven or a casualty of the lobster's freefall? Donovan didn't spot the small leg nearby and was about to widen his search when Roderick groaned and shivered, his large tail convulsing abruptly and almost knocking Amad over.

"Good lady . . . so nice to see you." Roderick's words came out slow.

"What happened, warlock?" Aunt Esmel said.

"The hybrid woke up, took me down with some ice knives." He peered at his missing appendage. "Good thing I have plenty more."

Lut signed quickly and placed a hand gently near the missing limb: *It'll grow back. Be glad you didn't lose an eye.*

The lobster nodded and used his magic to right himself. He floated over to Donovan. "And it wasn't just her. She had help. Her associate showed up. Threw fire at me. I lost consciousness, and they must've flung me over the edge thinking that would finish me off. Little did they know I'm a stubborn one."

"We need to tell the others," Aunt Esmel said. "This is escalating."

Donovan remembered that the magic wouldn't let anyone leave until the Convocation was over. "But one of them might be working with the Twilight Monarch. Shouldn't we just try to speed up the Convocation and then send everyone through their gates?"

The lobster flexed each running leg. "He has two hybrids and is here for you, Donovan. He can't initiate the prophecy until he has the fourth. Won't he likely leave once he has you?"

"Hey," Donovan said.

"I didn't mean we'd let him take you, just pointing out that the prophecy isn't going to happen here."

Amad said, "We don't know that for sure. He could have the third one already or . . ." He looked around at everyone. "Or one of the emissaries is a hybrid."

They sat in stunned silence.

Aunt Esmel said, "A possibility, but in all my business with each, I've never seen any work two affinities."

"So Joven deals with water and air. I do stone and fungus. The guy who helped Joven escape worked fire. That leaves earth, flora, and fauna. Does that mean either Knord, Brin, or Ny could be the hybrid?"

Lut offered her thoughts: *We must tell them, gauge their reactions. Maybe one will step forward and confess their dual nature.*

"Or it could still be the hybrid is somewhere else," Roderick said.

"We must tell everyone now and be prepared for a more direct assault," Aunt Esmel said. "If his two enslaved hybrids are here, and he knows the identity of the fourth, he's going to be more aggressive."

Gregor's head slid into view above the trees. It looked like his spirit form was passing through the foliage overhead. "I've been here all this time. No need to catch me up. There is a way for us to determine if the last hybrid is on the isle. I can sense the dual nature of the magic. I detected it in Donovan."

"And Ny can, too," Donovan said. "When she touched me, she commented on my two pools of magic." He regretted using her exact words. It sounded too fancy.

His aunt widened her stance. "Then it's decided. We gather everyone together, tell them the threat, let the dragon sniff out if there's another hybrid on the island, and go from there."

It all sounded so neat and tidy. All except for the go-from-there bit. That part of their plan was vague and a big question mark.

"We must be prepared for the worst," Roderick said.

The dragon retracted his head. "I will fly back. See you soon."

The rest found another path home that didn't involve climbing up the rocks, much to Amad's dismay.

The earth emissary teased Donovan as they marched through the woods. "You're lucky, boy of stone and fungus. I'm much speedier on the climb up. Our rematch will have to wait."

Donovan grinned.

But his merriment soon faded. He had a bad feeling. His gut told him the bad guy was about to make his move. He really believed that the last hybrid was among them. Suddenly, the idea of playing the hero in a grand adventure felt all too real.

Chapter 21
Coming Clean

When they returned to the bed and breakfast, the dragon spirit was already there and visible. Knord was outside, enjoying a relaxed conversation with him.

"I'm sorry you lost your watchtower, Gregor. I can't say I even knew one was here." He glanced over at Donovan's group. "And you say Lady Esmel will be sparing no details in revealing just how your recent homelessness came to be and why she looks so fraught with worry?"

Gregor nodded. "Yes, but you must summon everyone outside." He looked over at Aunt Esmel for confirmation.

She nodded.

The front door opened, but no one came out. No one visible, that is. The troll's heavy footfalls sounded as the steps creaked. "Lady Esmel, everyone is at a loss as to why a dragon spirit is on the grounds. What should I say?"

While his aunt conferred with the chef out of earshot, Donovan focused on the dining room window. Brin and Reena looked out, their eyes wide.

Announcing his task, he ran back inside. "I certainly can send them all out. The fresh air might dispel some of the tension in my beloved dining area."

The door opened and closed.

Lut walked over to Donovan, signing slow and steady: *Fear not. You have many allies here. We will not let anything foul befall you.*

Donovan wondered if anything good ever 'befell' anyone.

The emissaries slowly emerged from the house, many looking put out that their meal had been interrupted. A few minutes later, all the emissaries milled about except one.

"Where's Ny?" Donovan looked at the house.

Egon said, "She's gone. Nowhere in the house, and I didn't see her leave. Did she mention wanting to get away to anyone?"

The other emissaries shook their heads.

"What is going on, Esmel?" Reena pushed past the rest of the emissaries to put herself front and center.

His aunt made calming gestures before drawing in a long breath and launching into everything: her nephew being a hybrid, the attacks, the Twilight Monarch likely being on the island, what happened to poor Gregor, and ending with finding Roderick wounded. The lobster made a show of exposing his injury to everyone.

"And Gregor believes he can detect if any of us might be the final hybrid? And the princess could also confirm this?" Knord spoke slowly, as if wanting to make sure he himself had said it right.

"Yes, but she's not here. We'll have to go on what Gregor says," Aunt Esmel confirmed.

"And you suspect one of us to be in league with this villain?" Reena uttered in disgust.

Grandl said, "Well, that may be, or the Twilight Monarch might have gotten lucky that Donovan would flee to the nearest worn spot. This is the closest to his uncle's place, yes?"

Aunt Esmel nodded. "The traitor is the least of our worries now. The villain is likely to attack, and we need to know who to keep away from him. Let's find out if any here are the hybrid. Of course, that person could just come clean and tell us."

No one stepped forward. In fact, Brin shuffled back a few paces and muttered to himself. The fungus emissary was truly awkward and off-putting. Did that make him the traitor? Or could it be Frayson? Donovan's head hurt from not knowing. He was letting his paranoia get the better of him.

"We'll go first." Grandl sauntered forward with Frayson right behind.

The dragon dropped to the ground and placed a clawed hand inches from their faces. He closed his eyes and concentrated. A few seconds later, he opened one to squint at Donovan. "Not these two."

Reena stepped up next, keeping her arms crossed the entire time. The dragon spent longer on her, but he still delivered a no.

Lut and Amad went together. Neither proved to be a hybrid.

Knord and Brin were next. The dragon checked, and they were also cleared. That left Lymol.

The air emissary floated over, a scowl etched in his face. "This is so beneath us. If one of us were a hybrid, their clan wouldn't have sent such to the Convocation."

"They would if that person kept it a secret," Donovan said. *Or if they didn't know they were a hybrid.*

The dragon scanned him. "Good news. He's not one. Nobody here is a hybrid."

His aunt stepped up. "Well, check me."

He did, promptly confirming that she also only held one magic within her.

"That leaves the princess," Roderick pointed out. "She's either the hybrid or . . . the traitor."

The second notion was impossible. No way could she be working for the bad guy. Donovan felt too connected to her. They both kept to themselves and felt drained when out in public. He had to admit to being utterly exhausted at the moment. "She couldn't be the traitor."

"How can you be sure?" Roderick said. "You just met her today. You really think you know all there is to know about the fair princess?"

"He doesn't, but I do," Knord declared. "Princess Ny wishes no one ill will. Our clans have always worked closely with each other. I have spent many a day with Ny. She would not betray Lady Esmel and hand her nephew over to evil forces." He raised an eyebrow. "As to her hybrid status, that I can't say for certain. Our clans have always had a close connection. Maybe she is special and has ties to both forms of magic. What a wondrous thing. I've never understood why all Fae view hybrids as dangerous and disowned them so."

"Because of the prophecy," Aunt Esmel said.

Donovan didn't like the direction of the conversation. He stepped in. "Maybe she's a hybrid. If so, we need to find her. And we need to be ready for when this Twilight guy strikes."

Roderick said, "The boy talks sense. He may not be much in the brains department, but his honor and ambition are unquestionably on display. Might I suggest we split into teams to keep an eye on one another?"

They all agreed and soon divided themselves into groups of three. Donovan liked that his team contained the chef and Knord. Roderick was partnered with Lut and Brin. Reena and Grandl, along with Frayson, wound up together, but they gave assurances they could work as a team. Lymol and Amad joined Aunt Esmel, while Gregor volunteered to fly over the island and attempt to keep tabs on everyone. His aunt produced several maps of the island and handed them out. They divided the island into four quadrants and dispersed.

While nervous, Donovan felt good about their chances. They'd find Ny and quickly resolve whether she was a hybrid. After that, they'd deal with the villain.

His party headed out. Their first stop, after combing a large section of the forest, was the gateways clearing.

Chapter 22
Magical Ties

No sooner had they entered the woods than Knord raced over to a family of squirrels and took a knee to engage them in conversation. At least that was what Donovan thought the fauna emissary was doing. The bald man tittered and clicked right along with the rodent trio. The animals drew closer to the Faerie, appearing quite comfortable with his presence. The smallest even nuzzled against Knord's grounded knee.

A branch snapped to Donovan's left, declaring the troll had stepped closer. Egon spoke in a deep whisper. "Knord is one of my favorites. He preaches the virtues of a meatless existence a little too much, but he never frowns when I serve game to the others and myself."

One of the squirrels glared at them as if it heard and understood the troll.

The chef sucked in a quick breath and broadcast an announcement seemingly directed to all in the general vicinity. "Not that I get any of my food stores from these woods. It's all shipped from the mainland, my fine woodland friends."

Donovan imagined the troll hunching and looking about the woods rather sheepishly as if trying to project that he wished no attacks on his invisible person.

Knord finished his conversation with the squirrels and waved them away. They scampered up the nearest tree, disappearing into its upper branches. Thankfully, none pelted them with acorns or twigs from above. The chef sighed. Donovan took that as meaning Egon was relieved he hadn't upset the creatures.

Rejoining them, Knord smacked the troll several times on his back. Or at least that was how it appeared to Donovan. How the Fae so confidently seemed to locate the invisible troll was impressive.

"It would appear my island eyes haven't seen anyone about in these parts. Maybe further in we might come across someone who has." He strode forward, heading deeper into the woods.

Egon clomped after. Donovan decided the troll was making far more noise than was necessary to let them know where he trekked. In several places, footprints pressed into the softer terrain. Donovan followed far enough back to avoid the chef's tail. It swished to and fro with a comforting regularity, occasionally sending airborne the leafy debris of the forest floor.

"Did those squirrels know who to look for or did they just tell you they hadn't seen anyone human in the area recently?" Donovan spotted another cluster of morel mushrooms. He winced, realizing he should have said Fae.

Knord responded, "They are acquainted with the princess. She makes herself known to both plants and animals." He cocked his head. "Come to think of it, she's quite good with any fauna she meets. That could indicate she works that magic in addition to flora. Why she would keep that from me is disheartening."

"Well, we don't know for sure she's the final hybrid."

"No, and even if she held such a secret tight, I would not think any less of her. Homeland is not kind to those with more than one affinity."

This saddened Donovan. Here he was a magical being, and his fellow Fae might not be so welcoming of his dual nature.

Knord stopped and studied him from over a shoulder. He frowned. "My most profound apologies. I did not wish to diminish your spirit, young Strong. Your magic self is a wonderous thing. Never feel shame for who you are."

Donovan nodded. "It's okay."

The older Faerie darted back, steering clear of the troll and his tail. He walked alongside Donovan, matching his pace. "Now, now. There is much that awaits you. This prophecy nonsense will be settled soon enough, and Homeland won't have a reason to not trip over themselves to welcome you."

Egon said, "There might even be parades and banquets." He uttered the last word with such adoration.

Donovan said, "I just wish . . ."

"That your parents were still at your side?" The troll said.

Donovan stiffened, but knew the troll wasn't being hurtful.

Dropping back to walk on his right, Egon placed a meaty hand on Donovan's shoulder and squeezed ever so gently. "My people commune regularly with those in the Great Beyond. It helps us stay tied to our roots. I could show you how sometime."

As he looked at the troll, or at least where he thought the chef's face might be, he imagined the troll's expression was as sincere as his words. "I'd like that."

Egon thumped Donovan on the back and surged ahead. "Then let's be on with this business and rescue the princess."

"Yes, let's. Your blustery friend is so direct and supportive. You are surrounding yourself with a delightful new family, young Strong." Knord winked. "Your parents would be . . . *are* . . . so proud."

* * *

Knord checked in with a hawk and then a porcupine. He relayed what the animals had to say to the rest. The porcupine had seen a treacherous two-legger sneaking about and wielding a flame. The animal was quite bothered by how careless the Fae had been with his fire, pointing to a scorched patch of ground that he'd stomped out after making sure the fiery fellow wasn't coming back.

The porcupine glared at them, then waddled off into the woods.

Egon said, "He's not the friendly sort, is he?"

"His family takes fire very seriously, Knord replied. "He lost his father to a blaze, so you can see why."

Egon's tone softened. "Oh, that is unfortunate." He raised his voice and directed it to where the porcupine had disappeared. "Fare thee well, prickly soldier. We will not let your wooded haven go up in smoke."

Knord snickered. "Good troll, I don't think your words come across as reassuring as you intend. I already swore an oath to Yark that I would not allow one so careless with flame endanger his woods." He pointed to their left. "Now let us press on with a quickened step. It's clear the fire hybrid is heading to the gates. Maybe all the villainy on the island is converging on that spot."

"That would be a stroke of good fortune," Egon commented.

"Would it?" Donovan said as he accelerated to keep up.

"Of course. You could take care of everyone, all at once."

"I didn't do so well against Joven. Not so sure I could take on two hybrids and the Twilight Monarch. And if he's gotten to Ny, I'd have to face her, too." He squeezed his eyes shut. "I couldn't throw stones at her." He blinked several times and focused on the slight incline ahead.

"You are not without your own army," Knord said. "Don't fret of the battle ahead. Take in a breath and soldier on. You write your journey. Trust that you will not bend to prophecy but break it and shape it into a brighter path." He tapped Donovan's chest. "I have a sense about these things. You have a wealth of optimism within, Donovan. That is magic our adversary can never know."

They worked their way through the woods until they arrived at the gateways. All eight stood in attendance over an empty clearing. They investigated, hoping to reveal evidence Ithor had been there but found nothing burned or on fire.

Donovan gravitated to the stone gate and stared at its opening. "Did they go through one of these?"

Knord shook his head. "No, Roderick and your aunt's spell prevents any from activating until after the Convocation is done and all emissaries are no longer on the island."

A horrible idea entered Donovan's head. "Wait, if all the emissaries were killed, would the gates work then?"

The fauna emissary gasped. He collected himself and tried to appear once again serene. "I suppose that would have such an effect, but that's highly unlikely. All of us are quite capable of defending ourselves."

Donovan hated being right. He had no idea how ruthless the Twilight Monarch could be. But if the villain was desperate . . .

"Let's not speak of such. It's only a wild theory. A slaughter is not in the cards." Egon clapped his hands together. "We should head back and let the others know we came up empty handed."

Donovan stared at the gate that led to the stone territory. It called to his magic, stirring the coiled stone energy in his chest. If the gates were down, should he be sensitive to it at all? He really didn't know how magic worked. He took a few steps toward the stacked archway, lifting a hand to it.

"Are you okay?" Knord said. "You look as if you've brokered a deal with the Ghost Traders."

Placing a hand on a stone at his eye level, Donovan registered the magic contained in the gate. It flowed into him, sending faint vibrations from head to toe. A pleasant numbness occupied his mind.

Red energy flared from the arch, and the interior of the gateway filled with spiraling plumes of black and white discharge.

Donovan gasped but maintained his concentration.

"You shouldn't be able to do that." Knord went to pull Donovan's hand free of the gate. The red magic shot out and slapped his hand back.

"Sorry." Donovan grimaced. As he settled his gaze on the fungus arch, he raised his other hand in its direction, feeling something there as well.

Excited at the idea he was finally experiencing his father's magic, he reached out with his essence. The fungus gate glowed orange, and the mushrooms adorning it swelled to twice their size. Its interior also filled with black and white spirals. They didn't look as solid as those in the stone's opening, but Donovan assumed that was because he was farther away. The fungus magic stretched out to reach him, forming an orange strand no thicker than rope.

Donovan took a step away from the stone gate. He stayed linked to it by a wiggling tether of red magic.

"Fascinating," Knord said, eyeing the magical tethers.

Feeling energized, Donovan glanced at the earth archway situated between the two active gates. Surprisingly, he registered its magic.

He shrank back, afraid of the new connection. How could he interact with three forms of magic? It didn't make sense. "Why is the magic visible?"

Knord said, "Because you're tapping into the purest form of it from Homeland. You've increased your magic, and it will show more now." He approached. "Something bothering you about the earthen gate?" The Fae's yellow eyes darted to the archway in question.

When he concentrated on the third gate, it glowed a pale blue in response. A questing tentacle of the earth magic formed and swam toward him.

Egon gasped.

Donovan lost his nerve and shut down all the magic. He dropped his arms and slumped to his knees, both mentally and physically spent, gulping in air as if he'd forgotten to breathe for the last minute or two.

Each type of magic snapped back to their respective gates, and the energies within dissipated, revealing empty gateways once again.

Knord fell to the ground and gripped Donovan by his shoulders. "That shouldn't be possible! Not only did you circumvent your aunt's spell and trigger a gate, you interacted with three of them. I don't quite understand . . ."

"That makes two of us." Donovan wiped a line of drool from his chin. "How did I do that with the earth? My parents didn't give me that gift."

Egon entered the discussion. "Perhaps you are special. Perhaps you can work more than two, maybe even all."

Donovan looked at the fauna emissary. "Have you ever heard of someone like that?"

He shook his head emphatically. "Never." He smiled. "This is miraculous, but also troublesome. The Twilight Monarch might only need you to bring back the dark magic. He might have no need of the other three hybrids. If he somehow watched us just now . . ."

"Then Ny and the others are of no use to him. Would he throw them aside without a second thought?"

"Yes," Knord huffed.

Donovan searched all about. "I don't see any of those Scrutiny Roses." He peered into the woods. "And nobody's around that I can tell."

"We must get you back to your aunt and far from here. I suspect our adversary intends to use these gates to link all the eight magics. You can't be here, Donovan!" Egon said.

"But the bed and breakfast isn't far enough away," Knord said. "We need you somewhere farther out and more secure."

Egon said, "I know of such a place." His voice was filled with dread.

"Where?" Donovan asked. No way would he leave the island.

"The caves my ancestors carved out. We have to tuck you away underground, Donovan Strong!"

Chapter 23
With This Gauntlet

They arrived at a cave without incident. The opening was tall and narrow. Moss clung to almost every rock. Someone had erected a door frame from several tall stones. *The handiwork of trolls*, Donovan thought. Or someone adept with moving about large blocks. Could his aunt have done this?

This entry was new to Donovan, a fact he was quick to point out.

"I entered with Roderick another way. The entrance with the waterfall is just over that rise, right?" Donovan pointed to a rocky hill.

Knord nodded. "Yes. Your sense of place is impressive. Of course, with this island being so rocky, that also helps." He faced the large cave opening, his hands on his hips.

"What do you mean?" Donovan kicked at a few blue pebbles that had skittered over to him and were determined to cling to his shoes much like the gravel back at the grocery mart. A small brown snake slithered out from a nearby crevice and hissed, upset that the rock-strewn ground it traveled over was unsettled by his magic. Maybe it knew he was responsible for the stony upheaval.

"The stone magic aids your sense of place." Knord casually picked up the snake and rubbed noses with the serpent. "I've seen your aunt even tune into the stones of the island and construct a small-scale model with floating pebbles. It's quite impressive." He gently deposited the snake near a large crack, and the reptile disappeared in a flash.

Looking down at the stones spread out before him, he asked, "Should I try that now?"

Egon nudged him forward. "This is not the time. What purpose would it serve? We are here. Let's get you underground. Maybe the earth and rock magic will hide you more than just hanging out up here."

They entered and traveled through a wide tunnel with plenty of headroom. The walls of the passage were lined with a glowing lichen or moss. *Ny would know the exact species*, he thought. Without the lobster's glowing claws that had helped light his way on the first trip underground, the brightness of the growths was more noticeable.

Donovan brushed his fingers against a long stretch of the radiant vegetation. "Is this something that was brought over from Homeland?"

"Yes, it's brightcreep. Fast growing and a hallmark of any cave network tunneled by my people." Egon's booming voice echoed through the open space. He sounded louder, his tone more vibrant, like he was happy to be here, an earthen roof over his head.

They continued, letting the invisible troll lead the way. Twice Egon stopped at forks, causing Knord to trip over his tail with each instance.

The slope grew steeper and the walls much slicker. Donovan streaked a hand across the ceiling, causing a drizzle to wet his hair and shirt.

"We're close to a waterway," Egon said. "Not the one that leads to the waterfall. We're much too deep for that. This one flows into an extraordinary lake tucked away in a decent-sized grotto. That's as good a destination as any."

Donovan tried to picture the island. Would they run into his aunt? Would she investigate underground? The air emissary had gone with her. The snooty Fae might not want to traipse about away from open skies.

The deeper they went, the colder the air grew. Donovan shivered and tried to downplay how much his teeth chattered.

Knord noticed. "Once we have you safe. I can go back and fetch you a jacket."

"My apologies," Egon said. "forget how cold it can get down here. Us trolls don't mind it in the least, but you tiny Faeriefolk have much less blood pumping through your slender limbs."

"It's okay. I'll manage."

The troll accelerated his pace. The brightcreep gave away Egon's position simply by how often the large troll brushed up against the walls and scraped it off here and there. Some of the bioluminescence clung onto the brute, revealing hints of Egon's elbows and forearms.

"I can see a bit of you," Donovan shared.

Egon laughed. "Yes, so you can." The glowing residue flew off his invisible hide, the sound of him brushing it free echoing faintly in the narrow passage.

When the troll was completely undetectable once again, they resumed walking. He clearly was being more careful as he incurred much less brightcreep on his arms.

This got Donovan thinking. "Could you paint your body so it would be visible?"

"Tried that. It worked but gave me a horrible rash and was quite itchy. Don't worry yourself. I've adjusted to being unseen."

Knord added, "Might tattoo ink be the answer? Have you considered that?"

Egon replied, "Your tattoos are tied to your bond with the animal kingdom and are quite fetching on you, Knord, but trolls don't believe in marking up our bodies. Please know I mean no offense."

"None taken, good fellow. Are we anywhere close to our destination? The few moles I've come across are rather tightlipped and not so free with any valuable info. Now, they do have quite a bit to say about the mighty root god they worship. They gush about lore on that one."

Since entering the network of tunnels, the Fae had grown distressed that they'd only come across worms and insects and nothing he could have a conversation with.

A few minutes later, they spilled into a large cavern, its upper reaches lost to shadows. Its walls were riddled with brightcreep, but Donovan couldn't detect any overhead. Odd how it didn't seem to grow on the ceiling. That had been the case all throughout the numerous passageways they had traversed as well.

A large lake filled the majority of the space, hemmed in by a narrow shore of stones. The lake glowed too but not nearly as bright as the walls.

Knord walked over to a large boulder and sat down. He patted the black stone and nodded at Donovan to join him.

He scooted onto the rock, pleasantly surprised at the comfort he drew from the stone's magic. It almost canceled out the extreme chill to the air. "How long do I have to stay here?" he asked.

"A day or two. Let your aunt and the rest of us deal with your villain. One of us can go back and bring you provisions, a change of clothes, and some proper bedding," Egon said.

"It might be wise for you to do that, troll. I'm sure Donovan would appreciate dining on what you concoct for him. My skills in the kitchen are lacking. I do make a lovely triz root salad, but I would think young Strong requires more nourishment than that."

"Absolutely, but I brought you here," Egon said. "Without me, you'd be quite lost."

Donovan smiled. "I think I paid attention. Plus, with all this stone around, I shouldn't get out of sorts."

"True." The sound of Egon clapping once reverberated through the large space. "Then I will set forth with great speed. I should be back in under two hours. Can your stomach wait that long?"

"It'll have to. Thanks, Egon." Donovan watched the pebbles and small rocks move about as the troll marched toward him. Seconds later, the chef's thick arms wrapped around him and squeezed hard.

"Be smart. Any whiff of trouble comes your way, flee. You are not equipped to take on our adversary by yourself." Egon cleared his throat. "Knord is certainly an excellent defender, but we're quite far from the woods, and not many living creatures call this place home. Down here, he's at a disadvantage."

Knord scanned the cavern. "Yes, mostly worms and some spooked insects. I'd have to backtrack a bit to access the bats we passed under earlier. Pity, as their echolocation talents are such fun to indulge."

Egon left. Although, he could easily double back and eavesdrop on them and they'd be none the wiser.

Knord slid off the rock and looked around.

"What's there to do?" Donovan asked.

"Maybe reach out. I imagine you might encounter some rarer stone down here compared to topside." He marched to the lake's edge. "I'm going to see if there's any aquatic life around that could hold up their end of a conversation." He squatted, closed his eyes, and dragged his fingers through the water.

Donovan left the large rock and walked along the lake's edge, situating himself well away from the Fae. The water was quite clear, and he could see hundreds of pebbles lined its bottom. He reached out and sorted through them, registering their magic. He really didn't find them all that different and wondered if he lacked the ability to see the variations in magic. All the energy presented as red and didn't stand out.

He pulled back, disappointed more in himself than the rocks. Surely there were rare ones mixed in, but he just lacked the finesse to detect them.

He spotted something brown wedged in a crevice near a section of wall that was absent of brightcreep. It was a little surprising anything had caught his attention, what with so little light in the vicinity. He walked over to the shadowy area, scraping off some of the glowing vegetation and holding it out to better light the darkness.

There was something shoved into a vertical gash. He tugged at it, losing some of his light in the process. The object gave after three sharp pulls, and Donovan walked it out into a more well-lit area.

He held an oversized glove. It was dark brown with black stitches. The fingers were segmented and tipped with lethal points. He slid his left hand in and found that his arm sunk in well past his elbow. He made a fist with the glove, and yellow light flared from its stitching.

Knord rushed over. "Do you know what you've found?"

Donovan shook his head.

The emissary said, "A gauntlet, likely one used to dig sections of this network of tunnels."

"Oh, so a troll gauntlet. But Roderick stated they wouldn't leave one of these behind."

"Well, evidently they did."

"Will it work for me? What can it do exactly?"

The gauntlet seemed to have developed a mind of its own. It dragged him toward the nearest wall.

Donovan tried to stand his ground, but the glove was insistent and yanked him even harder. He sent Knord a pleading look as he tried to shake his hand free. "It won't let go of me!"

"Interesting! If I recall, the trolls use them. They're magically augmented to work for Egon and his brood."

The gauntlet lifted itself high, resulting in Donovan being raised a few inches into the air. He kicked about, trying to come in contact with the ground again.

"I don't like this," Donovan said.

The glove flexed its fingers and then dove into the cave wall, scooping out a large gouge with three quick swipes. The dirt and rock Donovan excavated dropped to the ground, some landing on his toes.

Hoping to cancel out the gauntlet's magic with his own, he urged his stone magic to expand.

The glove's glow dimmed slightly, and it dropped just enough for him to regain his footing. He pried with his free hand, managing to liberate his captive limb by about half. After managing to wiggle his fingers, he tried to remove his arm completely.

The gauntlet's glow intensified, and he felt his fingers being dragged back into place.

Knord grabbed at the glove and attempted to pull it off. It gave a little but quickly had itself fully enveloping Donovan's hand and forearm once again. The fingers of it curled into a fist, each of his digits growing frighteningly numb. For a moment, he feared the gauntlet would pummel him in the face.

Donovan shouted at the gauntlet, "Let go of me!"

The glove did just that. It flexed open, and his arm slipped entirely free. Donovan dropped to his knees and drew the recently imprisoned limb close to his stomach, kneading at each finger to dispel the numbness.

The glove hung in midair, its fingers groping slowly toward the ceiling. Donovan moved away from it, and the gauntlet followed.

Unnerved, he scooted swiftly back. The levitating glove matched his move, keeping itself an arm's length away, at the ready.

"It seems you've acquired a friend." Knord smirked and nodded at the floating tagalong.

"What do I do? I don't want it sticking around." He thought for a moment, then wagged a finger at the gauntlet and pointed swiftly at the crack where he'd found it. "Tuck yourself back in there please."

The gauntlet stayed put.

"Move it! Go back to your hole in the wall!"

It didn't flinch.

Despite the accessory not having eyes, Donovan got the distinct feeling it was looking at him expectantly.

"Some have enchantments that allow them to talk back." The fauna emissary crossed his arms and shot him a considered look.

Donovan addressed the glove more politely. "Can you talk? That would be nice."

The glove just hung there, no reaction.

"Any words at all?"

Nothing.

Suddenly, a gout of fire shot past them only inches from their heads, blasting them with superheated air.

Both Donovan and Knord ducked and spun around.

A boy with long white hair, dressed in all black, marched toward them. He glared and threw another stream of flame.

Donovan jumped aside, narrowly avoiding being burned to a crisp.

This had to be the other hybrid, Ithor. What other ability did he have? If Ny was both flora and fauna, that left earth.

Donovan stiffened and gawked at the earthen surfaces of the cavern, their hiding spot clearly a poor choice.

The gauntlet flew over to Donovan and slid onto his arm.

Ithor grimaced. "What? How can you wield that? Only a troll or one tied to earthen magic can."

The glove dug into the ground and scooped out a huge ball of earth and stone. It jerked back, sending Donovan spinning on one foot to regain his balance. Then it flung the mass at Ithor.

The young Fae stabbed both hands forward, and blue magic shot forth, cleaving the ball in two. Ithor waved his hands all around, and the divided earth hanging in the air swirled about to match his movements while the stones clattered to the ground.

Ithor shaped the airborne soil into a thick spear, almost a log with a nasty point, and sent it back at Donovan with a flick of the wrist. Knord stood off to the side, uncertain how to help. He couldn't work much fauna magic if there were very few living things nearby. Donovan dodged the shaft of dirt, taking a second to watch the projectile slam into the ground behind him.

Ithor didn't let up. Three blasts of fire flew at them. Donovan sprinted left, while Knord slid across the ground a surprising distance.

After scampering to relative safety, Donovan concentrated on the rocks at his feet, scooping them up with the gauntlet along with a healthy amount of dirt. He compressed the magic, forming it into what looked like a dirty snowball the size of a beachball.

A plume of flame struck the rock.

Donovan waited for the fiery deluge to die out. A few seconds later, he popped up and returned fire, knocking Ithor on his back.

As he raced forward, Donovan scooped up another two balls and heaved them at his attacker. One overshot, but the other smacked the boy hard in the face.

Closing the distance in two swift bounds, Donovan landed atop him. He elbowed Ithor in the gut, barely holding back the gauntlet from wringing the boy's neck. To keep the eager gauntlet at bay required a good deal of stone magic and his significant attention. The hybrid took advantage of the distraction to swat at Donovan's legs with flaming hands.

His touch burned.

Wincing in pain, Donovan tried to squirm free. Ithor grabbed his pants and applied even more heat, keen on setting the clothing and the boy on fire.

He had no choice but to roll off the Fae and retreat, smacking at the smoking material threatening to ignite.

Rock in hand, Knord leapt at the young Fae, causing a ball of flame meant for Donovan to fly wildly into the ceiling. Rock and dirt rained down on them.

Ithor funneled a column of both earth and fire at the fauna emissary, driving him hard into a wall. Knord landed and crumpled into a ball, unmoving.

Infuriated, Donovan swept up a wave of earth and rocks and angled it at Ithor. It was an impressive attack, certain to smother him.

The hybrid saw this as well. He thrust his hands behind him, and a mass of earth flew into view. It was Ny wrapped in a cocoon of dirt, and Ithor had placed her in the path of Donovan's onslaught.

Needing to redirect his own attack, Donovan flung his hands to the right and implored the magic to veer off course. This sent the wall of stone and earth into the lake, with only a fraction of its mass striking Ny and her captor.

Ithor huffed and puffed, summoning flame to envelop his hands. He drew in several ragged breaths and just stared at Donovan.

Why wasn't he talking? Come to think of it, the Fae had only spoken a handful of words at the beginning. He'd been quiet since. Was he being controlled by the Twilight Monarch and the villain was distracted by having his attention split among all their groups? Was he in the middle of throwing Joven at his aunt's crew or another party?

Ithor's gaze hardened, and he stood with more authority. "You grow swiftly in your abilities, young Strong."

The villain's definitely present. Donovan hoped that didn't mean any of the other groups had been dealt with.

"I'll come for you shortly." Ithor winced and seemed distracted. The perils of directing more than one of his puppets at a time!

Donovan glanced over at Ny, who was awake but couldn't speak thanks to her mouth being covered by an earthen mask. That didn't stop her from trying. She strained to break free, shaking her head about in frustration.

Ithor smiled. "I thought it best to hide her away, far from the woods and woodland creatures, deprive her of her dual magic."

Donovan didn't know what to do. A direct attack could hurt the princess.

Ithor nodded. "Ah, you're not surprised at this revelation. So you knew she was a hybrid?"

He didn't answer.

"It matters not." The boy tapped at his temple. "I don't suppose you'd hand yourself over? No. It's clear you can work three affinities." He nodded at the gauntlet. "Could you wield the rest? Maybe I don't even need this one."

Donovan didn't like where this was going. "Let her go and I'll come with you."

The monarch considered this. "No, I think it best to stick with the original plan. I've never heard of someone wielding more than two. There must be another reason you can work earth as well as your other gifts."

Donovan noticed Ny was fixated on where Knord lay. Out of the corner of his eye, he thought he saw movement. Maybe it was the fauna emissary back on his feet.

Ithor said, "Your aunt is quite a fighter."

"If you've hurt her . . ."

"Oh, I tried, but she is a stubborn one."

Ny closed her eyes and furrowed her brow. She was up to something.

"You can't get away with this."

"Oh, but I will."

Ny's eyes glowed green.

"You don't need to do this." Donovan tensed, detecting a low rumble and vibration.

Ithor registered it as well. He glanced over his shoulder.

Donovan risked a peek at Knord. The emissary was now in a new position, sitting with his back against the wall, his head slumped to the side and his eyes closed, a sliver of green light leaking out.

Ny and Knord were working in unison, bringing something here.

The vibrations grew stronger.

Suddenly, from the tunnel they'd come through earlier, dozens of mice, rabbits, and birds flooded into the cavern. Some badgers, a few foxes, and a handful of deer crashed the party.

They stampeded toward Ithor. The hybrid flung his hands high and glared at the ceiling. He wrenched his arms downward, triggering an avalanche of earth and rock.

The animals scattered as hunks of ceiling fell.

Thinking he could rescue Ny, Donovan tried advancing on her. But a sizable rock and curtain of dirt slammed into the space between them, driving him into the lake and toward Knord instead.

The animals raced away from the earthen downpour, many heading back up the tunnel. Several found themselves buried in the deluge. Ny appeared heartbroken she'd led them into such a deathtrap. Her eyes glowed a brighter green as she shook her head and sent the nearby fauna frantic looks.

Likely telling her army to escape, Donovan thought. He scrambled out of the water and onto the shore to unearth a pair of rabbits.

Ithor howled, and more of the ceiling collapsed.

Knord snapped to his feet and raced over to Donovan. The emissary pulled him away from tugging at a large stone that had landed on a deer.

Donovan used his magic to sweep the stone aside and dropped down to help the animal to its feet. Only it was beyond hope. Its entire torso was flattened. He looked away, wiping tears from his eyes with his free hand.

The falling debris kept coming, thundering louder than the earlier animal stampede.

Knord pulled him back and directed him to the far end of the chamber, well clear of the falling ceiling and the rising cloud of dust it produced. Donovan couldn't see Ny or Ithor anymore but managed to hear the boy's howls over the crashing sound of the collapsing grotto.

"Time to go," Knord said, squeezing Donovan's upper arm.

"But Ny . . ."

"The villain won't let her perish. I'm sure they're already back in the tunnel, heading for the surface." He shot a look at the encroaching dust cloud.

They were trapped. No way could they get out through the tunnel. What had fallen already cut them off from the only exit.

"How?"

Knord lifted Donovan's arm wearing the gauntlet and pointed to the wall. "Be a troll. Dig us a path out of here."

A section of ceiling far too close crashed to the cavern floor, sending a spray of rocks and grit their way.

Donovan turned and faced the wall. He tore into the earth and rock with the gauntlet, mixing his stone magic with the earthen magic that he was now more readily able to perceive. The energies intertwined, supercharging the glove and provoking it to tear into the wall with impressive power. He flung what he carved from the earth behind them.

The ceiling continued to fall, but a dozen handfuls had them in a passage of Donovan's making. He worked with a frenzy, assaulting the earth and stone before him, all the while trying to keep the angle of the shaft heading upward.

He toiled and toiled, pausing to look back when they were a good ten feet in. Very little light from the cavern's brightcreep reached them. From what he could see, the cave was almost filled in. When a huge stone landed directly in front of their freshly dug escape route and plunged them into darkness, he gasped.

Hesitating, Donovan suddenly feared their tunnel would also collapse and crush them. It felt like everything would squeeze him into a tight ball. Suddenly worried about their air supply, he assumed a fetal position.

Knord placed a hand on his shoulder and spoke softly, as if anything above a whisper would spur the earth to swallow them completely. "Easy. You got this. We can get out of here." Several tattoos of worms and insects glowed green on his arms, affording them a pathetic light, but light just the same. "And I have it from good company you don't have to get us all the way to the surface. Just another few feet, young Strong."

Donovan took in several breaths, saddened that the underground lake was no more. Despite his muscles ready to revolt, he resumed digging. They had to escape. Ny was still a prisoner, and there was no telling what had happened to his aunt. He feared the worst.

A few minutes later, weak and wheezing, he broke through and into another tunnel. Fresh air rushed in, and Donovan and Knord lapped it up.

He worked carefully to strip away the earth and rock enough to yield an opening they could exit from, and soon they stood in a much shorter passage. Donovan only had to duck his head, while Knord hunched over rather awkwardly.

The emissary consulted with a large beetle waddling along the tunnel floor and guided the pair to the left. They reached a fork and took a right. The incline grew steeper, and the tunnel height also enlarged enough for both to walk fully upright.

At a three-way intersection, they went right and soon surfaced in the den of a fox. The critter struck a defensive pose and backed her tail up to hide her three kits from them. Knord assured the mother they meant no harm. The animal was on guard but let them hasten from her home without a fuss.

They stretched and brushed themselves off in a small clearing. Donovan looked back at the cave. "What now?"

"Back to your aunt's place. It's not ideal, but stashing you away underground isn't the answer. The villain knows what you can do now."

"Yeah, but he's not all that impressed."

"Is that what you took from the conversation?" Knord pressed at the small of his back, dispelling a tight muscle.

"He didn't take my offer to swap."

"Donovan, he may have seemed calm and unconcerned, but you have him worried. You're an unknown. He's quite spooked. I know what a cornered animal looks like. He's scared and desperate." Knord drew in a long breath through his nose, reacting as if what he smelled pleased him. He sniffed around until he spotted a few droppings on a narrow path.

"How does that help? You heard him. He did something to my aunt." He whispered a request for the gauntlet to let him take it off. It complied and slipped free. When he resumed walking, it followed a few feet behind. In the light of day, the floating glove was unnerving.

"That might just be to rattle you, which appears he has done rather successfully. I doubt your aunt faltered. I'll alert the locals to keep their eyes and ears peeled for her. They know her well, as do I. Esmel is fine. Now, let's talk strategy. Something tells me Ny being with the enemy is to our advantage."

They worked their way cautiously onto a game trail and trekked left. Donovan thought he heard crashing waves from somewhere ahead.

"I don't see how. He'll make her a puppet like the others."

Knord stopped and looked over his shoulder, frowning. "Knowing the princess, do you really think that?"

Donovan paused and squashed his rising paranoia, urging his thoughts to be more clear headed. He knew Ny pretty well, at least more than he did the other emissaries. "She's what my uncle would call a 'firecracker,' isn't she?" He grinned at Knord.

"If by that you mean she's about to spark chaos, then I wholeheartedly agree, young Strong. A firecracker, she is. Just don't ever say such in her presence."

Donovan laughed and let the gnawing worry and fear rolling around in his stomach lessen ever so slightly.

Chapter 24
Opening the Floodgates

They made it back to the bed and breakfast without incident to find his aunt's group already there and licking their wounds.

As they entered the kitchen, it was clear from the melting ice dagger stuck in the air emissary's left forearm that they had encountered Joven. Amad had nothing poking out of him, but his face was bruised, and he limped over to hand Aunt Esmel several rolls of bandages. She appeared unharmed. Had the Twilight Monarch lied about engaging her in battle?

Egon brushed past Donovan, offering a clipped apology as he darted into the kitchen proper.

"Aunt Esmel, what happened?" Donovan watched a cabinet door open. Several towels flew out and floated over to his aunt. She took two and thanked the invisible troll.

Knord stayed in the hall, continuing his chat with four crows perched on his shoulders. Since setting eyes on his aunt's home, the fauna emissary had waved the birds over and conferred with them about enlisting their winged fellows in patrolling the area around the house.

"It wasn't a fair fight," Lymol complained. "The foul villain has no regard for the rules of engagement."

Aunt Esmel looked up at her nephew as she repositioned Lymol's arm. "Let Amad fill you in. I need to concentrate."

She took the towels and slid them under the air representative's forearm as she began mumbling a spell and directing her attention to the bandages. She unspooled two and left the third wound tight. The unrolled pair covered the length of the table and draped over the edge by a few inches. Faint symbols glowed blue just barely above each laid-out bandage. *Magical glyphs or runes, maybe.* In *Goblin Cauldron*, runes were the preferred method of embedding magic into objects.

"Wait, I thought Fae didn't work with spell magic," Donovan said.

His aunt huffed and drew her hands up to hover close to the dagger. "We use them if we have to. Some purists refuse to, but thankfully our family has not counted ourselves among that group. If so, I'd never have made the acquaintance of Roderick. Associating with warlocks is forbidden by the narrow-minded dullards."

Amad cleared his throat. "Maybe the intricacies of spellcasting prejudices could be reflected upon at a later date. May I proceed with enlightening your nephew on what transpired?"

His aunt nodded as she recited another spell, this one rhyming. She moved her open hands up and down along the dagger, always keeping them inches away. Blue magic radiated from her open palms, and the ice dagger melted even faster.

"We found no signs of the villain or his puppets along the coast and worked our way inland," Amad related. "The ambush happened as we trekked through a very small canyon. It was foolish of us to travel its narrow confines, though."

"It was the most direct route, and I elected to float above you two and keep watch." Lymol winced, and sweat gathered along his dark brow.

The dagger was now half its size. Having been shaped by magic, it clearly took longer to melt it. His aunt no longer spoke, but kept her hands moving up and down, the heat magic still doing its job.

"Yes, well, see what expediency got us?" The earth emissary sent Lymol a lingering look, but eventually shifted his gaze back to Donovan. "As I was saying, we walked into a trap. Only it wasn't just the air and water hybrid who besieged us. The Twilight Monarch is here on the island, in the flesh as much as he can be."

A flood of panic struck Donovan, and he wobbled. The bad guy was here! He suddenly felt overwhelmed. Fighting off the hybrids had kept the big threat at a distance in his mind. To have the Monarch freely moving about here felt like a violation. And judging from his aunt's sour expression right now, she felt the same. Donovan wasn't equipped. It was all too much.

Egon's strong hands clasped his upper arms, and the troll whispered to him alone, "Steady."

To stop the room from spinning, Donovan shut his eyes hard. He blinked them open and fought off the vertigo, taking in several breaths before he felt on solid ground once again. Lymol caught his panic attack and scoffed.

His aunt melted the last of the ice dagger and patted the wound with the towels. There was some blood, but she applied pressure to slow it. Eventually, she removed the towels. Satisfied with how the gash only leaked slightly, she wound the magic-infused bandages several times around the forearm.

Amad continued, "Lymol and I found ourselves fending off a blizzard and an ice dagger barrage, while your aunt squared off against the foul villain. She beat back his dark magic with nearby stones."

Lymol added, "That young Fae is stronger than she has a right to be. I could never summon such winds at her age. I suspect the villain boosted her talents with his dark magic."

His aunt squinted at Donovan. "There's always rock at our disposal here on this island, Donovan. Seems foolish of the Monarch to attack in such a place of power for you and me, but he's desperate." She tightened the bandages and eyed Donovan's crew, even knowing where Egon stood despite the troll having stayed rather silent. "It was clear his attention was split. We escaped, but just barely. If we had been the only battle he waged, it might have gone worse. Was he occupied with your party or one of the others?"

Donovan looked at Knord, hoping he would catch everyone up, but the fauna emissary simply waved the crows off and gestured with a head tip that he wanted Donovan to fill everybody in.

He shared what happened at the gates and how it seemed he had an affinity for earth as well. His aunt nodded but didn't act as surprised as he thought she should. Next, he detailed their brush with Ithor and their narrow escape thanks to the troll gauntlet.

Egon jumped in at the end. "Donovan is being too modest. Only those of troll blood can work the gloves. I don't know how he did it."

Knord entered the conversation, sending Aunt Esmel an intense look. "But *you* do, don't you? You know why Donovan can move earth so well."

His aunt nodded. "I'm afraid it's time for my nephew to learn about secrets long hidden."

His frustration and anger surged. So his aunt *had* kept him from important details. "Is it you that planted the memory block in my head?"

Aunt Esmel appeared mildly shocked. She calmly discarded the bloody towels in a waste can under the sink and sauntered back over. "Yes, and just how did you find that out? Gregor?"

"No, Ny. She sensed it and tried to crack it open."

His aunt gaped. "She didn't succeed, did she? The protective wards I fortified that spell with have horrible consequences if one isn't careful."

"She couldn't, but you can," Donovan said. "I should know what you've been hiding from me."

Aunt Esmel replied, "Yes, it is time, but please know, nephew, I was only honoring your parents' wishes by shielding you from the truth."

"So do it!" Donovan could barely keep his fury in check. He wanted to throw something. Those lost memories had to involve his parents. The stones making up the shelf above the fireplace shifted about, threatening to break apart and shoot across the room. Thankfully, they were well mortared, and Donovan calmed himself and his stone magic enough to keep that disaster from occurring.

"What about the villain? I sense his next move is imminent." Lymol inspected his bandages, deeming them sufficient with a smirk.

His aunt marched out of the room and down the hall toward the stairs. "In due time. Right now, Donovan should know who he's truly up against and how things went the first time his family confronted the Twilight Monarch, no matter how much pain it will bring."

Fighting back the tears that threatened to burst forth, he rushed to catch up with his aunt.

* * *

Aunt Esmel brought him to his attic room and heaved the locked travel trunk onto his bed. The frame squawked in protest but didn't break. She pointed to the lock fashioned to look like a lion's head. When he'd been younger, his uncle had convinced him the trunk would bite if he tried to fidget with the lock.

She tapped the lock and didn't incur even a nibble from the trunk. "Please understand, you were eight. Your parents wanted to spare you grief, and they hoped to never have you know the specifics of how they died."

"It was on water in a boat." Donovan suddenly didn't trust his own memories. Had his uncle told him a lie? He didn't think the man had it in him to do such.

As if sensing what he was thinking, his aunt said, "Your uncle told you only half the tale. He never lied to you."

It was embarrassing that she could read him so easily. He crossed his arms. "Still seems wrong."

"And maybe it is, but your uncle and I were hoping to never have you meet the Twilight Monarch a second time."

"What? So I was there?"

"You were, but it's better for you to see it for yourself rather than me just explain." She wagged her thumb and index finger at the lock. It slipped open rather unspectacularly. His aunt lifted the trunk lid.

He leaned in to see the trunk that was heavy whenever he'd helped his uncle slide it around was mostly empty. It contained two objects: a black oval stone, and a short sword with a red gem in its pommel.

His aunt picked up the stone and closed the trunk. It locked with a sharp click.

"I don't need the sword?"

"Not yet. And not for battle. Its purpose is not to draw blood. Let's save that for after we deal with our current problem." She held out the stone, nodding at him to take it.

His fingers slipped around the smooth, heavy object, though not as weighty as the trunk had made out its contents to be. He must've had a questioning expression because his aunt said, "The protective spells on the trunk make it heavy and not what's inside."

He rolled the stone around in his hand. It didn't feel warm or cool at the touch. He inspected it and saw his own reflection.

"Place it against your forehead. The walls within will drop away, and you'll experience the lost memories as if you were there."

"Like I'll see things from a little kid's angle?"

She nodded, doing a poor job of hiding the worry that frayed at her expression.

Suddenly afraid, he paused. His parents had thought it best that he not see this. But that was only as long as the bad guy had stayed out of his life. He needed to know.

Donovan bit his bottom lip and pressed the black stone to his head. Everything came tumbling down.

Chapter 25
Saved By Blood

Donovan's mind collapsed inward, a whirlwind of remembrances crashing into each other—his time with his uncle in Maine, the lonely weeks just after his parents' demise, and the few memories of happier times with his parents that he only recalled thanks to his uncle retelling them over and over just before bedtime. The beach house years and all the rest flowed together, forming an angry ocean of crashing waves and churning currents. The recollections raced toward sheer white cliffs in the distance.

This had to be the closed-off section of his mindscape. His swirling memories built to a gigantic wave that crashed into the stark landmark.

The cliff broke into smithereens, the fragments glowing equal parts blue and red as they rained down, sinking into the unsettled waters of his thoughts. So the wall had been constructed of earth and stone magic. No orange, so no fungus. Donovan was a little sad that his own father's magic wasn't involved. But it made sense. Who would ever construct a barrier of fungus?

He felt himself pulled down, drawn to the sinking cliff debris. It formed a massive ring, and he plunged through its center. The magic flared and went from red and blue to white.

Donovan pawed at his eyes, worried he'd been permanently blinded. Something had gone wrong, and the block in his head had taken his sight. He rubbed with the heels of his palms until he saw black spots. When he opened his eyes, the scene around him resolved slowly into detail, gray at first, with color and shadow creeping in toward the end.

He was on a boat, buckled to a chair. His parents were both at the wheel and staring out the front window at the rain and winds assaulting the cabin.

Donovan tried to make his arms reach down and unhook himself, only he couldn't get either to respond. He felt hot tears streaming down his cheeks and realized he was just a passenger along for the ride. His younger self wasn't going to do anything that he hadn't done before. He couldn't race over and save the day—not that he could do much in the body of an eight-year-old.

He calmed himself and decided to be as observant as he could.

"We'll never make it to Esmel's in time. He knew we were coming," Donovan's father said, his voice screechy and laced with fear.

His mother wrestled with the wheel. The boat bounced around on the rough waters, threatening to capsize. Twice she was knocked to the ground but got back up.

A deep voice from behind Donovan entered the conversation. "It's my fault. I should never have risked a visit to see you. He followed me."

Donovan looked back to see a huge brute of a creature, green-skinned and with four horns jutting from the sides of his head above his small ears. His brow was thickset and his white hair pulled into a ponytail. He held a hammer at the ready and peered out the windows along either side of the cabin. Lightning slashed through the dark skies, making his appearance even more terrifying. Surprisingly, young Donovan didn't cry but actually reached toward the beast and gurgled, his tears momentarily forgotten.

"What's done is done. I don't fault you. I'm glad Donovan got to spend time with his godfather." His father flinched as a sudden gust smacked the boat, sending him crashing into a window.

"Yes, you Fae and your family traditions. Why I agreed to such a title is beyond me, but you had me in a bind. I was oath bound to you, Coyle, and what sort of troll would I be if I didn't honor such a pledge?"

"Don't worry, Duke Niall. We will take care of this and have you back for your son's lifeday," his mother said.

Suddenly, a bolt of lightning struck the front of the boat, splintering a large section of the deck.

A dark cloud massed in front of them, its edges seeming to erupt in inky extensions forming shadowy tentacles. They stretched and reached toward the boat. The two largest cloud tentacles latched onto the front of the ship and jerked it upward. Everyone except Donovan went crashing into the back of the cabin. The boat stayed vertical.

Donovan began to cry.

His mother was unconscious and wedged against a back window whose glass had spiderwebbed and looked to be on the verge of collapsing and sending her out into the chaos.

Duke Niall saw this and crept across the back of the wall to reach her. He grabbed her wrist and pulled Donovan's mom away a split second before the window and part of the rear wall collapsed.

His father hung onto the other seat next to him, giving his son a wide-eyed look. He barely held on. The front windows shattered, and a strong wind knocked free one of his hands. He held on with the other and managed to hook one leg on the armrest.

The chair was bolted to the floor, but the wind picked up, threatening to rip even the furniture from its moorings.

The black cloud slithered into the cabin and flowed together to form a human guise. A man made of quivering shadow floated before them, hundreds of shadowy spikes protruding from his shoulders and back. Two main spikes near his neck reached toward Donovan just as yellow eyes opened on the darkened surface of the creature's face. This was immediately followed by a crooked smile, revealing black teeth held in place by festering purple gums.

There was no doubt this was the Twilight Monarch!

Donovan shook and wailed. His father tried to calm him even as he barely held onto the armrest.

"Your child shall be mine!" The Twilight Monarch slung two tentacles, latching onto Donovan's legs. His touch burned. The dark magic leaked into his younger self, invasive and corrupt. His blood seemed to flee from the villain's presence throughout his arteries and veins, retreating inward and seeking refuge in his beating heart. The pressure was excruciating. His heart would surely burst. Donovan shrieked. He knew he wouldn't die here, but the agony almost convinced him otherwise.

His father hurled himself at the Twilight Monarch, knocking the fiend away from Donovan with a massive fungus axe. The weapon sliced through dozens of snaking limbs, but the villain simply produced more.

The Twilight Monarch stripped the axe from him and wrapped tentacles around his father, delighting in constricting and making the Fae struggle to breathe.

Where was the troll and his mom? Donovan so wanted to see where they were, but he couldn't stop wailing and squeezing his eyes shut, opening them only fleetingly.

He caught only snatches of the confrontation. Even bound under all those tentacles, his father grew a variety of capped brown and blue fungus and bigger pale ones the size and shape of melons on the ceiling and sent them at the villain, who batted them away. The larger, orb-shaped mushrooms exploded, spraying a fine gray dust on the Twilight Monarch that disintegrated any tentacles it touched.

The villain howled in pain and slammed his father into the spikes jutting from his back.

His father went limp. The last vision of his death was of the Twilight Monarch sliding the lifeless body from his spikes and hurling it out the shattered front window to be swallowed up by the storm.

Donovan wailed and closed his eyes, shock overwhelming him.

A scream of rage echoed through the cabin, but he had no idea what was happening. His eyes were sealed shut, and his younger self was losing consciousness.

No, stay awake! Open your eyes! I don't know what happened to Mom! Stay awake! I need to know!

His eyes fluttered open long enough to witness the enraged troll—-with his mother slung over Niall's back—fling his hammer at the villain, knocking the monarch completely off the boat.

Duke Niall scrambled over to Donovan and freed him from the chair. The troll, with two in tow, vaulted out of the cabin and fell into the choppy waves.

Donovan lost consciousness.

* * *

He awoke on his back, staring at a cloudless blue sky. He sat up and patted his body, finding he still inhabited his younger self. *So another memory!*

Waves lapped against the rocky shore. He was on his aunt's island.

Aunt Esmel, a slightly younger version, walked into view and dropped to her knees next to him. "Finally awake, are you?"

Vertigo smacked Donovan back down when he tried to stand. "Mom?"

His aunt nodded beyond him. "Farther up the beach, being tended to by Niall."

He sobbed. "Dad . . ."

She put an arm around him and drew him close. "Gone. Gave himself to save you."

Donovan buried his face in her shirt. The tears wouldn't stop. His stomach heaved and rocked, every gut muscle protesting. He pulled away from his aunt and threw up.

She rubbed his neck and stroked his arched back. "You're okay. The transfusion saved you."

"What?" He wiped a strand of drool from his bottom lip.

She rose and helped him to his feet. "Come. You need to know."

She walked him up a dune, each step becoming less and less shaky as the dizziness lifted. The sun seemed much too bright, but at least he wasn't as out of it as before. While his chest still hurt, his circulation felt clean of the villain's prickly dark magic.

At the top of the rise, he spied his mother and was flooded with relief.

A few yards away, she lay on her back, her head propped up by a thick piece of driftwood. The troll kneeled at her side, cupping her small hand in his massive ones.

She was pale, her eyes so sunken and rimmed in shadow.

He pulled free from his aunt and stumbled hurriedly through the sand and stone, falling twice. "Mom!"

"Oh, Donny!" She squinted and stiffened in pain.

He ached. It had been so long since he'd heard her call him that. He dropped to his knees, not caring that the rocks scraped up his legs. "What's wrong with you?"

"She took on too much, young Strong." Duke Niall's voice was soft and distant. The troll came off as huge, likely because Donovan was small as eight-year-olds go. Even without having ever seen Egon, the troll chef just came across as not quite as colossal as the duke.

"What? I don't understand."

"You were hurt, dying from what the Monarch's magic did to you. I used my stone magic and Niall's blood to purge the darkness from you. It was the only way."

His mom struggled to speak. "But before we made it here and I saved you, Donny, we were attacked one more time. The Monarch struck hard." She hugged her midsection as if reliving a traumatic blow.

The troll offered, "Being who I am, I was no help. Just dead weight in the water. Your mom had to send the Twilight Monarch away alone. She did so, but not without incurring dire injuries herself."

"What do you mean? Magic? What's a Twilight Monarch?" Donovan sucked in a panicked breath.

He knew about magic now, but experiencing the jarring understanding that the world was so much bigger and more menacing than it was before with his younger self was not a feeling to be endured more than once. The color in the memory started to dissipate. He felt himself retreat slightly and suddenly feared his cowering would cause the memory to be ripped from him. He focused and tamped down his twisted emotions.

His aunt said, "And this was after she beat back another attack and found the strength to use her stone magic to bring you three the rest of the way to my island. I don't know how she did it with such grave injuries."

Her words strained, his mom spoke, "It was only when Niall gave of his blood and own magic that the dark magic was expelled." She gasped. "I'm afraid my own injuries are too extensive. His darkness shredded my magic, my very spirit." She looked at her sister. "Promise me, Esmel. Take Donny far away from Homeland. His uncle's home—it's so remote and the last place anyone magical would look. Lose my son among the humans so the monarch can never find him again."

Aunt Esmel nodded, wiping tears from her eyes. "I will, but you can't go. You can pull through, Klara. You're stronger than anyone I know."

His mom looked at Donovan, her gaze penetrating. "You deserve to live free of pain. Your uncle will see to that. I love you."

"Mom, no. You're fine. Use whatever magic to fix yourself." Donovan felt anxiety permeate the memory.

Waving him back, his mother sat up slightly as she gestured for Aunt Esmel to approach. He stepped back, hating that he couldn't force his younger self to stay close.

His mother whispered something to her, and then his aunt solemnly nodded for Donovan to return.

As soon as he was again by her side, his mother fell back and placed a hand on his knee. Donovan dropped his own hands atop hers, alarmed at how cold it was.

"You will do great things, lovely boy. You will always be in my heart." She coughed, and her eyes slid closed. Her smile withered, and her hand dropped from his knee as her chest fell and was still.

Donovan screamed and thrashed. His aunt tried to calm him, but he punched her in the jaw by accident. Niall stepped in and restrained him, drawing the boy into a tight embrace.

Sobbing, he beat at the troll's chest until he couldn't lift his arms anymore. Donovan turned and stared at his mother, the wind tugging at her red curls the only movement on the rocky beach.

The colors drained from his surroundings, and everything faded to gray. In seconds, he blinked open his eyes and was back in the attic with his aunt, the black stone no longer affixed to his forehead.

He clutched the stone, unsure whether to embrace the numbness and rage that wrestled with his insides. Wiping at his wet eyes didn't help him settle on how to feel.

Time stood still. The light streaming in from the moon-shaped window warmed his cheek and collarbone. He drew small comfort from it.

His aunt let out a slow breath. "You saw all of it? The attack on the boat? Your mother's final moments?"

He nodded.

She sat with him, her closeness appreciated but also resented. He pushed the dueling notions deep.

"I have troll blood?"

"Well, maybe not anymore, but the magic in the blood transfusion is clearly still with you. Trolls have a connection to the earth. It's different than what a Fae with an affinity for the soil has, but no less powerful. You can work three forms of magic, Donovan."

He shrugged, not impressed at all. "What did she whisper to you?"

"To block out the memories associated with magic and your parents' deaths. I didn't want to, but she felt it was for the best. She wanted any ties with magic to be buried in the hopes that it would keep the Twilight Monarch from finding you. Just knowing who he is might be enough to set him hot on your trail. It worked until it didn't, and now here we are."

"I don't know what to do."

She smiled and awkwardly hugged his head. "Lucky for you, I do."

"What?"

She stood and put her hands on her hips. "Be a Strong."

Chapter 26
A Trinity of Magic United, Sort Of

Donovan's aunt stowed away the stone in the trunk and prodded him to head downstairs with her. Donovan didn't feel like moving. But when he saw the red eyes of Gregor peer into the attic through the half-moon window, he set aside his moping and bolted down the steps.

Lymol, Knord, Amad, and, he assumed, Egon were already outside as the spectral dragon flickered into being, his appearance much more transparent than before, his glowing outline slightly faded. The reptile landed and issued a strained smile at Donovan as the boy leapt from the porch directly to the yard.

"I'm afraid I didn't do so well with keeping track of everyone," Gregor said. "I saw Donovan head underground but lost track of your party when you entered a very dense part of the woods." He pointed at his aunt and then continued, "I just swooped down and checked on Reena's group. They're on their way back, maybe fifteen minutes out."

"What about Roderick's group?" Aunt Esmel asked.

"I didn't spot them anywhere on the island." Gregor frowned. "And there's something else."

"What?" Donovan said.

"The villain is at the gates with Joven and some boy wielding flame. He actually sensed me and threw a fireball my way. The nerve. I was almost tempted to char him but didn't want to escalate matters as they had the princess."

"He's plotting something," Donovan said.

"He's setting a trap. He wants you to come to him. I hate to put you in danger, but I think you have to go. It's your decision." His aunt scowled.

"What choice do I have? He could hurt Ny." The stones around Donovan responded to his growing agitation by floating a few inches off the ground and hopping about. "I can use my magic."

"Only your earth and stone magic. You've yet to manifest anything with fungus." His aunt paced. "And it's not like we can ask the fungus emissary to help bring that magic out in you. He's with Roderick."

"What does he want with the hybrids?" Lymol interjected. "I've not paid much attention to the prophecy. My people really don't entertain such notions as fate or magic that can map out future events."

Aunt Esmel rubbed her chin. "The Twilight Monarch needs four hybrids manifesting all eight affinities in order to tap into each magic and bring about ruin with them. I'm not sure how exactly, but I suspect it boosts his dark magic. He's a Fae with no claim to any particular magic. I'm sure there's a story to why that is, but the villain hasn't exactly shared his dark intentions with anyone."

Knowing what he said might provoke his aunt to keep him out of the line of fire, Donovan still weighed in. "My magic powered up the gates even though you had the spell in place that kept them from working until the Convocation was over. What if he needs to open the gates so he can suck all the different magics from Homeland?"

"All the more reason to keep you as far away from there as possible, but I know that's not the answer. This is your fight now." She added, "And your magic is impressive to override my spell."

"But if I can open all the gates, can't each emissary access more of their brand of magic and we use that to throw everything at the bad guy?"

"It's risky," Knord commented. "The Twilight Monarch might have already considered that and schemed accordingly. He may have a plan to neutralize all on the island except the hybrids."

Donovan felt his aunt was rethinking encouraging him to go. To sit on the sidelines wasn't an option. The vile thing that killed his parents was out there, intent on something awful. He had to face the Monarch. He looked at his aunt, resolve—along with his stone and earth magic—building in his chest. "You said I needed to be a Strong. You know that it has to be me. I'm going."

His aunt paused, doing her best to hide her admiration, but Donovan caught the nodding respect she gave him. "You're so young and inexperienced. You can't even wield all your gifts. This is too much."

"I'll have all of you at my side, while he has no one, just unwilling slaves. Let me do this."

She edged toward the dragon and placed a hand on his snout. It passed through the creature's muzzle despite her trying to hold it in place. "I made a promise to my sister that I would keep you safe . . ."

His aunt was having second thoughts. It was important she knew he wasn't going to run and hide. "*This* will keep me safe. Doing nothing is what's dangerous for me . . . and for Homeland."

Despite his brave words, it didn't feel like he was winning the argument. He needed to show her he meant business. A kernel of an idea crept into his head.

Donovan assumed a wider stance and concentrated on his magic. He held his hand out, palms down and fingers clenched. It was easy to coax the stone magic out. Red energy tumbled forth from his chest and hands. The rocks from far and near flew through the air, forming an ever-thickening ring around the entire group, including the dragon. The floating structure was impressive.

He then summoned the earth magic, ignoring the gauntlet that had floated behind him ever since he'd used it to dig them out. The glove hung in the air, slumped over rather than its normal rigid vertical self, almost as if disappointed to not be of use.

Blue energy clawed its way out of his chest, acting like it wanted to stay hidden. He concentrated, willing it to fully emerge. It flopped about, swirling wildly until he exerted enough control to forge it into a somewhat restrained mini-tornado. He nudged it to the center of the ring, causing the invisible troll to bump into Donovan as the chef moved out of the way. Lymol and the other emissaries also took a few steps back. All switched their gazes from the ring of stones to the earthen magic and back again, uncertain which to be mindful of.

The bottom of the blue funnel struck the ground, and tons of earth sprang up and added their mass to the magical cyclone. It doubled in size, darkening and growing predominantly brown with occasional streaks of blue.

"His control is impressive," Knord said.

"Surprisingly so for such a youngster," Lymol said with judgmental envy.

Donovan wiped the sweat from his brow, trying to ignore his growing hand tremors. "Not . . . done . . . yet."

His father's gift needed to be called forth. Donovan slowed the earth tornado's spin to a crawl and urged the fungus magic to manifest. He sent his demand inward and registered a tiny orange spark. Instead of his will giving the magic fuel, the spark shrank. Frightened, he hastily implored the magic to bloom. It dimmed even more. Being so forceful wasn't working. Magic didn't like being ordered around. He needed to access it another way.

He settled himself, checking to see that his other forms of magic also hadn't flinched or dissipated. Both the ring and tornado appeared to have unraveled slightly, but he sent them a wave of confidence and their configurations tightened up.

He turned his attention back to addressing his father's birthright. Maybe the magic would respond to the bond he felt with his dad. It had been so long since he'd played through any memories from his childhood. Maybe the fungus needed to see how he was connected.

Donovan sighed. What good would merging the three energies be if it took him so long to do it? It wasn't like the bad guy would wait for him to arrange his attack just right.

His doubt sparked a memory. To block out any distractions, he closed his eyes and focused on the remembrance.

His father had always been a patient teacher. Donovan saw himself astride a bike, looking down at the back tire as his dad removed the training wheels. His father was all smiles, twinkling reassurances, and radiant confidence as he talked his nervous son into believing he could conquer Bikeriding 101, a label his father had been playfully namedropping the past few days.

Donovan took a deep breath and pushed off the concrete, propelling himself forward. His father's gentle hand kept contact with his back for a few seconds, and then he was adrift, in charge of his own cycling destiny. He scrambled to place his feet on the pedals as the handlebars wobbled. His bike helmet felt askew on his head. He focused and steadied his inertia.

The bike coasted for several feet before he lost control and tumbled into the yard, luckily avoiding hard contact with the sidewalk. He landed on something soft, a cluster of mushrooms, rather big ones. His father rushed over and commented on his good fortune to have stuck such a soft landing. Donovan brushed bits of fungus from his legs and elbows before getting up, righting his bike, and insisting they try again.

And they did, over and over, until he didn't fall, until he didn't need a conveniently arranged soft landing.

The memory evaporated. His father had slyly used his fungus magic, and he hadn't realized it back then.

Several gasps forced his attention to return to the real world. He opened his eyes.

A giant mushroom sprang out of the top of the earthen cyclone. An orange magic tether extended from his right hand to the top of the fungi's cap, its gills underneath glowing orange as well.

Remembering his original intentions, he concentrated on uniting the three. The ring of rocks darted forward, merging with the earth cyclone. Everyone ducked to avoid being smacked in the head.

Donovan snickered but maintained his concentration. *Great work, everyone. Now let's come together and show them what a powerhouse looks like.*

The mass expanded, and two trunk-like legs erupted from its bottom. Dozens of smaller green mushrooms sprouted all along the whirling soil. Arms assembled from stone sprang forth from its upper half, which shaped itself into more of a broad torso using a mix of earth and stone. The mushroom cap elongated and took on the lumpy dimensions of an oversized head. It was a little absurd, a magical bobblehead. To make it more intimidating than comical, he spurred twin horns of fungus to curl upward. He envisioned two eyes and a large mouth. Instead, only one eye, no more than a slit, appeared on his creation's face.

His magical monstrosity stood before them, its head teetering under its bulk.

"Here's a warrior to aid us in battle!" Donovan waved at his creation.

To drive home the point that it was designed for combat, he projected into its head what possible duty it could execute. "Jump and hammer the ground with your fists!"

The construct swept its arms back and crouched, its legs bulging as it readied itself to leap forward. It pushed off the ground, heaved into the air by just a few inches, and toppled backward from the weight of his raised and overextended arms.

The earth, stone, and fungus magic rushed back into Donovan as the entire thing came apart. Stones bounced and rolled away, while earth deposited into numerous mounds and the smaller mushrooms rapidly decomposed. The large one split in two and slowly liquified. It was a sad end to such a grand warrior, Donovan thought as he tried to hide his disappointment.

Everyone stared at him, at a loss for words.

It was Lymol who broke the silence. He took to the air and floated over the ruins of the creature to settle at Donovan's side. "A disappointing first attempt, young Fae." His expression was stern. "But a magnificent achievement nonetheless." The air emissary smiled and patted Donovan's shoulder. "I've never seen anyone attempt to wield three affinities. You are quite impressive as champions go."

Donovan mouthed a thank-you. No one else approached, and neither did they chime in with their own praise.

Lymol added, "I would follow such a warrior into battle. Anyone else?" He punched toward the sky, and a dramatic gust flew upward, billowing his immense sleeves.

Amad and Knord raised their hands. The dragon added an uplifted wing to the mix.

Egon's invisible hand tousled Donovan's hair as the troll declared, "I also am raising a clenched fist in allegiance to the young Strong."

His aunt nodded once, spun about, and hastened up the porch steps. "Then let us beat out a decent plan of attack. Egon can fix us something to eat. An army always fights fiercer on a full stomach."

The others drifted inside as Donovan lingered, casting his gaze over what was left of his creation.

Gregor smiled. "You are mighty. I can stay for just a few more hours before I must depart. It is my hope that it will be enough time to witness your monumental victory over evil, Donovan Strong."

You and me both, he thought as he sent the dragon a sheepish grin and then hustled inside, doing his best to ignore the sinking feeling that he was in over his head and no amount of magic could change that.

Chapter 27
Clash of the Frightened

Everyone gathered in the dining room. Egon brought out sandwiches along with a fruit salad. His aunt led the discussion, with all the emissaries pitching solid suggestions, especially Lymol, who seemed to be treating everyone much nicer than before. And all it had taken to tear down his snobby demeanor was Donovan whipping up a failed monstrosity.

Whether it was getting some much-needed food in his belly, or the sense of solidarity that radiated from everyone else, his mood lifted. Donovan stopped being so hard on himself and was soon in the thick of strategizing. Half his ideas were shot down, but a surprising number were deemed acceptable, with Egon always labeling those as either 'genius' or 'groundbreaking.'

Donovan appreciated the troll's genuinely kind and supportive nature. Everyone else was also Team Donovan, just not as gushing or as vocal as the chef. For someone never seen, he sure liked to be heard.

". . . is a surefire solution. How do you keep coming up with these gems, Donovan? Such a problem-solver, you are," the troll said as he refilled the strawberries in the large serving dish.

The front door burst open, and Reena's party spilled into the room. The fire emissary looked battle-weary. The two water representatives appeared slightly less downtrodden, although the younger one, Frayson, clung to his right arm as if it were badly sprained or broken.

"Oh dear," Egon said.

"What happened?" Aunt Esmel asked.

"We ran into the Twilight Monarch," Reena said. "He had Lut and Brin wrapped up in his dark magic and was heading toward the gates. He attacked."

"The villain would've defeated us if he didn't have to contend with those he captured." Frayson rubbed at his arm. "Lut broke free and escaped. Did she make it back here?"

Nearly everyone in the room shook their head.

"Was Roderick with them?" Donovan asked.

"No, the warlock must've escaped as well. I take it he's not here either?" Reena touched her bruised cheek and winced.

Grandl placed a comforting hand on the fire emissary's shoulder. Instead of slipping out from under, Reena gave him a weak smile.

"He has three hybrids. Joven and Ithor are his puppets. We don't know if he's got full control of Ny." His aunt's expression reminded Donovan of how he looked when he tried to finger solve an algebra problem by writing it out in the air.

Amad said, "I would bet she's still free. Bound but not doing his bidding."

Donovan found himself nodding, which was noticed by Amad, who grinned at his supportive take.

"So the two wild cards—where are Lut and Roderick?" his aunt said. "I don't like having the lobster sidelined. He's a huge asset."

Donovan pointed out, "Well, we hadn't included him in our big plan."

"Yes, but I was counting on him showing up and throwing some of his magical weight around." His aunt frowned and rubbed at her chin.

"We should stick with the plan. Add fire and water to our group and head to the gates," Lymol said, floating toward the front door.

Reena raced right behind the air emissary. She locked eyes with Donovan. "We will be by your side." She then looked at Frayson and Grandl. "We are always ready to lend a hand to the Strong family."

Grandl remarked, "If we could be apprised of the specifics of the attack plan on the way, it would be appreciated." He, along with Amad, charged out the front door.

Knord patted Donovan's back and slipped between him and the gauntlet that hung in the air behind his chair. "I have many eyes out there. We'll find Lut and your lobster ally." The fauna emissary rushed to join the others outside.

Egon spoke up. "It appears your army is at the ready, awaiting your go ahead."

Donovan looked at his aunt, uncertain who the invisible troll was addressing. Surely his aunt.

After a long pause, Egon exhaled and said, "*Donovan*, your fellow Fae are at the ready along with this old troll. We place ourselves in your capable hands."

Donovan smiled. The troll really knew the right thing to say. He charged out of the bed and breakfast, his magical troll gauntlet nipping at his heels, with his aunt and the troll bringing up the rear.

It was 'make or break' time. Donovan gulped in a deep breath and awkwardly climbed onto Gregor's back.

The dragon had made himself semi-solid now, a state he had related to them that used up a good deal of his magic and reduced how long he could stay on Earth by half. But Donovan leading the charge from the air was a key part of their plan. Thankfully, he didn't sink into the reptile. The area in and around Donovan looked more there than the rest. Gregor's head, tail, and wings were still quite see-through.

He didn't feel secure at all and tried to stabilize himself, which meant hugging the dragon's lower neck quite severely. His clingy pose must look ridiculous. To compensate, he sat up straighter, only wobbling slightly.

Everyone stared at him as if it were in his second nature to declare words of wisdom in instances like this. He swallowed and clamped his legs tighter against the dragon's scales.

"Time to fly," he said and punched the air.

Gregor took off, and the others hastened into the woods as they headed out to confront the Twilight Monarch.

The land raced by below. It was all happening so fast! He could barely believe he was about to fight, using magic. Doubt gnawed at his insides, but everyone was relying on him to pull off a victory. That seemed awfully daunting. Suddenly aware he'd been holding his breath since climbing aboard, he blew out a rushed breath and inhaled just as rapidly.

Gregor commented, "Fear not, young champion. You have the mettle and the magic to succeed." The dragon stared at him, making his eyes more solid to drive home his point. "And most importantly—the heart."

* * *

The dragon slowed and circled lazily back until they spotted part of their group. Reena and the two water emissaries climbed along a rocky ridgeline, positioning themselves to rush into the clearing from the west. Frayson waved, which Donovan found impressive, considering the dragon was mostly invisible and the fire emissary could only see Donovan against the backdrop of dark clouds.

Gregor swooped low and zoomed over a thickly wooded stretch. He abruptly pulled up and circled again, tipping his wing toward a snaking river below.

Aunt Esmel made her way along the riverbank. Egon was with her, or at least he was supposed to be. They would converge on the clearing from the east.

Donovan and his scaly steed raced up above the clouds and traveled over the gateways, descending well out of view to check on the party coming in from the North. Amad and Knord ran along a narrow path, a motley crew of forest animals racing along behind them.

"That leaves us to tackle the southern approach. Everyone should be in position in the next few minutes. I'll let loose with the signal in five, just to be certain." The dragon veered right and accelerated, keeping his flight low so that he would remain unseen if any at the gates looked in their direction.

Several minutes later, they flew high, and Gregor glanced back at Donovan. "We're all in position by now."

He nodded to the dragon.

Gregor dove and flew so close to the treetops that his arms and legs passed through the uppermost branches. He was careful not to let his more solid body get near the trees, which Donovan appreciated, as he didn't want to be plucked from the dragon's back by a randomly extra-tall tree limb.

The clearing appeared before them, and the dragon flew straight up. The wind threatened to pull Donovan off, but he tightened his grip and looked down, his red curls whipping all about.

A figure made of shadow stood at the center of the clearing, the Twilight Monarch somehow smaller than he had been in the boat memory. Three people were bound with dark magic, which the villain seemed to be adding to. His fellow hybrids. Two others, Lut and Brin, were cocooned in dark magic and lashed to a fallen tree that bisected the gates between the earth and fungus arches. That was new. Had the tree been knocked over in battle with his aunt?

Gregor cleared his throat. "It is time."

Donovan thudded his hand against the dragon's scales, a better cue to proceed than having him trying to yell over the winds. The dragon's voice was far more powerful than Donovan's, and he doubted he could match Gregor bellow for bellow.

His ride snaked his neck about and aimed directly below, expelling a long purple flame that was intended to be their signal and not actually an assault on those in the clearing.

They turned about and plunged. While the flame had long dissipated, the air they passed through was still rather warm. Donovan winced but didn't incur any actual burns. The dragon landed in the clearing opposite the fallen tree. A wise move to keep the two captives out of the line of fire.

The dragon belched a plume of flame that produced a huge cloud of smoke between them and the Twilight Monarch. The smokescreen was a minor distraction so that everyone could converge on the villain. Of course, while it impaired their target's vision, it also kept them from seeing what the Monarch was up to. Donovan had to hope that wouldn't prove to be a failing in their plan.

He dismounted and summoned his earth and stone magic. Rocks flew to him, forming a shield about as big as a manhole cover. Several earthen mounds welled up in front of him. The gauntlet flew onto his arm, magnifying his control of the earth. He coaxed the piles into merging and forming a cresting wave and hopped atop it. The earth rumbled forward as the shield kept pace and afforded him protection from a frontal assault.

The smoke was clearing, letting him see that the Twilight Monarch rushed toward them, his expression one of glee. Ithor flew alongside as well, while the other two hybrids remained encased from neck to toe in dark magic back at the center of the clearing.

An intensified aura of dread radiated from the Monarch compared to Donovan's first encounter with the villain. Much larger and with more shadow spikes and tentacles radiating from his back and shoulders, his presence immediately triggered the maddening desire to flee. The appendages coiled and uncoiled slowly, drawing attention to the hundreds of nasty barbs sticking out from every inch of his blackened hide, far more menacing than the few barbs that had covered him in Donovan's restored memory.

His courage evaporated as Donovan looked all about. Where were the others? He couldn't spot anyone else rushing into the clearing from the three other directions. Something was wrong. He slowed his soil wave and gawked all around, resisting the urge to call out to the others.

"Where is everybody else?" he said.

The dragon blew out another flame, sending the Twilight Monarch back. "No idea."

The villain sidestepped the flame and surged forward.

Gregor spat out two more gouts of fire. "I'm afraid I can't do much more of this, Donovan."

Ithor threw several fireballs at Donovan. He maneuvered his rock shield to bat them aside. The villain had to be keeping the others out. How? A magical force field? Then how did Donovan and the dragon get through? He looked up at the sky. It just wasn't adding up.

Two shadow tentacles knocked Donovan from atop his wave and shoved him into the ground. It was almost impossible to breathe. He clawed at the tentacles, afraid they were pressing him into the ground so hard he would black out.

The Twilight Monarch laughed as he approached.

As the shadows constricted and crept all across Donovan's body, pinning his arms and legs, no amount of squirming seemed to help.

Gregor flew off. He couldn't blame the dragon. There wasn't much left of the spirit. He looked so immaterial. It was a miracle he had made it this far.

The Twilight Monarch drew up next to Donovan, kneeling to speak to him. Every fiber of Donovan's being screamed at him to run. The very air grew foul with the villain's presence, causing Donovan to emit a strangled cough as he fought to suck in an uncorrupted breath.

The Monarch narrowed his gaze at him. Shadows from the villain's neck reached out, licking at his own neck, Donovan's skin going numb where they made contact. "So you're what all the fuss is about. After all these years, you're finally in my grasp." He sneered. "And no overprotective parents around to come to the rescue."

He paused and motioned for Ithor to hang back. The boy complied.

The villain faked confusion. "You are all alone. How perfect."

"What did you do to the others?" Donovan said, trying to hide how hard it was to catch his breath.

"A little fear spell around the perimeter for those approaching on foot. After I get what I need from you, I'll command all four of my hybrid puppets to dispatch the emissaries and your dear aunt." He stretched his arm muscles. A host of shadow tendrils rippled outward from his forearms. "I knew you were coming by dragon and would be unaffected by that spell. I wanted you to myself."

It was important to keep the villain talking. For one, it was helping him understand the Monarch's plan. For another, it bought him time to think of a way out of this mess.

"The traitor told you what we were up to? How did they have time to? We only finalized the plan less than an hour ago. No one could have snuck off to contact you."

The Twilight Monarch laughed and gestured toward the fallen tree. From behind its leafy crown, Roderick flew out and raced their way. The lobster must've been hiding, awaiting the right time to attack the Monarch. His claws glowed with pent-up magic.

The warlock zoomed past the villain and loomed over Donovan, his eyes swiveling back and forth between the two.

Something was off about the warlock. Maybe he was enslaved. "I don't understand. You made it through the fear spell. Help me."

The Twilight Monarch said, "He's working for me. Always has. He's the traitor in your midst, child. So clueless." The villain tipped a tendril toward the lobster. "A stellar performance, warlock. You had them all fooled."

Donovan glared at Roderick. How could he? What would make the warlock betray them? Then it clicked. He tensed and strained against the shadows encasing him. "He knows where your real body is."

Roderick said nothing.

"He promised to put you back in it if you were his spy."

"Yes," the villain cut in, "he kept me apprised of all your comings and goings. And even installed a surveillance spell in the house so I could hear what you discussed. And your oh-so-capable aunt never knew." The villain spun around and walked toward the bound hybrids. Ithor hurried after him.

Roderick picked up Donovan and carried him over, placing him down next to Joven and Ny as delicately as possible with his huge claws. He whispered to Donovan, "I'm so sorry. I wish there was some other way . . ."

Donovan refused to look him in the eyes. Instead, he checked on Ny and Joven. Both were awake and breathing through their noses due to being gagged by the shadow magic. Joven looked slightly out of it, while Ny had a fire in her eyes. Both were fending off the Monarch's influence, but for how much longer? Donovan had the feeling that the Monarch would apply much more pressure to breaking them now that he had a complete set of hybrids. And it didn't help that Stonebridge was a worn spot and allowed greater access to Homeland magic even with the gates closed.

He needed to know more, so he ramped up his taunting. "You can't do anything with the gates sealed."

The Monarch crossed his arms and scanned the eight arches. "Yes, that pesky spell." He shot Donovan a lingering look. "A sure way to get around that would be to kill everyone. Convocation ended. But that's too risky. I don't yet have the magic to take on so many."

"Well, I can't help you." Donovan knew he actually could. Somehow, he had gotten around the spell and made the gates work, three of them at least.

"Ah, but you can. See, when I snuffed out your father's life all those many years back, I got a taste of his abilities. He worked fungus and capably so, but he also had a second aptitude, one I don't believe he was aware of and, I sense, he passed on to you."

Donovan had no idea what he was talking about. "I have earth magic thanks to a transfusion of troll blood and magic, but that's not what you mean."

"You're a spellbreaker. You have the talent to shatter cast spells and runes. It's why the gates worked for you and why I had the warlock make the fear spell a ring around the clearing and not a dome. If you'd flown through that, you'd have disrupted its effects."

Donovan grew lightheaded. So much magic swirled around inside him. It felt like too much. Stone, fungus, earth and now this.

"Fear not. When the warlock helps me weave the final spell to make all four of you hybrids completely under my sway, I'll take your magic and hopefully your spellbreaking talent and make them mine. But to do that, you need to be unconscious. Otherwise, your natural spellbreaking talent would play havoc with anything the warlock casts." He squinted at Donovan. "So this is goodbye. You won't be coming out of this on the other side, I'm afraid. I need all of your magic to link with the eight affinities in Homeland and open wide the access to the dark magic I've been so long deprived. And Fae tend to die rather quickly once stripped of our magic. Just ask your parents."

Donovan's anger and magic boiled up. The shadows imprisoning him buckled and started to tear.

The villain concentrated and funneled more shadow magic at him.

With the restraints reinforced, Donovan squeezed his eyes shut and unleashed a silent roar. He was a wreck. How could he fight feeling like this? He'd watched his parents die just moments earlier, and now to endure the monarch's cruel gloating . . . he just wanted to give up.

Suddenly, Roderick and Ithor went flying backward as if struck by a cyclone. The lobster slammed into the fauna gate and landed on his back. He struggled to flip over. Ithor smacked into a tree trunk stomach first. He crawled around, gasping for air.

Was it Egon? Had the troll come to his rescue? Or Lymol throwing around his air magic? Nobody else appeared to be in the clearing other than the hybrids and the Twilight Monarch, who assumed a ready stance and transformed eight long shadow spikes from his back into tentacles, holding them high like cobras arched to strike.

Invisible hands clamped down on Donovan and whisked him into the air. Only he wasn't hurled at a gate or cast against a tree. He went high into the night sky and knew who had come to the rescue—Gregor!

There was not a single trace of the dragon, not even his glowing eyes. That wasn't a good sign.

The dragon's voice barely rose above a whisper, and Donovan almost didn't catch it with all the air whipping by. "Thought . . . I could manage . . . a decent rescue."

They suddenly plunged, strafing a treetop whose spindly upper branches raked across Donovan. They didn't scratch him thanks to Donovan being still wrapped in shadow.

The dragon twisted out of the dive and flew higher, but his flight was erratic. Donovan did his best to quell the nausea brewing in his gut from all the bobbing. Thankfully, the shadows binding him unraveled the more distance they put between them and the monarch. The final lengths of dark magic dropped away, allowing him to take in a grateful deep breath. He was suddenly not as depressed as before. The foul magic must somehow magnify his sadness.

"You have to go, don't you?" he asked the dragon.

"I do. If I stay . . ."

"It's okay. You did a good thing. Set me down and go."

Gregor coasted and then veered toward an open area, roughly landing next to a small stream. He released Donovan.

He couldn't detect any of the dragon but sensed Gregor was directly in front of him. Donovan reached out a hand, making contact with nothing at all but still drawing comfort in the gesture. "It has been an honor."

"The honor . . . was all mine, Donovan." The dragon flickered into existence for a split second, and then there was the sound of air rushing in to fill a dragon-sized void. Then the forest was silent except for the faint gurgle of the nearby running water.

Sobbing, Donovan dropped to his knees. He was alone. Any second now, the villain would charge in and scoop him back up. He didn't know what to do. While his demeanor had improved with the shadow magic no longer touching him, he was still so overwhelmed.

He coaxed the magic buried in his chest to emerge and rally around him. A strand of red magic intertwined with one of blue and squirmed up and away from his chest. It rotated about in front of him, giving off a reassuring glow.

Donovan swept his fingers through the magic, drawing comfort in the icy tingle the move spurred. "You guys are here for me, aren't you? We can do big stuff together." *Big stuff? Wow, Donovan, quite a way with words there. Good thing none of the troops are around to hear that dud.*

But his allies were out here.

Somewhere, the others rolled around on the ground, grappling with frightening illusions. How on earth was he going to help them?

By breaking the spell. But how? Simply walking through some unseen ring of magic that ran through the woods? How was he supposed to find that?

Suddenly, a long moan cut through the air to his left. He rushed over to the stream, his ears perked. His magic retreated into his chest as he peered intently into the shadowy woods.

A high-pitched shriek sent him splashing downstream. It had to be one of his allies.

He leapt out of the water and quickened his pace along the bank of the waterway until he burst onto a scene that filled him with dread.

Thrashing around in the grass and knocking against the exposed roots of several trees that spiderwebbed across the rough terrain was his aunt. Stones clung to her, offering her a patchy armor. She punched and kicked at an invisible attacker. Was Egon her assailant? It couldn't be. The troll would never dream of harming his aunt.

The fear spell had to be making her see something that wasn't there, like some hideous beast from Homeland that had terrified her as a kid. He had no idea but suspected it must be an awful nightmare, based on the terror etched across his aunt's weary face.

He raced over, hoping his presence would cancel out the fear spell. It had to be around here if she was still caught up in its illusions.

Donovan fell to his knees. Stone and rock surged toward him, erecting a wall to defend him. The magic was more instinctual now. He didn't need to think about what he wanted it to do as much.

His aunt kicked and punched the air. He dodged a powerful uppercut and then grabbed her wrists.

Without warning, he was pulled into her head. It was not a pleasant feeling. His body, or spirit, funneled into a corkscrew ribbon that dove into his aunt's forehead. Everything went dark for a second, and then suddenly he was front and center to Aunt Esmel's nightmare.

And boy, was it a doozy.

Chapter 28
Wings to Go

The scene was unsettling. Several canyons radiated from the rocky plateau Donovan stood on. A sea of purple and blue rocks covered the terrain except at the center, where Aunt Esmel stood glaring up at the gigantic creature that occupied almost all the sky. There, the rocks seemed to be falling over each other to get away from his aunt.

The beast was a sprawling storm cloud of shadow magic. Hundreds of tentacles jabbed at his aunt. She evaded each thrust, kicking and punching at the dark magic as best she could. She dodged and rolled, sending the rocks shying away from her imploring looks. With her attention on the tentacle onslaught and the three victims trapped in the underbelly of the shadows, Donovan had gone unnoticed. His parents and his younger self were wrapped up in darkness, all withered and drained of their life forces. They sent Aunt Esmel looks of defeat and agony.

She kept gesturing at the rocks, trying to get them to respond. Her stone magic wasn't working.

Donovan raced toward her, relieved that the creature wasn't attacking him for the moment. Still, he kept an eye out for any aggressive tentacles.

His aunt spotted him and balked. She looked up at his emaciated younger self and then back at Donovan, unnerved that two of him existed.

He drew the stones up, forming a shield that he floated over his aunt. It was surprising his magic worked here while hers didn't. Maybe her nightmare was being unable to help her family.

The tentacles hammered at his shield, with quite a few snaking around it and taking shots at them from the side. One struck Donovan, its touch burning hot. He yelped and hopped back. A few stones in their shield dropped away, but he concentrated and built it back thicker and much larger, and more like a dome that enveloped them than just a slightly curved shell.

Aunt Esmel yelled at him, but there was no sound.

"I can't hear you." He couldn't even hear his own words.

Why wasn't her nightmare ending? Surely he had broached the fear spell. The Monarch had seemed so certain that he was a spellbreaker.

Maybe freeing his aunt from her nightmare would have a ripple effect and break the spell. Would it radiate and disrupt the nightmares of his other allies?

A tentacle broke through and lashed him across the face. He sealed up the hole with stones, severing the shadow magic. The appendage flopped about on the ground. His aunt stomped at it until it no longer moved.

He flung his arms out and hugged her, sending his earth and stone magic her way. He hoped his spellbreaker magic also went along for the ride but couldn't sense it in the least.

She pressed her face into his chest and whispered one word that this time he heard: "Donovan."

The scene exploded around them, the stones overhead along with the gargantuan shadow creature shattering and flying every which way. None of the debris struck them.

Seconds later, they stood in a white void, the sky and ground gone except for a few random blue and purple stones that hopped about at their feet.

The stones leapt up and floated between them, pulled in both of their directions. Donovan let the stones gravitate over to her, relieved that her magic was again working. The stones arranged themselves in a necklace configuration and looped over her head.

"You were stuck in a fear spell. Roderick made it to use against us. He's the traitor."

She scowled and sunk her shoulders. "I can't believe it."

"I escaped from the Monarch with Gregor's help. He had to go, though."

She nodded, looking wistfully at him. "Are you okay?"

"The Monarch says I can break spells, that I got the talent from Dad. Did you know?"

She shook her head. "Not really, but I suspected there was something else to you. It explains why you cancelled out the spell that kept the gates closed, but likely they only work for you. A spell woven by two is quite strong."

"Does that mean the fear spell is still up and running for the others?" Donovan hated that he might have to enter everyone else's nightmares to cancel out the spell.

"No, if it was only cast by Roderick, it would be weaker. You probably disrupted it completely, which means we have to find the others and make sure they're okay."

The void around them darkened, and he felt himself being pushed out of her mindscape. In an instant, he was back in the real world staring at his aunt, who was on her knees facing away. She stood, glanced over her shoulder, and smiled, still wearing the blue and purple stones from the nightmare as a necklace. They floated an inch from her person, with the center blue one angling slightly to the left.

His aunt pointed to the feisty stone. "Another aspect of our magic is we can locate anyone if they're in contact with any sort of rock. This will lead us to the nearest of our friends." His aunt walked in the direction the stone tugged toward.

"It wouldn't be taking us to the Monarch, would it?" he asked.

"Not a chance. I'm good at summoning lodestone magic. It can be very helpful in hunting animals for sport." She stopped by a tall, crooked evergreen and leaned against it, looking back to see if he was coming. "I've tuned it to find only our allies, no animals or villains this time." She grinned.

He scurried to catch up to her. "The troll told a squirrel all his meat is shipped in."

She smiled. "I said sport, Nephew. I've only caught and released, never brought any harm to those who call this island home. The foxes find it quite stimulating to play the role of prey for me. Now, come. Time is ticking. We need to reunite with as many of our friends as we can before the Monarch finds us."

They traipsed through the woods, a determined blue stone their guide.

* * *

A few minutes in, Donovan asked where they were going.

Aunt Esmel pointed to a rocky ridgeline barely visible through the leafy canopy. "Up there. Since we were to the east, that puts us closer to Amad and Knord."

He stopped and cast frantic looks all around. "Wait, Egon was with you. Where is he?" He immediately felt foolish. How had he forgotten about the troll? *Because he's invisible. Don't beat yourself up. He wasn't on my aunt's mind either.*

"I've got an eye and ear out for him. He was scouting ahead when we crossed through the fear spell."

Donovan dropped to one knee and peered intensely at a lower branch to their left that was waving. After a second, he dismissed it as the result of a breeze and not from a stocky invisible troll wading through the woods. "So we might even trip over or march past him if he's not moving or making a noise?" He resumed walking, taking more care in where he placed his steps and keeping his strides high and long to possibly avoid treading on an unconscious Egon. He must've looked ridiculous, as his aunt barked out a laugh.

"Likely already on the move and looking for the rest of us. Faerie magic doesn't work as well on trolls. He didn't get taken down by his own fears as much as the rest of us." She paused, cocking her head to listen. Something small crawled through the tall grasses to their right. Realizing that it wasn't the troll, she moved on. "Although, it is curious why he didn't rush back to check on me."

"Maybe he couldn't. Maybe he had to deal with another attack and couldn't risk circling back and exposing you to danger." He pictured the Monarch charging into the woods after he'd fled on Gregor and stumbling across Egon. The troll couldn't possibly deal with the villain by himself. Donovan hoped Egon had remained hidden if that had been the case.

"That does sound like him." She sped up and headed through the thinnest section of bushes to reach the base of the steep rock wall they'd spied earlier through the trees. She looked at Donovan and then at the long climb ahead. "We could use stone magic to scale this, but that would still take quite a while."

"Or?" He didn't know where she was going with her line of thinking.

"You've grown in your use of magic shockingly fast. The creature you built from stone, earth, and fungus was incredible."

"Yeah, but it fell apart."

"No matter. If you can do that, you're certainly ready to take on one of the more complicated bits of magic we do."

"Like what?" If she thought he could relocate the entire mountain of rock, she was crazy.

His aunt concentrated, and her entire body glowed red. A second later, she shrank to half her size. She paused and furrowed her brow and looked even more determined. Her glow doubled in size as she shrank to no taller than a pencil. Bright red wings riddled with yellow veins sprouted from her back, and she flew up to land on his right shoulder.

Surprisingly, her voice wasn't high-pitched at all.

"Now you try." She hopped off and hovered in place, inches from his nose.

He concentrated, inviting the stone magic to emerge and picturing himself half his size. The red energy flowing all around him buckled and expanded briefly before retreating back into his body. He frowned.

She said, "Try again, nephew." Her wings vibrated at an intense rate to keep her in one place.

He doubled up his focus and closed his eyes, willing himself to become smaller. He felt the magic expand and risked a peek to see it was twice as thick as before. Everything around him had a slight red cast to it. He once again visualized himself smaller, thinking of the Marvel character Antman.

His entire body went briefly numb, and then he was shrinking. It was bizarre. He felt it the most in his bones, not so much a pain as they seemed somehow softer. Everything vibrated, like he was holding onto a jackhammer, then a little nausea struck. Even with his eyes shut, the change in height was the most detectable. Surprisingly, shrinking provoked a minor earache. Thumping his hands against the sides of his head got rid of the pain.

When it felt like his bones, muscles, organs, and skin had stopped shifting and relocating, he whipped open his eyes to see he wasn't simply half his size but just as small as his aunt. He stood on the ground, the pebbles all around as big as boulders. Even the gauntlet had shrunk with him.

She flew down and landed next to him, nodding and smiling in approval. "Nice work. You might feel a little pressure, like a headache is trying to get your attention. That's your mind wanting you to revert to normal size. When you want to do that, focus on the slight pain and you'll be back to your normal self."

He did notice what she was talking about but quickly tried to think of something else, fearing that if he fixated on it, he might pop back up to full size unintentionally.

His aunt patted his back. "Now for the wings. Extend out the stone magic and shape it to your liking. Mine are basic moth wings, but you can also do ones that are bird or even bat inspired. Maybe this first time out, keep it simple."

Bat wings would be cool, but he studied his aunt's and coaxed the same from his magic instead. The wings appeared, slightly taller but not as wide a wingspan as Aunt Esmel's.

She clapped her hands together. "Excellent! Now, flying is very intuitive. It doesn't take much. Just think about it and let your wings do all the work." She pointed to the top of the cliff. "Race you there."

Before he could protest, she tore off, streaking so fast that she was a red blur of magic.

"Don't make me look bad, guys," he muttered to the wings.

He leapt upward and shot into the air, his wings flapping furiously. The air blasted his face, and his cheeks tugged slightly backward. *Wow, so like a little g-force.*

Realizing his aunt was more than halfway to the finish, he accelerated, marveling at how the wings really did work without much effort. They were fully a part of him, as easy to use as his arms and legs, responding instinctively and with no real learning curve. His uncle would've likely pointed out how the magic was being directed more with his brain stem than his cerebellum, which meant faster reaction time.

He scolded himself for getting too caught up in the possible science of the feat and enjoyed racing past his aunt and landing atop the cliff at a breathtaking speed.

She dropped in next to Donovan and gave him a partial hug, steering clear of squeezing his new wings. "You're a natural. So good." She looked around. "Now, don't ask me how, but our vision is radically improved in this form. We should be able to spot Amad and Knord rather quickly. C'mon!" She took off and raced toward a raised ridgeline.

Astonished at how he could see everything so clearly, he followed. And it didn't seem as dark as before, even though it was still obviously night. So maybe he had some form of night vision. "I can see so far! And it's not as dark."

She smiled and nudged as close as she could get without risking their wings knocking into each other at their downward extension. "Just know that while small we burn brighter, so we can't hide as well in this size."

"That's messed up. One of the advantages to being this tiny is you should be able to be stealthy."

Aunt Esmel shrugged and pointed to a cave entrance fairly obscured by the pines that loomed over it. Rabbits and birds huddled together at the mouth of the cave. He wouldn't have spied any of that with his regular vision. Definitely not the tiny mice darting around the slightly larger fauna.

"They've got to be with Knord," he said, zooming toward the unusual gathering.

They glided into the cave to find Amad and Knord staring at them. Both emissaries grinned and waved at Donovan. A robin perched on Knord's shoulder, chirping incessantly.

Amad said, "Young Strong, why am I not surprised to see you've mastered yet another aspect of Fae magic? You are a wonder."

His aunt hung back and transformed, growing at a much faster rate than she had shrunk. Her wings retracted. Oddly, her hair stood briefly on end as if responding to a build-up of static electricity. She touched the damp cave wall, and her upright follicles settled down.

It was now his turn. Donovan focused on the dull ache at the back of his head, and he reverted to his normal size. His hair also held a static charge and only dropped down when he too touched a wall. A bout of dizziness caused him to lean against the rock for a bit until the cave stopped its impression of a Tilt-a-Whirl.

Knord waved for the bird on his shoulder to fly off. The little robin did, racing past the other animals outside and out into the night sky, which Donovan noted had returned to its normal amount of darkness. He already missed the keen eyesight of his little self. *Tiny me will never need glasses*, he idly thought.

Aunt Esmel filled the pair in on the fear spell and how Donovan had escaped the Monarch and freed them from the nightmare magic.

Amad hugged him, squeezing him rather tight. "My gratitude, Donovan. So glad to be out of that nightmare loop. I was trapped in a third marriage to Sylph. Her fits of rage are not what I wish to revisit."

Knord grinned. "A spellbreaker? Met one a while back. Peculiar fellow. Always afraid he was undoing magic at every turn. Then again, I'm sure you already have much better control of it."

Donovan didn't know how to respond. He didn't want to be paranoid about negating spells he wasn't supposed to.

Knord sensed his worry. "Don't fret. It's a gift. You will make it so." He pointed to the mouth of the cave. "Now, the robin who had my ear did say she'd spotted an unruly Fae setting fire to the woods nearby. You didn't notice any blazes on your flight here, did you?"

Both shook their heads and looked at each other.

"Probably the hybrid with fire magic trying to flush us out." Knord exited the cave, the animals hopping out of the way with reverence.

They all fled the cave and spotted the fire immediately. Red flames ignited several pines to the west.

His aunt said, "That's where we were going next. Frayson and Grandl's group. Could be Reena fending off an attack. Although, she's so precise with her flame, I doubt she started such. Likely, Ithor's doing."

Knord frowned at the fire. He spun about and clapped his hands. He shrank all the way, skipping the halfway stage his aunt had done earlier. His wings glowed brown and were feathered. He hovered in front of them, showing off his impressive wingspan. "Time is of the essence. Several of our fellows are in jeopardy."

Amad transformed next, also executing his change in one fluid move. His blue wings were more like a butterfly's, their yellow veins forming more rigid geometrical shapes than Donovan's.

His aunt also skipped the secondary stage and fluttered among the others with her less eye-catching wings. She nodded for Donovan to follow suit.

The threesome winged toward the fire, his aunt in the rear and waving for him to get on with it.

The change happened much slower than before, and he even underwent the second stage. More time between transformations might be required to recharge in order to shrink in one fell swoop. Donovan shrugged at being half-sized and then urged the transformation to finish. He coaxed out a pair of bat wings to make up for his initial change having to be done in two stages and chased after the others. The wings were much larger than his previous flight gear, but he quickly grew right at home with them, finding he could go much faster than before. *I'm almost supersonic.*

As they zoomed through the night air, a stampede of all sorts of animals wove through the woods below, defying their instincts and racing toward the blaze. Donovan knew they were following Knord's orders and felt a little sorry for them. Wouldn't they normally turn tail and get themselves as far away as possible?

Then again, Knord didn't work that way. He just wouldn't force anyone to do something they didn't want to do.

His aunt flew next to him. "The Monarch may also be here or close by. Gird yourself, nephew."

He nodded and put on his most serious game face, as if he were taking on a level 36 boss with a character who was a dozen levels below that. He chastised himself for thinking that their plight was anything like *Goblin Cauldron*. The stakes were serious, and none of them had any extra lives to fall back on.

Donovan swallowed and flew with confidence. He wouldn't let his friends and family down. *That's not what a Strong does.*

Chapter 29
Boulder Moves

In minutes, they were over the forest fire. Four pines were engulfed, with much of the underbrush spawning tall flames that threatened to ignite even more trees. Frayson and Grandl flung water at any fire approaching them. The emissaries had their backs to a huge boulder.

The giant stone was a good sign. Plenty of magic to draw from for him and his aunt.

Reena darted through a wall of flames, slinging fireballs at Ithor. The villain stood inside a fiery cyclone hurling fire, all about, hitting more of the forest than anything else. The boy, even without the villain's influence, liked chaos far too much. It was hard to tell which of his callous actions were self-inspired or directed by the Twilight Monarch.

Ithor roared, "Surrender, and maybe I won't burn down the whole island!"

No one had noticed Donovan's group yet. They hung back, Knord zipping toward his approaching fauna army. He gestured and likely sent them some sort of mental warnings as the animals gave the fire plenty of distance.

Two more pines close to Frayson lit up. The boy flinched and retreated. But then another tree that had been on fire, likely one of the first to be lit, fell toward him. He leapt out of the way, sending a wave of water at the blackened wood as it struck the ground. He concentrated on dousing it so the fire wouldn't light the sparse grasses near the boulder.

Sweating profusely and white-faced, Grandl furrowed his brow and moved his hands slowly forward. A small pond of water moved in overhead. Donovan and his fellow airborne Fae would be caught in the massive downpour if they didn't move fast.

Grandl spied their bright glows at the last minute and grimaced, summoning what little strength he had left to hold back the water.

Donovan and company flew right. Once in the clear, Grandl let go and the water fell, extinguishing almost all of the flames on the ground. The trees still burned, though. Another looked ready to drop, its trunk charred and dangerously destabilized.

Ithor unleashed a huge fireball. It knocked Grandl to the ground and caused him to roll frantically on his burning robes while trying to summon enough water to extinguish the rest of the flames.

Furious at the villain's ruthlessness, Donovan flew at the evil hybrid. Realizing his small stature would have very little impact, he triggered the change at the last second and slammed into Ithor as his full-sized self.

They landed in a heap on a patch of smoldering grass. Donovan pummeled Ithor with his gauntlet while summoning stones to race over and entomb the boy. With Donovan's emotions running so hot, the rocks dug into Ithor's skin, provoking a painful howl.

"Get off me!" Ithor landed a punch to Donovan's jaw.

He ignored the pain and dumped more stones on the boy, succeeding in pinning Ithor's arms. Donovan took a second to scope out what the others were doing. Reena helped Grandl to his feet, while Frayson ran around putting out fires with small quantities of water his white magic pulled from the air.

Amad, Knord, and his aunt also helped. Amad sent a plethora of earth to smother the flaming trees. It was awkward and slow going but seemed to be working. His aunt did the same with her stone magic, tightly packing hundreds of stones to the burning wood and depriving the flames of oxygen. It was impressive how she managed such a tight seal with the interlocking stones. Donovan imagined his precision wasn't there yet.

Ithor spat at him. "You're nothing! I wish he didn't need you. For the longest time, it was just me by his side. I earned his trust so he didn't have to take control of me."

"He wants to strip us of our dual magic to gain access to more shadow magic!" Donovan said. "You're crazy if you think he cares about you. All he wants is power!"

"He'll pick the rest of you clean of yours, but he promised I could keep enough of my magic to rekindle it. He won't let me die."

"And you believe him?"

Ithor gritted his teeth. "My parents abandoned me the minute they realized I was different. Everyone saw me as worthless or some freak to avoid, like me being a hybrid was infectious." He glared at Donovan. "I had to fend for myself in Homeland. I didn't have parents that ran off to Earth to hide me away."

"Stop!" Donovan didn't know what to say. Ithor was crazy but also a little sad. Would Donovan have turned out the same way without his family? "Just stop."

Suddenly, another fire-damaged tree fell, sending leaf matter and dust high into the air. Many around him, including Donovan, coughed and wiped grit from their eyes.

Despite his hands being covered in stones, Ithor summoned a fireball inches from Donovan's face. The heat was blistering, and Donovan had no choice but to jump back. The fireball followed him, crashing into his head.

He screamed and fled, swatting at the flames all around his face.

Frayson ran over and hit him with a wall of water, extinguishing the fireball immediately and soaking him from head to toe. Donovan pawed at his face, relieved to not feel charred flesh. It hurt but no more than a bad sunburn.

He spun about. Ithor stood, free of the stones. He brushed a few stubborn rocks away and summoned a fireball for each hand. Both blazed with far more intensity than any of his previous magic. His entire body glowed a bright yellow.

"You're super easy to distract." He stalked toward Donovan. "Twilight Monarch needs you in one piece, but nothing says you can't be hideously fried to a crisp with your magical insides intact." His eyes narrowed as his flames swelled. Ithor threw his hands up, preparing to hurl a full-fledged inferno at Donovan.

Suddenly, Roderick dropped out of the sky and landed between them. The lobster glanced at Donovan before facing the fire and earth hybrid. "Ithor, that's not going to happen."

What was the warlock doing? Donovan retreated a step. Out of the corner of his eye, he caught his aunt motioning for the others to hang back.

"Get out of the way." Ithor kept his voice at a low growl. "If I don't bring him back, he'll make me a puppet and never trust me again."

"I won't let you harm him." The lobster held up his claws. Blue magic leapt between them.

"You can't protect him. He won't find your body if you do. Move aside." He bared his teeth.

Roderick fired his magic at the boy. Ithor leapt clear, and the blast hit the base of the large boulder.

Wanting to fight but afraid he'd be in the way, Donovan moved back.

Ithor threw one of the fireballs at Roderick, hitting the lobster's tail and leaving a blackened mess of the shelled segments there.

Roderick swept his tail around and struck Ithor hard. The hybrid flew through the air, ramming into the boulder headfirst. The stone shuddered and shifted forward a few feet but stopped before it fully toppled.

Furious, Ithor threw two more fireballs, which Roderick deflected with his magic, one landing deep in the woods off to the left. The second flew back toward Ithor, who once again dodged it. The fire struck the boulder and dissipated.

Summoning a stone shield large enough to protect both, Donovan ran toward the lobster. "What are you doing?"

"The right thing."

Ithor screamed and hurled flame after flame at the shield.

The lobster continued, "I'm so very sorry. I knew it was wrong to help the Monarch, but I . . ." He lowered his head. "It was a moment of weakness. It will not happen again." A fireball punched through the rock shield, and Roderick drove it into the ground with his magic. "We need to knock him out."

"Let me." Donovan gestured and swept the rock shield forward. It fell atop the enraged hybrid, a more massive amount of stone than what he'd heaped on the boy earlier. He controlled it just enough to not cover Ithor's face.

"You're nothing." Ithor struggled to draw in a breath.

Worried the stones were too heavy, that the Fae couldn't fill his lungs, he used his magic to start removing rocks.

Roderick placed a claw on his shoulder. "Not yet, let him lose consciousness first."

Donovan didn't like that. It felt cruel and risky.

Ithor took in short raspy breaths, his eyes revealing a restless panic.

Suddenly, yet another fire-damaged tree fell, this one striking the large boulder with a loud crash. The stone teetered forward and then toppled.

Roderick snatched Donovan and flew high into the trees. The huge stone came down atop Ithor, who let out a faint shriek. Then the boulder thumped into the forest floor, sending dust everywhere.

The warlock flew him back to the ground, mere feet from the boulder. His aunt rushed over and snatched Donovan out of the lobster's claw, sending the warlock a harsh look.

Sobbing, Donovan tried to use his stone magic to remove the huge rock, but his emotions were so floppy that he couldn't get it to do more than vibrate. Next, he resorted to earth magic and began digging away at the ground under the rock, sending dirt flying.

Roderick drew closer. "Donovan, stop. It's over. He couldn't have survived that."

Tears streamed down Donovan's dusty cheeks. "No, he's under there. My stones protected him. He's going to run out of air! We have to help!" He whirled around and held out his hands to the others. "Please, you have to. We can save him."

A keening howl cut through the forest, sending chills down Donovan's spine.

The Twilight Monarch charged onto the scene, his shadow-shrouded face one of maddening fury. "His magic is gone. You took away two. I need all eight."

Everyone tensed and drew forth their magic, sliding into heightened battle poses, Aunt Esmel included. Several large rocks hovered above her, at the ready to become missiles.

The Monarch glared at Roderick. "I saw the whole thing through Ithor's eyes. You betrayed me!"

Dozens of shadow tentacles shot at the lobster. Roderick flew higher and batted away the few that snagged him by the tail.

The Monarch shouted, "You've served your usefulness to me! And don't worry about finding your body. After all, the dead have no use for one." He flung a massive tentacle at the warlock, who shredded it with a magical blast. The lobster raced off into the night sky, abandoning them and fleeing for his life.

The Twilight Monarch turned his attention to Donovan. His tentacles slithered over and wrapped him up tight.

Donovan knew he should've fought back, that he was just giving up, but his mind was so fogged.

Ithor was dead. He'd been crushed.

And Donovan had a part in Ithor's passing. He felt nauseous as he watched his aunt and his allies attack the villain and attempt to free him from his clutches. They failed miserably, and soon all were being dragged through the woods toward the gates.

Donovan's mind was sluggish. He really wasn't paying attention. What was going on? The villain no longer had all the hybrids he needed.

He listened, thinking maybe the bad guy would ramble about his intentions, but the Twilight Monarch didn't say a word.

He just dragged them on, his expression that of rage.

Chapter 30
Separating Shadows

Donovan only caught snatches of their trek through the woods. He tried to focus on his surroundings, but his mind wouldn't cooperate. Despair clawed its way to the surface and wouldn't let go. He was a failure and had doomed everyone. Ithor's death was on his hands. He could've stopped the boulder, redirected it. With how well he was using his magic, he should've been able to toss it aside, even if it was twice as big as the one he'd held in place on the beach.

At some point it began to rain, and he let himself be distracted by how the water soaked his hair and then ran down his face to gather at his nose and chin before splashing to the ground.

The villain didn't care if any arrived injured. While they were mostly wrapped in shadow, their heads and feet were exposed and constantly being knocked into trees, rocks, and the ground along the way.

He lifted his head to check on his aunt. *She's definitely unconscious.*

Could he make himself small and slip free of the shadows? Aunt Esmel would still be a captive. And he had no idea if the rest were alert and able to shrink as well. What good was it if only he escaped? He couldn't fight the Monarch alone.

He wanted to curl into a ball and give up. No avenue seemed to lead to success. The bad guy had won. Maybe if the villain took his magic and the others', they'd wind up a spirit like Gregor and could go on to the next plane of existence. Donovan didn't have a strong belief in any sort of afterlife, but the dragon surely had. And the fact that he had stuck around as a spirit seemed to confirm there was something beyond death. Maybe surrender was the smart thing to do. Would that mean finally being with his parents again?

The cold rain caused him to shiver, bringing him a respite from his intense sadness.

They were at the clearing, and Donovan pushed himself to focus on what was happening. It wasn't easy, He was at war with himself. Give up or fight? Right now, his curiosity kept his fighting spirit burning ever so slightly.

The Twilight Monarch secured his aunt, Amad, Knord, and the two water emissaries amid the tangled mass of shadows holding Lut, Lymol, and Brin. None put up a struggle, which upset Donovan. If they would break free, maybe he could do that too. Several sent him serious looks, with Lut and Amad conveying silent support his way.

It didn't matter that they might believe in him. He knew he was outmatched. This was the end.

The Monarch bound Donovan and Reena to Joven and Ny at the center of the clearing. Joven was unconscious, while Ny sent Donovan imploring looks. Reena appeared as out of it as Donovan, her expression blank and resigned to whatever fate the Monarch had in store for them.

Why was Reena here? She wasn't a hybrid.

The Twilight Monarch drew in a measured breath and looked up at the night sky, almost as if his intense gaze could stop the steady downpour. When the rain didn't lessen, he scowled and began moving his arms about as if executing some form of martial arts. Donovan knew that wasn't the case. He was initiating the spell.

"What are you doing?" Donovan said.

The Twilight Monarch paused and glared at him. "Taking your magic. Now curl up and still your tongue lest I do it for you."

Suddenly, dozens of animals raced into the clearing. Deer, raccoons, squirrels, and other furry inhabitants of Stonebridge poured in along with hundreds of birds. Lut and Knord broke free and dashed toward the gathering animals.

The Twilight Monarch paused in his spell and charged toward the growing crowd. He summoned shadow magic and whipped the tentacles about, striking the animals half as much as he missed. The amount of shadows he used was far less than before, which made sense as he had so much of his magic tied up in those still bound by the dark energies.

A voice next to him said, "You must fight your apathy and depressive thought, Donovan."

It was Egon. He could just about make out where the rain struck the troll's broad shoulders.

"The shadows sap your will and cast thoughts of despair into your head. You must resist."

"Where have you been?" Donovan asked.

"By your side since you saved your aunt."

The animals scattered, efficiently evading the Monarch's attacks. The villain cursed and grew more frenzied in his assault. Lut threw stones at the monarch and was just as spry as the birds that flew all about. Knord was also equally acrobatic, springing all around and avoiding the tentacles.

"Then why didn't you announce yourself? We could've used your help." His anger simmered.

"I thought it best to wait, engage at a time when I could do the most good." He cleared his throat. "Lut and Knord are executing the perfect distraction like we discussed moments ago. I jogged ahead once I saw the Monarch had you in his clutches and set this up."

A thick tentacle struck Knord, sending him flying. Luckily, he didn't crash into any of the stone arches but did slide a good distance through the mud.

"Set up what? The original plan won't work."

"That's the shadow magic influencing you. It robs you of your spirit and forces you into the doldrums. You don't feel like yourself, do you?"

He really didn't. An overwhelming sense to give in latched hold. Maybe he should simply go along with whatever fate had in store. A tiny part of him rebelled. Donovan gritted his teeth and sucked in a deep breath. "The Monarch is making me feel this way."

Reena stirred, lolling her head toward him. Her fiery spirit there, but reined in. She burned away enough of the shadow around her mouth to speak. "I feel it, too. We have . . . to resist. We have to care."

"Why is she bound with us?" Donovan tried to pierce his mental fog, seeking a reason why the fire emissary was lumped in with the hybrids. An idea flopped to the surface. "Because Ithor controlled fire and earth. She satisfies the fire affinity . . . and my troll magic transfusion means earth is also covered. He's going to go ahead with the spell."

Dread rose. Would the spell even work if one of the hybrids was swapped out? Would they burn up because of a magical substitution?

Egon sounded further away. "You have to break free and open the gates, not for the Monarch's sake, but to give the others access to Homeland magic."

He knew what the troll said was true, but he still hesitated.

The villain pinned Lut down and stalked toward Knord, looking quite ready to be done with such foolish distractions.

Seeing such abuse flipped a switch inside of Donovan. His resolve, which up until this moment had been squirreled away in a dark corner of his psyche, broke loose and roared to the forefront.

A focused blast of air alerted Donovan to the fact that Joven was awake and up to something. "He's not in my head for the moment but will be soon. You have to push yourself, Donovan. Open all the gates."

"And don't forget your spellbreaking abilities," Egon said. "The Monarch needs you unconscious for that ability to not be a factor. Don't let him knock you out."

That's true. Then why even risk letting him stay alert this long? Because it's the villain's way of gloating. He wants me to see just how bad everything is going.

Donovan clenched his fists.

The Monarch had Lut subdued. He hurled the stone emissary at the nearest gate, the one covered in fungus.

Donovan reached out with his father's magic and stirred the smattering of mushrooms growing from the arch to action. They swelled in size and expanded their population so fast that when Lut hit the arch she bounced off the soft, thick blanket of fungus and landed on her feet, spared a concussion or any broken bones.

The villain raged and manifested dozens more tentacles from his back spikes. This significantly depleted the shadows binding the emissaries and his aunt but not Donovan and his fellow hybrids.

Egon shouted to be heard over the heavy rain, "Off to help Amad and the others!"

Huge footprints sank into the ground, revealing the troll racing toward the still-trapped emissaries. Donovan risked a glance at the Twilight Monarch, fearful he had also witnessed the evidence of the troll's mad dash.

The villain's gaze was on the trail left behind by Egon. The Monarch roared and hurled shadow tentacles at where he thought the invisible troll would be next.

Hoping the troll could fend for himself, Donovan focused on the stones and earth all around, requesting they slip under the shadows enveloping him and form an armor. They did just that, and he flexed, trusting that the dual magic would magnify the movement.

The shadow tentacles buckled and sloughed off as the blue and red magic flared, leaving him with a swirling violet aura almost a foot thick.

His ploy loosened the tentacles holding the others, giving them the chance to escape.

Reena burned the few shadow limbs still encircling her and sprinted away from the center. Joven slid free and lifted into the air, her expression one of rage. She was once again the Monarch's puppet. Donovan readied a large rock to cast at her, but a flock of birds, many raptors, flew at Joven, engaging her in battle. She flung ice daggers at her feathered attackers, but they easily evaded most of her icy missiles. It saddened Donovan that Joven was still not in control. He believed she was trying her best to fight off the Monarch's influence but had been his captive too long and had little resistance to his dark hold.

Meanwhile, Princess Ny summoned vines to pry herself free. She stepped clear of the writhing shadows and sent Donovan a determined look.

He accumulated still more earth and rock until his armor was quite thick. Free of the shadow tentacles, his mind rapidly cleared. He reached out to the stone cores of each of the eight gates, opening them far faster than before.

Reena raced over to the other emissaries, flinging fireballs at the tentacles the Monarch tossed their way. The villain glared at Donovan and charged toward him, waving his arms about as if casting a spell.

With renewed determination, Donovan flung a wall of earth in front of the Twilight Monarch, who just vaulted up and over it, while he directed all his shadow magic at Donovan.

A mass of tentacles held onto nothing, but Donovan knew that wasn't it. They had Egon!

Grinning, the Monarch swung around his invisible captive until finally releasing him. Donovan had no idea where to place a soft landing for the troll. He tossed his fungus magic at where he thought the troll might land, but he failed to see the mushrooms compress under impact. Sadly, he did hear a loud snap issue from a nearby tree. Several of its upper branches crumpled, and then there was a horrible thud near the pine's trunk. Donovan thought he saw the mud around the roots cave in, but he had to switch his attention back to the Monarch.

Ny charged at the villain, carried forward by an impressive surging carpet of thorny vines. The plants looped around the villain's arms and pulled in opposite directions. Ny concentrated. Donovan worried she was being too ruthless, that she intended to pull the Monarch apart. But he soon realized she was just preventing him from finishing the motions of his spell.

The Twilight Monarch directed shadow tentacles at Ny. Dozens of animals raced to her side, gnawing and clawing at the dire limbs to keep them at bay.

Aunt Esmel charged toward Donovan, vaulting over a large shadow mass that had almost driven her into the ground. She threw her stone magic about to defend herself. "Once every emissary is in front of their gate, they'll funnel their magic to you. You have to use it to purge the villain of his shadow magic."

"But what if I simply end up feeding him exactly what he needs?"

She swatted an aggressive tentacle aside with a giant airborne fist of stone. Donovan liked that tactic and was itching to try it himself.

"As long as you stay awake, your spellbreaking should stop his spell from succeeding." She glanced over at Ny, who still had the villain occupied, but it didn't look like it would be for much longer. His shadow attack was thinning the animal reinforcements, hurling feathered and furred soldiers into the woods. Donovan feared not all would make it out alive.

He watched the fighting all around, lending a hand with his earth and stone magic, at one point hammering a stubborn tentacle into oblivion with his own attempt at a fist of stones. It collapsed after the pulverizing was over, but Donovan drew satisfaction at holding onto its basic shape for so long.

All the emissaries made it to their respective gates and began drawing their magic from each arch. The many colors of the different energies created a rainbow strobe effect in the clearing, the constant flickering from the various sources causing every move to appear herky-jerky.

Howling, the Twilight Monarch yanked his arms free of Ny's vines. He batted her aside with one tentacle as he spider-walked toward Donovan on four long shadow appendages.

His aunt would've helped, but she was tangling with Joven, keeping the hybrid from attacking Reena and the others. It was clear Joven's orders were to try to take out the emissaries while her boss focused on Donovan.

Donovan fashioned fungus grenades and tossed them at the villain.

He knocked them aside with a tentacle. This time, they exploded rather than produce a smokescreen, dealing extensive damage to the shadow magic. The appendage was shredded, and the villain abandoned it, letting it die on the vine.

The Twilight Monarch fell on Donovan, screaming inches from the boy's face as his shadow magic spiderwebbed all around, forming a sphere trapping the pair inside. The shadow tentacles spread like blown-upon globs of ink, crisscrossing and merging with each other until Donovan could no longer see out.

His blue and red glow lit the fresh prison.

The Monarch stood over him, glaring. "I don't require air. My shadows provide. But you do. I simply need to wait you out." He seemed to think better of his plan and pummeled Donovan with several tentacles. "Or . . . I could simply speed up the process and knock you out."

Donovan's stone and earth armor protected everything but his head. He prompted it to flow over his skull to form a crude football helmet. One punch made him see stars. Even with the added head protection, the villain would eventually land a telling blow. He had to try something different.

He thought, doing his best to ignore how each breath felt more and more strained. The air couldn't be running out this fast.

It dawned on him that the sphere was contracting, speeding up the loss of oxygen. He felt lightheaded.

Another tentacle hit him square in the nose. Blood trickled from his left nostril.

"No one can race to your side. I've cut you off from your allies."

His panic intensified. He didn't see a way out. *Wait, cut off?* That gave him an idea. The shadow sphere cut him off from pulling more earth and rock into the mix. He'd have to lose his armor. Would that leave him too exposed? He had to try. Already, he was seeing spots and feeling fainter and fainter.

He released the stones and earth from their protective duties and shoved them at the villain. He needed a way past the shadows covering the Monarch. The earth found slivers of openings, no more than fractures, and funneled in. The hairline cracks grew, allowing him to insert the smallest of rocks.

The Monarch didn't seem to notice his ploy. He probably thought that the sudden loss of armor meant the boy was giving up, and he struck at him with even more zeal.

Donovan endured blow after blow as he shepherded the earth and stone to slide between the evil Fae's body and the coat of shadows that protected it. He briefly wondered if the Twilight Monarch was shriveled up within the shadows, having been drained of almost all his mortal energies. Was he kept alive simply by the dark magic?

It seemed like minutes, but it had to be mere seconds. The earth and stone forged a shell around the villain's inner self. Donovan felt the last rock slide into place, and instantly there was a reaction.

The Twilight Monarch stiffened and paused in his attack. He went to shout, but all he could manage was a muffled shriek. Donovan had him sealed tight.

The villain thrashed his arms and legs as the tentacles retreated, returning to being long spikes along his back. He convulsed and flailed.

The shadow magic tried to pierce the shell Donovan had erected. He kept it together, impressed by its integrity.

Suddenly, the shadow sphere fell apart, and they were exposed.

Keeping his focus on his magic, Donovan watched his aunt rally the troops. All eight emissaries pulsed with their unique magic for the briefest of seconds, then stabbed their arms forward, sending their magic at the shadows encasing the Monarch. The combined effort blasted the shadows away. They didn't resist. Maybe because they were no longer connected to the villain. Lacking cohesion and a mind to unite them, the dark magic ruptured and flew in every direction, disappearing into the dark clouds and the dim recesses of the woods all around.

Donovan gulped in several breaths as he dropped to his knees. The Monarch lay curled up in a ball, still covered by stone and earth.

His aunt and Ny approached, the princess kneeling next to Donovan and placing a hand on his shoulder. Several rabbits and mice scurried around at her feet, which amused Donovan so much he snorted.

The villain didn't move. Not even his chest rose nor fell. Had he killed him? Donovan fought back tears. He hadn't meant to take the Fae's life.

"Did I kill him?" He looked into his aunt's eyes, letting the warmth radiating from them lessen the stark notions flying around in his head.

His aunt's fingers grazed his cheek. "Donovan, let us see."

He coughed and wiped at his nose as he prompted the magic to abandon the evil Fae. The rocks and earth fell aside, revealing a frail wisp of a man. He was all skin and bones, knobby-jointed and so wrinkled. His eyes were squeezed shut.

Several other emissaries approached, with Brin the only one close enough for Donovan to register. The emissary held three purple mushrooms.

The Twilight Monarch's eyes snapped open, and he wheezed. He swiveled his head to glare at Donovan. "You . . ."

Brin dropped to the ground and pressed the mushrooms together, producing a gray cloud of spores that he used his magic to corral. The orange energies directed the spores into the villain's flared nostrils and gaping mouth.

The Monarch gagged and thrashed, but then went limp.

Donovan sent Brin a panicked look.

The Fae rose and smiled. "Worry not. It will keep him under until we can get him back to Homeland and figure out the best way to prevent him from summoning his shadows again. As you saw, he is quite harmless without his dark magic."

His aunt hugged him. Donovan felt numb. It was finally over. The threat to his family was just a weak, old man. He patted Aunt Esmel on her back and slipped free of her vice-like embrace.

He registered everyone gathering around, including the many fauna. A small brown bird dropped onto his shoulder and chirped in his ear before flying over to nuzzle and tweet in Ny's curls.

The princess grinned and nodded as if agreeing to what the bird was saying. "She's very thankful you sent the evil away from Stonebridge. She wishes you many springs and many seeds."

He laughed and then grew serious. "Wait, is Egon okay?"

Everyone looked around. For all they knew, the troll could be lying somewhere, breathing his last breath, and none of them would be the wiser.

A faint cough caught everyone's attention. Donovan bolted over to where he thought the sound had come from. He slowed when he suddenly realized his brashness could lead to him tripping over the invisible troll. "Egon?"

"To your left, under this big branch." A large tree limb stood at an odd angle, literally floating as it teetered back and forth slightly.

Donovan drew up beside the troll and gently felt around until he located an arm and then a shoulder.

"Careful of my spikes," Egon said. He coughed and grunted. "I think just a few broken ribs. No bleeding that I can tell."

His aunt joined him, and they lifted the branch free with their magic.

Egon said, "Thank you. I might be in need of Brin's medicinal magic. Would it be a bother to call the grumpy Fae over here?"

Donovan did just that and watched the fungus emissary minister to the troll. Brin fretted and cursed at the troll's uppity manner but let everyone know the chef would recover in time.

Egon begrudgingly thanked the Fae and called Donovan over. "It looks like I might be unable to fulfill my duties as cook for the next few days. Would you be my hands, and I can walk you through enough meals to keep this bunch from starving to death?"

"I'd love to."

His aunt whisked Donovan away, assuring him the others could get the injured troll back to The Sleeping Dragon without them. He said his goodbyes and thanks to all and joined his aunt as she struck out through the woods.

Aunt Esmel didn't take him home but to the rocky beach where she'd given him his first official lesson. Although, he realized he'd been learning from the moment his uncle had dropped him off at Stonebridge.

She made a staircase out of stones and walked up it to sit herself down at the top of a very upright boulder. She motioned for him to join her.

He scrambled up the stairs, noting how they fell apart after he fled the last makeshift step.

The sun was coming up, dispelling the gray shadows of the night.

Sitting with his legs dangling, Donovan eyed the waves breaking just below.

"You did good. Your mom and dad would be so proud." Her voice caught on her last word.

"Thanks," he said. "What's next?"

Repositioning herself to take in the sun, she said, "Up to you. Stay here or go back with your uncle. Or . . ."

"Or what?"

"Or journey to Homeland, tour your birthright." She placed a hand under his chin. "You are quite impressive. It might be fitting for those who frown on hybrids to see the wonders you can do. And I'm not just talking about your magic. You are something, Donovan Strong. So much of your father's impulsive joy and your mother's spirited kindness. Homeland needs to see that. They need a direction, a fresh take on their tired ways. And who better than a Fae that spent so much time among humans to bring a new perspective to our realm."

"I think I'd like that. But would I have to go alone?"

Aunt Esmel smiled. "I think not. You probably have quite a few back there that would want to walk your path, some who might surprise you." She tousled his curls and went to stand.

He reached for her hand and gently pulled her back down. "A little longer. Let's just enjoy the moment. And maybe you could tell me a story only you know about my mom."

She wiped a tear from her eye and made a point to declare it the fault of allergies before sharing a ripe tale from his mother's childhood, one that made Donovan laugh so much he almost fell off.

Once the sun no longer touched the horizon, they left to return to his aunt's house. They passed by the sign on the dock, and Donovan wanted so badly to magically alter it to say: Faeries Do Exist!

For him, that would be the case from this day on. A world of magic beckoned, and he owed it to himself to find his role in such a crazy place.

Donovan picked up a stone and skipped it across the surprisingly calm waters, boosting its journey with a healthy dose of stone magic. After its tenth bounce, he realized it wasn't curving back to return to him. He followed its path until it disappeared from sight. He wondered if it would bounce along the water forever but quickly dismissed the idea. Still, he drew comfort in knowing that it might just keep going and going and going.

Author's Note

Fairies Don't Exist! is my second novel focusing on the Fae. *Arcana Creek* is the first and has some similarities with this one. I wanted to tell a story about family and secrets. There needed to be dark faerie magic. Where this—my 35th novel—is different, lies in the eight magical affinities. I wanted the Fae to each work different forms of magic but felt just using the four elements was so overdone. Enter: flora, fauna, fungus, and stone. I loved the variety, and it expanded the story a great deal.

And for those of you left wondering what the red sword in the trunk was for, that will have to wait for the sequel. I have some fun ideas about where the sword will take Donovan, but that's all I'm saying right now. If you want to see a tale of him in Homeland, then get to work helping me make this one a bestseller. I'm sure I can be persuaded to write a follow-up adventure if this tale garners a nice amount of passionate fans.

If you liked *Faeries Don't Exist!* might I suggest you hunt down the *Emery Fogg* series, *Arcana Creek*, and *Ghost Coast*? These titles explore family and rebuilding after a loss. They also delve into what it's like to have magical powers suddenly thrust upon you. I guarantee you'll love them all!

Thanks for reading, and do spread the word about my novels. I greatly appreciate you as a reader and fan of my work.

Building a Brian Bookshelf

novels by Brian
Faeries Don't Exist!
This Lemon Saves the World
Emery Fogg Takes to Magic (Sort Of)
Emery Fogg Conquers the Warp Dragons (Mostly)
Emery Fogg Defeats the Shadow Swarm (Pretty Much)
How to Survive a Magical Quest (Emery Fogg 3.5)
Irving Wishbutton and the Questing Academy
Irving Wishbutton and the Revision Ravine
Irving Wishbutton and the Tomb of Tomes
Irving Wishbutton and the Domain of Sagas
Graham the Gargoyle 1: Graham's Grief
Graham the Gargoyle 2: Flenn's Folly
Graham the Gargoyle 3: Ot's Ordeal
Graham the Gargoyle Omnibus
Here Is Where I . . . Wield a Really Big Sword
The Powers That Flee
Ghost Coast
Bring On the Magic
Tagalong
Flame and Fortune
Ned Firebreak
The God Wheel
Arcana Creek
With a Side of Universal Destruction
Heroes of Perpetua
Turncoats Book One: Overrun
Turncoats Book Two: Overwhelmed
We Kill Humans Book One: Offshoots
Angus Farseek Book One: Untimely Agents
Monsters in Boxers 1: Chaos At the Door
with Keith Robinson
Fractured
Unearthed

Books Brian Wrote Under a Pen Name

as D. Spangler
We Three Meet
Decisive Magic
as Landon Alspiret
Burnt Jesus

Printed in Great Britain
by Amazon

29018221R00115